MURDER ON TOUR

MURDER ON TOUR
A ROCK 'N' ROLL MYSTERY

BY DICK CLARK
with Paul Francis

THE MYSTERIOUS PRESS
New York • London • Tokyo

The Mysterious Press, 129 West 56th Street, New York, N.Y. 10019

Printed in the United States of America

First Printing: January 1989

10 9 8 7 6 5 4 3 2

Library of Congress Cataloging-in-Publication Data

Clark, Dick, 1929–
    Murder on tour : a rock 'n' roll mystery / by Dick Clark with
    ————., created by Bill Adler.

      p.   cm.
    ISBN 0-89296-286-0
    I. ————. II. Adler, Bill. III. Title.
PS3553.L2814M87 1989
813'.54—dc 19   88-14730
                                                      CIP

This is dedicated to the ones we love.

Part I:

First City on the Tour

1

f I've learned one thing in the music business, it's never trust a guy who says "Trust me." But that's what Max Horton kept telling me as we approached the departure gate at La Guardia Airport to catch our flight to Minneapolis.

It was Friday, July 13th, a bad day to fly if you're superstitious. I'm not superstitious. But I'm deathly afraid of flying, and Max knew it.

Despite my inclination to distrust people, I was willing to make an exception in Max's case. Not only was he a guy you could trust, he once saved my life.

I know there are good people in the music business, but I've got good reason to be suspicious of all of them. I went from rock top to rock bottom all because of a guy I couldn't trust. His name is Del Barnes. My name. I'm the guy.

Ten years ago, in 1969, I had a band called Meet the Press. If you've never heard of it, you probably don't pay much attention to rock music. We had a hit song called "Rock 'n' Roll Register," a historical opus that paid tribute to the legends of rock, from Chuck Berry and Elvis Presley right up to the Jefferson Airplane and the Grateful Dead. To this day it still gets airplay on quite a few FM stations. It's a good song, if I do say so myself, but you probably shouldn't trust me on that. After all, I'm the guy who wrote it.

We released a single of it for AM airplay, and it spent the summer nestled in the number-two slot on the charts. The number-one hit was "In the Year 2525," by a duo named Zager and Evans. Theirs was one of those novelty songs about the apocalypse that seems to come along every few years. Surely you remember "Eve of Destruction," by Barry McGuire, from the summer of '65.

In the parlance of the music business, Zager and Evans are known as one-hit wonders. My band was light years better than they were, but I had a lot in common with them. I was a one-hit wonder myself.

It didn't have to be that way, and I've got only myself to blame. My shrink convinced me I'm a better man for admitting it. But that's not much of a consolation in the dark of night, when you're lying awake wishing you could have another shot, wishing you could go back and do it right this time, wishing the demons would go away and leave you alone, wishing you could finally put the past to rest and go to sleep.

Unlike other one-hit wonders, Meet the Press didn't die of natural causes. It got killed, and I'm the guy who killed it.

To understand what happened to us, you've got to understand what was happening on the music scene in 1969. There was a big concert in upstate New York that summer. A *big* concert. It was called Woodstock, but it actually took place about fifty miles from the town of Woodstock, which is where we were living at the time.

Before our recording contract came through, we spent a few years working straight jobs full time and playing music part time. We played at parties, at picnics, in small clubs, in people's garages. We played for spare change, for free, for the fun of it. Sometimes we played for drugs.

Our big break came in 1968. We made the jump from small time to the big time faster than you could say Do-Wah-Diddy-Diddy. It happened, of all places, at an outdoor wedding. We usually just played oldies at weddings, but we were feeling loose that day and did "Rock 'n' Roll Register." After the song, a short, chubby guy in sandals and a suit came up to us and said he liked our sound. He said he could get us an audition. The guy's name was Max Horton.

We didn't believe him, and that was the last time I didn't

believe Max. He proved true to his word, which is more than you could say for the two newlyweds. Six months later, when they were in divorce court, we were in the recording studio cutting our first—and last—album.

It took us about five seconds to quit our jobs and move to Woodstock. Three of us were college buddies who worked at a newspaper, which is how we came up with the name Meet the Press in the first place. The other member of the band, our chick singer, was a waitress named Karen Conner. When people asked if she was a journalist, she'd smile and tell them she only knew how to write checks. She had a beautiful smile and she sure knew how to sing. I thought she sounded like Billie Holiday, but maybe I was a little prejudiced. Karen was my fiancée.

We rented a huge yellow house, not too far from where the guys in Bob Dylan's band lived. They had an album coming out in '69, too. They called themselves simply The Band. They lived in a large pink house, and they had called their first album *Music From Big Pink*. As a joke, we called our house Big Yellow.

It was one wild summer. We played music, as the Kinks song goes, all day and all of the night. We took a lot of drugs. We didn't have a care in the world. We were living in a dream.

It seemed like the dream turned into a nightmare all of a sudden, but looking back later I could see it started to go bad the moment we hit the Top Ten. It was Max's idea to release a single. He was our manager and our producer, and we did pretty much everything he told us to do. Putting out a 45 seemed like a good idea at the time. The record company went for it, deejays went for it, the public went for it. We just went crazy.

For the first time in our lives, we had more money than we knew what to do with. We thought nothing of getting on a plane and flying down to New York City for lunch. We'd throw parties that lasted for days and invite the whole town. One day I bought six custom-made guitars. We were stinking rich. You don't realize what that phrase means until you've made a mess that you can't clean up.

I had smoked some marijuana in college, but I didn't really get into drugs until a few years after I graduated. I tried LSD, PCP,

MDA, and mescaline, but pot was the main drug of choice. We burned more grass in a week than suburbanites mow in a lifetime, but I had always thought I could handle it. I thought I could handle anything.

Until I got hooked on speed.

If you've never taken amphetamines, you don't know what you're missing. The bottom line is: not much. But it takes some people a while to get to the bottom line. It took me a long while— too long. When you take a hit of speed, your heart starts pounding like a big bass drum. You feel happy, energized, ready to boogie. You feel like nothing could ever go wrong. You think you're invincible.

Then you crash. Whoever thought up that word for it knew exactly what he was talking about.

By the time we went on tour in the fall of '69, our album was rising on the *Billboard* chart with a bullet, as they say in the record business. But the bullet was lodged in a gun that was cocked and aimed at my head. I was a total wreck. I had burned the candle at both ends for too long and was running out of wick. It seemed like the only way to keep the flame burning inside me was to take more speed. That's exactly what I did.

I finally hit rock bottom in Chicago, the third city on our tour. I hadn't slept for three days, and my body just refused to take it anymore. To say that I was irritable is like saying Attila the Hun had a bad temper. I was okay when we were playing, but offstage my buddies and I weren't buddies anymore. We weren't even on speaking terms. Karen and I were on more than speaking terms— we were shouting at each other. The wedding plans were all but dead. Max tried his best to keep things together, but he must have been wondering if it was all worth it.

We were supposed to play in Cleveland that night and our plane was scheduled to leave in two hours. I told Max I couldn't make it unless I got some rest. He arranged for a later flight. When the time came to leave, guess who still wasn't ready.

It was decided that the rest of the band would go on ahead. Max would stay behind and help me get my head together, and we'd take a later flight. I was asleep when he pounded on the door of my room and told me we wouldn't be making the trip to Cleveland after all. Three quarters of Meet the Press had met their maker five miles out of O'Hare. All the while the leader of the band was sacked out in a posh hotel room, a pathetic wretch. I hadn't hit bottom yet, after all. I was only beginning to crash.

Some people will never understand why I didn't attend the funeral. Karen's mother and father, I'm sure, will never forgive me. I'm not sure I'll ever forgive myself. My parents tried to understand, but they were understandably horrified by what had become of their son, the former "A" student who once had a promising career in journalism. They live in a world where r & r stands for rest and relaxation. Only Max Horton understood. He lives in a world where it stands for rock 'n' roll.

Max took me back home on a plane—not to Big Yellow, but to the split-level where I had grown up. For the shape I was in, he might just as well have shipped me home in a box. I went into a severe depression and didn't utter a word for three days. The doctor persuaded my parents to put me in a hospital, where I was treated and cured—with drugs, of course.

When I got out I set up living quarters in my old bedroom, the one that still had a New York Yankees pennant and a Chuck Berry poster on the wall. I was better. At least that's what my parents thought when they went away for a weekend and left me alone for the first time in two months. They had no way of knowing I had stolen the pills from the hospital.

I swallowed them as soon as I got back inside the house, moments after waving good-bye from the front porch. I'll never know why I began having second thoughts. It probably comes down to not having the guts to go through with it, but I like to think it was because I didn't want to let my parents down.

I called Max in New York and told him what I'd done. He told me to get to a hospital right away, but something in my tone made him think I wasn't going to take his advice. The next thing I remember, after passing out, is waking up in the hospital. Max was sitting at the foot of the bed, smoking one of his stinky cigars and reading a copy of *Rolling Stone*.

He called me a bunch of names and shouted and cussed at me

until a panicked nurse arrived with the doctor. I told them it was all right, I had it coming to me. He called me a coward and a selfish brat and told me it was time to get on with my life.

"Your problem is you went to college and got a degree, but you never learned one of the basic lessons of life," he said.

"What's that?" I asked.

He smiled and spoke through a purple haze of cigar smoke. "You never figured out that it's only rock 'n' roll," he said, beating a philosopher named Mick Jagger to the punch by a few years.

"I thought that *was* my problem—that I did think that way."

"Bullshit," he said. "If you thought that way, you wouldn't be drowning in self-pity, taking yourself so damn seriously."

I can't say that I actually believe in Max's philosophy. I'm not even sure that he does. If he did, he'd be a lot richer and wouldn't have the respect of so many people in a business where the first definition of the word is "tune by Aretha Franklin." But the sentiment works for him, and it worked for me. The only difference was, I never went back into rock 'n' roll.

When I got out of the hospital, I sold my guitars and donated the proceeds to an outfit that counsels people on drug abuse. I spent a year living with my parents until I moved out and landed a job at a weekly newspaper in New Paltz, a pretty little town in upstate New York with a hippie enclave that will last forever—or at least until the year 2525.

It's not the kind of place you should live if you want to stay away from drugs. I think I chose to live there because I wanted to make it harder on myself, to do my penance and pay my dues. I don't lecture people about drugs, but I tell my story to anybody who's willing to listen. I haven't taken anything since I got out of the hospital, but sometimes I go down to a bar at the end of Main Street and drink until they shut off the lights. Then I stagger home and sit in the dark, chain-smoking and drinking until the lights go out in my head.

No matter how bad I hurt the next day, I don't allow myself the luxury of taking an aspirin. In my mind, there's no such thing as a free concert.

I used to have nightmares all the time, but they eventually became less frequent. Basically, the dream was the same old song, with variations on the theme. I'm on a runway, carrying my guitar and chasing a plane. Sometimes Karen is standing on the wing reaching out to me, other times she's looking out the window and waving good-bye. I'm running so fast that I overtake the plane, but as I'm about to hop aboard, it lifts off and the handle to the door is just out of my reach. I'm left standing alone, watching as the plane bursts into flames against a sky of ominous black clouds.

I haven't had the dream for more than a year now. My shrink said that's a good sign. For that I was paying him seventy-five bucks a session. I never objected to spending the money, but when I told him I was starting to, he said that was a good sign, too. It meant that I was getting restless, that I was finally ready to get on with my life.

Four months ago, I got a call from my old friend Max Horton. We'd kept up with each other over the years, but it had been a while since we'd talked.

"You ready to make a comeback, Thelonius?" he asked. Max had given me that nickname after coming up to visit me once, because he thought I was living like a monk. Thelonius, he said, was the only Monk he ever liked.

"Not if it involves playing guitar," I replied.

"You? Play guitar? No offense, Del, but the only thing you and Eric Clapton have in common is you both have ten fingers."

He was right, of course. Max knows about musical talent. My skill was writing songs, not laying down licks. Nonetheless, I've never let him get off a wisecrack without returning the favor. "And the only thing you have in common with John Hammond is that your last name begins with H," I said.

"Why don't you come down from the monastery, Thelonius, before you've got no sense of humor left at all."

"Why don't you say something funny, and maybe I'll laugh."

"I'm starting a magazine called *Rock of Ages*."

"That *is* funny," I said, and started to laugh.

"Yeah, well, before you die laughing, let me tell you

something funnier," he said. "I need a staff writer and I'm thinking about you. You interested?"

"I'm on my way."

The woman at the check-in counter announced the final boarding call for the flight to Minneapolis. Her voice reminded me of Patti Page doing "Tennessee Waltz."

"Well, time to face the music," I said.

"Trust me," Max repeated as we walked toward the boarding tunnel. "There's nothing to be nervous about."

"I'm not nervous, Max."

"That's the spirit, kid."

"I'm petrified."

Max laughed, but he knew I wasn't joking. The last time I'd flown on an airplane was when he brought me home from Chicago. I had sworn off flying, just as I had sworn off taking drugs and playing guitar. The time had come to break one of my resolutions.

I guess one out of three ain't bad.

2

"See, what did I tell you?" Max said, lunging for a cigarette the moment the NO SMOKING sign went off. "There's nothing to be afraid of. It's much safer than driving a car."

"Don't give me statistics, Newton wasn't lying," I replied, borrowing from a Loudon Wainwright III song. It had seemed clever when I heard it, but the version now playing back in my head wasn't as funny as the original.

"You'll feel much better as soon as we get a drink," Max said, craning his neck in search of the flight attendant.

"Not for me. I had a beer in the lounge, that's plenty."

"Suit yourself, Thelonius. You've turned into a regular Boy Scout. I wish Marcy was with us. I'd have a lot more fun talking to her than you."

"The feeling's mutual," I assured him.

Marcy Hopkins was the staff photographer for *Rock of Ages*. Thirty years old, she was quickly becoming one of the best in the business. Max was lucky to have her. She also was drop-dead gorgeous and knew it, which made her the object of unrequited lust and the subject of idle speculation around the magazine office. Marcy was married, so most of the guys who hit on her knew they were exercising their libidos in futility. But lately the speculation had been that she and her husband were on the rocks. If they split up, people would begin hitting on her in earnest. I had been earnest about her since we met. That might explain why I never tried to hit on her. It also might explain why Marcy seemed to like me.

11

"I hope she got some good pictures," Max said. "I heard they practically had a riot there last night."

Marcy had left New York a day ahead of us and stopped over in Chicago. She had gone there to shoot a bizarre radio station promotion—a "disco demolition" at Comiskey Park, where the White Sox play baseball. Between games of a doubleheader, a deejay named Steve Dahl, who had a band called Teenage Radiation, blew up disco records brought to the ballpark by his listeners. The event turned out to be a huge success or an unmitigated disaster, depending on your musical tastes.

The promotion attracted a sell-out crowd, and few of those in attendance had come to see the game. Thousands of kids had charged into the field, and by the time they were done stampeding around, the place looked like it had been sacked by the Visigoths, or at least trashed by a heavy metal band. The second game was canceled, and the White Sox had to forfeit. I know I've got a bad attitude about Chicago, but it seems to me that they have more riots in that city than the Beatles had hit records.

I assured Max that Marcy had gotten plenty of good shots. I knew this for a fact because she had called me and told me so the night before. I didn't tell Max that part.

"If this doesn't put the final nail in the disco coffin, I don't know what will," Max said.

"I don't know," I replied. "I hear it's just starting to catch on in Iowa."

Max chuckled. Although he comes off like a seasoned New Yorker, he doesn't mind people knowing that he grew up eight miles outside of Des Moines. Back when he was managing my band, he once convinced a wide-eyed hippie girl that he was from a town called Resume Speed.

"Give Iowa a couple more years," he said. "I hear the Hula Hoop craze hasn't quite run its course yet."

Max had a martini while I nursed a ginger ale. I passed on the lunch offering, but by the time Max finished shoveling down something that the stewardess said was chicken, my nerves weren't as frayed as they had been. After ordering another drink, Max pulled an advance copy of the July issue of *Rock of Ages* from his briefcase. I had seen it in on boards, but this was my first look at the final copy. There was a picture of Bruce Springsteen on the cover, and feature stories on Blondie, Billy Joel, Fleetwood Mac, and a new band called the Knack.

"Hot off the presses," Max said. "The printer dropped it off last night after you left. I thought you'd like to see your first story. You did a nice job."

I shrugged. No matter how many pieces I write, I'll always get a charge out of seeing my byline. But this was only a short preview of a new band called Roots, and I had written it entirely from a press kit that was short on facts and long on hype. If one-tenth of the hype could be believed—and nine times out of ten it can't—Roots was the best rock 'n' roll band to come along in ten years. We would find out for ourselves soon enough, because we were on our way to Minneapolis to witness their debut concert that night.

"There wasn't much writing involved," I said. "I picked up most of it from the press release."

"Well, I liked it. You used lots of adjectives."

"There were lots of them in the release."

"Hey, don't start acting like a journalist on me. You don't want me to give you The Speech again, do you?"

The Speech was a running joke between Max and me. My first day on the job, he gave me a lecture on what he wanted. Any time he thinks I'm being too serious, he repeats The Speech. It goes something like this:

"I want creative writing, not investigative journalism. We're not the fourth estate. We're just doing this until we get rich in *real* estate. Think of the magazine as a service arm of the music industry. If we play our cards right, we'll go arm in arm to the bank. We're not here to cure cancer. If you want to be Woodward and Bernstein, go work at *The New York Times*."

At the end of The Speech I always remind him that Woodward and Bernstein work for the *Washington Post*.

"Same difference," he says. "Just be sure and use lots of adjectives and adverbs." I usually refrain from pointing out that he wouldn't know an adjective from an adverb if it punched him in the nose. Max has a very large nose. He says it helps him sniff out talent.

"I just hope you do as good a job on the next one," Max said, "because this is the biggest story in years." He made a mock toast with his drink and grinned. "And we've got the exclusive."

Max is a businessman, not an editor, so he wasn't exactly right about the "exclusive." Other writers would be covering the debut of Roots, but we were the only magazine with permission to travel with the band and do in-depth interviews. I had heard that the folks at *Rolling Stone* and *Circus* were hopping mad about the arrangement. But Max was right about it being a big story, and it was his connection that made it possible.

Roots was the brainchild of Chuck Darwin, arguably the most successful executive in the music business. He was also one of Max Horton's best friends.

A few months before, Darwin had rocked the music industry with the announcement that he was stepping down from his $500,000-a-year job as head of American Records, the biggest rock label in the world. Darwin's departure had been preceded by rumors of internal squabbling between him and the number-two man at American, Gerry Stillman.

Stillman and Darwin had been lifelong friends and partners. This was quite an achievement in a business where the average friendship lasts about fifteen minutes. Between the two of them, they had signed more hit artists than Elvis Presley had jumpsuits. But the relationship began to sour when they launched a band called Survive, which had two major flaws: a bass player named Gerry Stillman Jr. and a rhythm guitarist named Chip Darwin.

Chuck Darwin and Gerry Stillman were geniuses when it came to spotting talent, but it didn't take a genius to realize that talent was something their sons were sorely lacking. Word was that the size of their egos was inversely proportional to the range of their musical skills. Nor had they inherited their fathers' fondness for each other. No matter how much of American's money Gerry Stillman and Chuck Darwin pumped into promoting the band—and rumor was they had spent a bundle—Survive achieved exactly what it deserved: immediate extinction.

Following the breakup of the band, reports about a possible management shakeup filtered out of American. Most people in the know were betting that Gerry Stillman soon would be ankling, as they say in the business, to another company. Chuck Darwin put an end to the speculation when he announced that he was leaving to start his own label, Evolution Records.

A day later, Gerry Stillman became head honcho at American. The friendship officially ended and the feud officially began.

Within a week, three of American's top bands announced plans to record on Chuck Darwin's new label. Stillman said Darwin had lost his skill for finding talent and would have been pushed out of American if he hadn't jumped first. Darwin said Stillman only got to where he was because he, Darwin, felt sorry for him.

Their sons got into the act too, trading public insults every time a music writer felt like quoting them. Gerry Jr. said Chip Darwin only knew three chords. Chip retorted that Gerry Jr. didn't know how to put on his guitar strap. It all seemed pretty juvenile, but it was the most talked-about breakup in the music business since Simon and Garfunkel filed for divorce.

But perhaps the most surprising development that came out of the whole affair was Chuck Darwin's announcement at a press conference that he was putting together another band featuring his son Chip. The name of the band was Roots. They would go back to the basics, playing pure, simple, good old rock 'n' roll. They were not an oldies band, he stressed, but they would be playing original music in the mold of Chuck Berry and Buddy Holly.

Darwin predicted that Roots would be the most successful rock band of all time. Even allowing for the usual music-industry credibility gap between truth and hype, this was an extraordinary claim. Pressed by skeptical reporters, some of whom were snickering openly, Darwin stuck to his guns.

"Laugh all you want," he told them. "But I guarantee that you won't be laughing after you've seen Kid Lee."

Kid who?

Kid Lee, according to Chuck Darwin, was a young black guitar wizard, the most electrifying guitarist since Jimi Hendrix.

When someone reminded him that Jimi Hendrix was better known for playing acid rock than for rhythm and blues, Darwin said the comparison had more to do with stage presence than musical style. Kid Lee was not merely a guitar player, he said. He was a guitar "sorcerer."

In addition to Kid Lee, the band featured a black drummer named Jack Mitchell, whom Darwin described as having no peer in rock music; and a young blond singer and bass player named Tina Darling, who Darwin said combined the vocal talent of Ronettes leader Ronnie Spector with the soulfulness of Janis Joplin.

As one music writer who attended the press conference later told me, "It sounded like a dynamite band, if only Chip Darwin wasn't in it."

People in the industry were somewhat dubious, but Chuck Darwin managed to arouse their curiosity. Except for the press conference and the news release that rehashed it, there was no other information available on the members of the band. They practiced in private in Darwin's sprawling, secluded house in Minneapolis, and reporters were barred from rehearsals. Their album, *Rock for Real*, was slated to go on sale the same day as their debut concert. Radio stations, which usually get advance copies of records for airplay, would all receive the album the day it went on sale. To promote and commemorate the event, Darwin distributed more buttons than the total population of the United States. The buttons said: ROCK FOR REAL, July 13, 1979.

Darwin ran the risk of pissing a lot of people off, and he did. The strategy turned out to be a masterful public relations tactic nonetheless. In just four months, Roots had become the most talked-about band that nobody had ever heard. And a slick new magazine called *Rock of Ages* was leading the PR drum rolls, hyping the band in its "Hot Licks" section in each of its first three issues.

At some point I mentioned to Max that we weren't just a service arm of the music industry, we were practically a promotional arm of Evolution Records. He laughed and gave me The Speech. My sense of journalistic ethics gave me reason for pause, but it was, as Max likes to say, only rock 'n' roll. And to paraphrase the Rolling Stones, I was getting to like it.

As our plane began its descent into Minneapolis, Max and I had another round of cancer sticks. He reached into his briefcase and pulled out a mock-up magazine cover.

"This is just a rough layout for the cover of the next issue," he said. "What do you think?"

The design was a sketch of Roots, which would later be replaced with a color photograph. The headline said: THE BEST ROCK 'N' ROLL BAND IN THE WORLD.

"Isn't that coming on a little strong?" I asked.

Max stuffed out his butt in the ashtray and leaned his head back. "Yeah, maybe you're right," he said at last. "We'll put a question mark after it."

"Good idea. That's the kind of professional restraint that will win you a Pulitzer Prize someday."

"Screw the Pulitzer Prize. All I want is some ad revenue."

3

By the time we got to the baggage claim area at Minneapolis–St. Paul International Airport, my knuckles had regained their color and my heart had stopped impersonating Ginger Baker. Marcy Hopkins was waiting for us, as planned, and seeing her helped calm my nerves.

One of the nicest things about Marcy is that she looks good without even trying. She has jet-black hair and ocean-blue eyes, making her a living argument for why Sicilians and Swedes should marry and breed. Her hair was tied in a ponytail that ended in the middle of her back, and she was wearing a tight cotton dress that matched her eyes.

As we stepped outside into the afternoon sunshine, it was just like the good old days. There was a black stretch limo waiting for us. Hail, hail, rock 'n' roll.

Marcy laughed as Max and I bumped into each other while trying to open the door for her. The chauffeur, whose name, if you could believe the tag, really *was* James, beat us to it.

Marcy entertained us with stories about the disco demolition as we cruised up Interstate 35W toward downtown Minneapolis. In the distance, the IDS building towered over the city, reflecting sunlight back in our direction. It's only fifty stories high, but that's taller than any building west of the Mississippi River until you reach the West Coast. Leaning back and listening to Marcy, I could feel my anxiety about the plane ride fading away. It was a nice sensation. I had faced one of my demons and won.

Going to Minneapolis was something of a homecoming for

me. I attended the University of Minnesota in the early Sixties. It was a swell place to be during that period. Folk music was big then, and I spent a lot of the time when I should have been studying sitting in the Scholar Coffee House on campus, listening to guys like Dave Ray, John Koerner, and Leo Kottke. The most famous of the locals was a songwriter from Hibbing with the voice of a cement mixer. His name was Robert Zimmerman, but he was better known as Bob Dylan. He had split for New York by the time I got there, but they hadn't stopped talking about him by the time I left.

When we reached our hotel off the Nicollet Mall, Chuck Darwin was waiting in the lobby. Max waved to him as we entered behind James, who insisted on carrying all the luggage himself, including about five hundred pounds of Marcy's camera equipment. I gave him a five for his efforts, but I think he would have been happier if I had slipped him Marcy's room number.

Max and Darwin shook hands, then followed up with bear hugs. It was funny to see the two of them pressed together, because they had the same build—short and plump. I'm only five-ten, but Max thinks I'm a giant. Except for their hair, of which Max had close to none and Darwin had a full head of satiny silver, they could have passed for brothers.

Max released his grip, stepped back, and said, "Nice to see you, Charles." Darwin responded with, "Likewise, Maxwell." Then he angled toward us while Max handled the introductions.

"Del Barnes," Darwin repeated after he heard my name. "Max has told me a lot about you. I'm glad you're working for him."

I didn't think it was appropriate to remind Darwin that we had met at the magazine office three months before. He paused uncomfortably, as if he wasn't sure he should say what he was about to say. He did anyway. It was almost word for word what he had said the first time we met.

"I want to let you know that I think 'Rock 'n' Roll Register' was one of the best songs from the 1960s. It was just remarkable how you put all that history together in one song."

"Thanks," I said. "That was a long time ago."

"I'm still burned up that this jerk"—Darwin pointed at Max—"signed you on Columbia instead of American."

"You didn't offer enough money, cheapskate," Max replied.

Darwin turned to Marcy and said, "So you're the famous photographer."

Marcy blushed. "I'm a photographer, but I'm hardly what you'd call famous."

"Well, you will be soon. Max has been singing your praises, too. Of course I can't repeat most of it." He poked Max in the ribs. "I should warn you, Marcy, that you're working for a dirty old man."

"*Fat*, dirty old man," I corrected.

"Hey, watch that," Max warned. "Writers are a dime a dozen."

We checked in and got settled in our rooms, then met again a few minutes later in Max's suite, where we ordered a late lunch. Darwin wasn't hungry, but he happily joined Max in what might have turned into a martini marathon if there hadn't been pre-concert business to attend to.

As glad as Chuck Darwin seemed to be to see Max, I couldn't shake the impression that his main purpose in being there was to work us over with superlatives about Roots. One of the first things I noticed was the gold lapel pin he was wearing that said: SURVIVAL OF THE FITTEST. It was clear that the pin was something you were supposed to ask about, but he didn't give us a chance.

"The original Charles Darwin said that," he explained, fingering the pin. "I'm not a descendant of his, but I wish I was. I've spent my life in the music business, and let me tell you, it's nothing *but* a game of survival. If you expect to do anything more than survive in this business, you're destined for a big fall."

"I know," I said.

Darwin's face began turning red. "Yes. I guess you do."

I told him there was no reason to feel bad, and Max piped up with, "Yeah, don't worry, Chuck, this kid's skin is thicker than an old seventy-eight."

Darwin smiled, excused himself, and went to the bathroom. When he returned, he was sniffling slightly and rubbing his nose.

"Tell us about Roots," Max suggested as Darwin began to sit down. But by the time the words were out of Max's mouth, Chuck had decided to stand up instead and had already launched into a speech that we used to call a "rap" back in the Sixties.

"I've told you about my interest in Charles Darwin," he said. "When I was in college, I studied anthropology. It fascinated me. I was even thinking of majoring in it, but I went into business instead. It's partly because of Darwin that I decided to name the new label Evolution Records. But it also has a double meaning. Roots, you see, is the cornerstone of the label, and the concept behind the band is that we're finally getting back to the *roots* of rock 'n' roll. To me, that's a natural *evolution* following what we've been through—the Brit invasion in the Sixties, the psychedelic period, glitter rock or whatever you want to call it, and finally, the scourge of disco.

"In the early Seventies, the producers took over, and music lost its vitality, its originality. There was no *spark* anymore. If you ask me, there should be a law against the electronic drum machine. I think it's time to finally get back to our roots, and believe me, when you hear this band tonight, I'm sure you're going to agree that it's a *very* good idea."

I nodded. That's all you could do in response. Darwin made a lot of sense, but he was talking faster than a wind-up doll and there was no sign that he was winding down. He had sniffled a few more times, which put up a warning signal in my mind. Some people would have thought he was just an enthusiastic guy with a cold or allergies, but when you've seen the trouble I've known, other conclusions spring to mind. Chuck Darwin had powdered his nose with cocaine when he was in the bathroom. This might sound unlikely for a guy who's over fifty, but in the music business nothing is unbelievable.

"Now, let me tell you about the band," Darwin said. "Did you ever hear the story about how I discovered Kid Lee?"

Marcy and I nodded, because we had already heard it from Max, but Darwin continued anyway.

"It's three o'clock in the afternoon, and I'm sitting in my office in New York. One of the perks of being an industry bigwig is that you get to have offices in New York and L.A. I'm reading a memo or something when my secretary buzzes me and says two black guys are waiting to see me. Their names are Kid Lee and Jack Mitchell. She says she told them they can't see me without an appointment, but they won't leave and she wants to know if she should call security. Now I've had all kinds of crazy rock stars come into my office, so nothing fazes me. I mean, the week before, I had a visit from that guy who likes to bite off a chicken's head onstage. So I told her to send them in.''

Darwin let out a chuckle. "Well, you should've *seen* these guys. The one looks like he's maybe fifteen years old. He's short, thin, and he's got this innocent look on his face. The other guy is much older. He's big and mean and looks like he eats nails for breakfast. I ask them what they want and the little guy says they want an audition. So I ask what kind of music they play, and the kid says, 'Rock 'n' roll.' That was one of the funniest things—the kid did all the talking, while the other guy just stared straight ahead.

"Well, I press the kid a bit because that can mean a lot of things, and when I'm done trying to explain that he has to be more specific, he just nods and shrugs and says, 'We play rock 'n' roll.' Well, we're getting nowhere fast, so I ask if they've got a demo tape. The kid looks at me like he doesn't know what the hell I'm talking about, so I ask if they've got a band, you know, to find out where they're playing or something so I can give them a listen. The kid says they don't have a gig, but they've got their equipment downstairs in a van or something, and they want to go get it and give me an audition—*right there in my office!*"

Darwin was laughing hard at this point, and Max joined in with him. Even though we had heard it before, Marcy and I were grinning too. It *was* a good story. And it could only happen in the music business.

"Well, by this time," Darwin continued, "the only thing going through my mind is how the hell am I going to get rid of these guys. So I tell them they'll have to make a demo tape, send it to me, and I'll see to it that I personally get the chance to give it a listen. And I meant it, that wasn't just b.s.

"Well, that wasn't good enough. The kid looks like he's about to burst into tears, and the big guy's looking even meaner by the minute. I tell them I'm sorry, that's the best I can do, then I notice that the big guy's got a knife in his hand. Then I see that he's got *two* of them—he's got a knife in each hand! Well, I've got a gun that I keep in my drawer because you never know what kind of crazies you're going to run into these days, especially in the music business. So I'm starting to reach for it real carefully and I ask him real nice, put away the knives, we don't want any trouble. And you want to know what the kid says?

"He says, 'Those are his drumsticks!' "

Darwin was sputtering with laughter now, and Max was rolling on the couch. Being built like Max affords the possibility of actually rolling with laughter. Speaking between guffaws, Chuck Darwin told the story for another half-hour. And all the while this dutiful writer was furiously taking notes. It went something like this:

When Darwin arrived home at his house in Westchester that night, Kid Lee and Jack "the Knife" Mitchell were waiting for him. As Darwin pulled into his driveway, he got the benefit of a free concert right on his front lawn. Darwin's terrified wife had called the police as soon as Kid and Jack got there, but by the time the cops arrived, Chuck Darwin was already convinced that he had made the discovery of a lifetime.

As soon as he finished the story, Darwin hurried off to meet up with the band. We were scheduled to join him backstage in a couple of hours. The martinis were taking their toll on Max, who decided to take a catnap.

As Marcy and I left the suite, Max, who was still chuckling, said, "Chuck's a helluva guy, isn't he?"

We agreed, but as we walked down the hall, Marcy confessed, "There's something I don't like about that guy."

"Maybe it's his insincerity," I replied.

"Maybe it's his coke habit," she said.

"Oh, you picked up on that, too."

"Who could have missed it?"

"Max, for one."

"Well, you know Max. He thinks he's seen it all, but he doesn't have any idea what he's missed."

I was enjoying talking to Marcy and suggested that we go downstairs to the cocktail lounge. She begged off, saying she had to call her husband. It didn't sound like something she was looking forward to. Saved by her better judgment, I went to my room and lounged on the bed.

As I stared at the ceiling in my temporary home away from home, the old feelings started to surface, the ones I used to have when *I* was a rising star. I dismissed them as a case of pre-concert jitters, but something told me I might have made a mistake by getting back into the weird, wild world of rock 'n' roll.

I took some deep breaths to relax, and it must have worked. I drifted off to sleep with Bonnie Tyler's song "It's a Heartache" going through my head. When I woke up an hour or so later, the tune had changed to "Do Ya Think I'm Sexy?" by Rod Stewart, and Marcy was pounding on my door.

I thought she looked sexy, but I doubt she was thinking the same thing about me. There was a concert to go to, and I was back to my old habits—sleeping through the curtain call.

4

The traffic on Hennepin Avenue leading to the Guthrie Theater was tied up for two blocks. James flashed our VIP credentials to a beefy guy in an orange parka who waved us over to the shoulder and directed us past the other cars. As we cruised through the drive-up, we could see thousands of people gathered outside, waiting for the doors to open. I used to be amazed by the inconvenience people were willing to put up with to see me play. Ten years later, I still found it baffling.

Given the advance hype, the Guthrie was a small venue for the Roots debut. But that was also part of the Darwinian plan. By booking the band at small concert halls instead of huge arenas, he had virtually guaranteed a series of sell-out crowds for the tour. Any concert promoter worth his weight in phony gold chains knows that it's smarter to fill a small house than play a large hall that's half full.

Chuck Darwin's other strategy was to start the tour in the friendly environs of his hometown. From Minneapolis, Roots would be going to Milwaukee and Madison, then on to Chicago. The band would play a few more stops on the Midwest circuit— St. Louis, Kansas City, and Omaha—to build up momentum before they headed for the West Coast. The big finale, in two months, would take place in New York. Then it would be back to Minneapolis for one last homecoming stop, possibly out at Metropolitan Stadium in Bloomington if things went well.

James knew a back way into the complex, which includes the Walker Art Center, so we were able to get into the building without having to fight our way through the mass of humanity huddled outside the main gate. Depending on your point of view, it was either the servants' entrance or the VIP gate.

Once inside the back door, Max got the attention of a big brawny kid with tattoos on both his biceps and a coil of electrical cord on his forearm. His muscles rippled under a cutoff T-shirt that said: TED NUGENT—1976 TOUR. Ordinarily I would have given a guy in that outfit a wider berth than a runaway garbage truck, but he was surprisingly cordial, and helpful as well. He introduced himself as Tommy Ventura, the head roadie for Roots. He led us down a long hallway to the dressing room.

If you've never been backstage at a rock concert, you don't know what you've been missing. There's a spread of food and booze big enough to feed an army and intoxicate a herd of elephants. There's also a feeling of electricity in the air, as if something really important is about to happen. Sometimes the mood is loose, which is usually a good sign. Backstage before the Roots concert, the atmosphere seemed tighter than the head on a snare drum.

A swarm of sound and tech people moved in and out of the room, all looking like they had pressing business to attend to. Chuck Darwin was armed with a cocktail, laughing and chatting with a small group of people in the middle of the room. He looked pretty relaxed, but I had a feeling it might have been his presence that was making the band's support staff so nervous. Darwin bounded over and put his arm around Max as soon as he saw us. They talked for a moment, then Chuck led us through the crowd to meet his sons.

The first one we ran into was Danny Darwin. He was as short as his father, and though he was only twenty-five, it was apparent that sooner or later he would resemble him right down to the pot belly. At that moment, he just looked husky.

Danny was the producer of Roots, which made him responsible for the overall sound of their album. A good producer can make a band. A bad producer can break one. Danny also was the manager of Roots, which meant that he supervised all their bookings. He had played the same dual role for the ill-fated

Survive. Before Chuck Darwin left American Records, it had been assumed that Danny would rise in the ranks and someday take over as head of the company. But, as David Bowie might say, there turned out to be some "ch-ch-ch-changes" instead.

Chuck Darwin explained to Danny that I would be covering the tour for *Rock of Ages* and Marcy would be taking photographs. He gave us a peremptory nod, then waved at us with a can of beer.

"Not now, man," Danny said. "I promise we'll get you some time, but right now nobody but nobody disturbs the band. Got it?"

We told him we did and I added that it might be a good idea to hear the band first anyway. I don't think he got my sarcasm, but it wasn't lost on Marcy, who shot me a knowing smile. Although she was relatively new to the business, she had already dealt with her share of spoiled rock stars and aloof managers.

Chip Darwin was a couple of years older than Danny and tall by contrast to his brother and father. He was quite thin, but I was willing to bet his trim figure was not the result of careful dieting. His eye sockets were dark and hollow, which indicated to me that he might be in the habit of substituting controlled substances for vitamins and protein. When his father told him that I had played in Meet the Press and written "Rock 'n' Roll Register," he shrugged and said, "Yeah, I think I might've heard it."

Unless he had been living *under* a rock all his life, I was sure he had. Maybe I was being too quick in forming an instant dislike for the Darwin brothers, but I thought to myself that if I wrote an updated version of the song, you could be sure neither of them would be in it.

Despite Danny Darwin's temporary restraining order, his father led us across the room to meet Tina Darling, the much heralded but still unknown singer and bass player for the band. On the way he stopped to talk with a tall, wiry guy in a Grateful Dead T-shirt. The guy looked fifty, but I had a feeling he was only a couple of years older than I am, which would make him thirty-eight. He was chewing on his thumb, holding a cigarette in his other hand,

and panning the room with his eyes, as if he was waiting for something to go wrong.

"How do things look, Artie?" Darwin asked.

"Fine, I guess. So far so good, Chuck," the man replied. "I'd feel a lot better if the concert was over."

"Come on, relax, Artie," Darwin said. "Enjoy yourself for a change." He turned and introduced the man to us.

His name was Artie Crosby, and he was the road manager for Roots. It was no wonder he was worried. Any time something goes wrong at a gig, it's the road manager's butt on the line. Needless to say, Artie wasn't exactly overjoyed to meet us. To him we were just three more people to worry about.

At that moment, Tina Darling got up off her chair in the corner and moved slowly toward us in a pair of black high heels. Next to me, I heard Marcy mutter, "How does she walk in those things?" I didn't know if she meant the heels or her jeans, which looked tighter than the cellophane wrap on an LP.

Tina was making her debut without a bra, in a blue T-shirt that was as tight as her jeans. She had a full mane of golden hair that was parted on the side of her head and flipped over the top. The color was as natural as her name, which she had adapted from Darlengato. A lot of guys would have regarded Tina Darling as a bombshell, and beneath the glitz she was a very pretty girl. I thought it was a shame that she was trying so hard to turn herself into a rock goddess. As far as I'm concerned, it's the sound that counts, not the look. But I guess I'm a little old-fashioned.

Tina gave Chuck Darwin a big hug, and I caught him winking at Max over her shoulder. She was pleasant with us, but she had a bad case of the heebie-jeebies. She was bouncing on her heels and shaking so much that she spilled her drink.

"I'm sorry, I'm just so *up!*" she told us.

"That's okay, I understand," I told her.

"Wait a minute," she said suddenly, snapping her fingers. "Del Barnes. You were with . . ."

"Meet the Press," Marcy completed her sentence.

"Yeah, yeah, right, I know the song. Wow, that's great." She turned toward Marcy. "Were you in the band, too?"

"No, she wasn't," a voice from behind us said. As I turned to see who was speaking, Chip Darwin circled our group and put his hand on Tina Darling's shoulder. "The whole band croaked in a plane crash."

I met Chip's eyes straight on and thought about ending my second career in rock 'n' roll and his first right there on the spot. He stared back, a smug grin spreading over his face. Apparently he had heard of my band after all. I felt Marcy's hand grasp my wrist, her way of telling me to stay cool. I looked at her and nodded. As I continued staring at Chip Darwin, I realized that I might have been looking into a mirror of myself a decade ago. That thought helped me control my temper. I glanced to see if Chip's father was taking the scene in, but he was chatting away at Max. Max, however, never misses a beat, and he sent me his sympathies with a roll of his eyes.

"Wow, is that true?" Tina asked me.

"Yeah, I'm afraid it is."

"Wow, I'm sorry. That's a bummer, man."

Chip tugged at Tina's arm and pulled her away. We watched as they walked to the far corner of the room. Chip was still holding Tina's arm with one hand. He whispered in her ear, then she opened her hand discreetly and he slipped something into it. Just then, Danny Darwin strolled over to them and put his hand on Tina's unoccupied shoulder. Danny and his brother exchanged cool glances, then Chip walked away and joined a pair of young girls who were stationed against the far wall.

"What a jerk," Marcy muttered, careful that Chuck Darwin wouldn't hear her.

"Which one?"

"Yeah, you're right. Both of them, I guess. It looks like some interesting dynamics going on with them and Tina."

"I picked up on that, too."

I kept my eyes focused on Tina. As I expected, she put her hand to her mouth, then took a mouthful of her drink. I didn't know what Chip Darwin had given her, but I was sure it was supposed to make her feel good. She probably thought it would help her play better.

Chuck Darwin ushered us past the buffet table to meet the stars of the band, Kid Lee and Jack Mitchell. At least in my book they were probably the stars of the band. I'm sure Chip Darwin would have given you an argument about that.

The Roots press kit listed Kid Lee as twenty-six years old and Jack Mitchell as thirty-six. To look at them, you would have guessed that the ages were off by about ten years in either direction. Kid, with a smooth baby-faced complexion, didn't look a minute over sixteen. Jack the Knife, with a few days of growth on his chin, looked to be in his mid-forties. He also had a long history of scars on his cheeks—whether from street fights or adolescent acne, I couldn't tell. And I wasn't about to ask.

Jack sat perfectly still, staring straight ahead and looking like the guy Jim Croce might have been thinking about when he wrote "Bad, Bad Leroy Brown." His demeanor was actually pleasant, despite the fact that he said very little and barely cracked a smile—except when he shook Marcy's hand.

Kid Lee, by contrast, looked happier than a kid who's just discovered ice cream. He wore eyeglasses with heavy black frames and pop-bottle-bottom lenses. He was rocking back and forth in his chair, apparently humming a tune in his head while eating a sandwich that looked like it had a slice of everything on the buffet table. When he stood up, I saw he was shorter than Max. But when he put out his hand, the fingers were long and strong, the kind that are custom made for playing guitar.

"Glad to see you're eating well, Kid," Chuck Darwin said. "If I ate as much as you did, I'd weigh three hundred pounds."

Kid's head bobbed up and down. "Food's great, Mr. Darwin," he said appreciatively.

"What all do you have in there?" Darwin asked curiously. That would have been my first question.

Kid grinned. "I like to put the potato salad and the cole slaw right on the sandwich. That way I don't have to use a fork."

"It's his third one," Jack said matter-of-factly.

"Hey, I know your song," Kid told me between swallows. "It's a good song. Real good song." He hummed a few bars to show that he did know it, then turned to Jack and asked, "Wasn't that a good song?"

Jack nodded. "Yeah, good song."

I thanked them and asked if they were nervous about playing their first concert.

"Nervous?" Kid asked, puzzled. "Why be nervous? Playing music makes you feel good." He looked at Jack and laughed. "You nervous?"

The Roots drummer answered with a deadpan shake of his head. He didn't know the meaning of the word.

Just then, I heard a shout behind us. The buzz of conversation in the room ended abruptly. We turned to see Chip Darwin gesturing at a pair of guys who had just entered.

"Out of here. *Right now*," Chip snarled, adding a choice selection of four-letter words and all their possible adverbial and adjectival variations for emphasis.

The two men stopped in their tracks, then took a couple of steps back as Chip advanced on them. One of them looked about fifty, and the other was about half that age. The older guy was dressed in a three-piece pin-striped suit, and his companion wore blue jeans and a Doobie Brothers T-shirt. They were pretty much the same height and build, size-40 regulars. In fact, except for the variance in age, they were almost identical, right down to their beards, the only difference being that the older guy might have been keeping his hair black with the aid of Grecian Formula.

Chuck Darwin rushed across the room and stationed himself between his son and the two men, and Max followed slowly behind. Danny Darwin left his two young companions along the wall and joined his brother.

"Is that Gerry Stillman?" Marcy asked.

"They're both Gerry Stillman," I replied.

"Looks like double trouble," Jack the Knife said.

5

In the days when they were business partners, Chuck Darwin and Gerry Stillman had been nicknamed the Minnesota Twins after the baseball team that played in their common hometown. There was no physical resemblance, however, and it was actually Max and Chuck who looked the part of twins. Back in the Fifties, during the early days of rock music, the three of them had been friends when they were independent agents, working primarily for Chess Records. Chess was started as a blues label by a pair of brothers who operated after-hours clubs in Chicago, but they got into rock 'n' roll when they signed Chuck Berry.

To hear Max tell it, those were the good old days. To hear Chuck Darwin's tone, the good old days were dead and gone.

"What the hell are you doing here?" he demanded.

Gerry Stillman Sr. put his hands up and said, "We're not here to cause any trouble, Chuck. We just wanted to wish you good luck and assure you that there are no hard feelings."

Chip Darwin laid down another track of epithets, and before he could finish, Gerry Stillman Jr. answered with a verse of his own. It was the same bad harmonizing that had driven Survive's only album right into the remainder bins of a record store near you.

"We don't need your damn luck," Danny Darwin piped up, borrowing a few X-rated lyrics from his brother's last solo.

Chuck Darwin held out his hand to demand silence. His sons obeyed. "Danny's right. We don't need your lousy luck."

Before Darwin's ex-partner could respond, Max stepped between them to play the role of peacemaker, King Solomon with a New York accent. "I want all of you to cut the crap right now," he shouted. "You're acting like a bunch of damn fools."

That got everyone's attention. Then he zeroed in on Gerry Stillman. "It was a dumb idea to come here, Gerry. You should have known that. Why don't you guys leave before things get out of hand."

"Yeah, get the hell out of here," Chip Darwin added.

Max wheeled and pointed with his cigar. "Put a lid on it, Chip. Go tune your ax or something."

Max turned back to Gerry Stillman. "Whaddaya say, Gerry?"

Stillman nodded. "Okay, Max." He looked angry, and his son's face seconded the emotion. But I had a feeling sheepishness was taking over for all of them.

The fathers and sons glared at each other for a few more moments, but the battle of the blands was over. The Stillmans scowled one last time, then turned on their heels and left. The Darwins' eyes escorted them to the door.

Max put his hand on Chuck Darwin's shoulder. "Come on, buddy," he said, "let's go out front and leave the kids alone."

Most of the other people followed their lead, and the room cleared out quickly. Artie Crosby urged the stragglers along, saying "Okay, people, the show's over. The real show's about to begin."

The road manager was referring to the concert, but Chip and Danny Darwin were in the mood to play a second number. All of a sudden they flew into a tandem rage, shouting and cussing for at least a full minute. Their outburst reached a crescendo when Chip Darwin overturned a tray of sandwiches. He then vented his wrath on Artie Crosby, yelling at him to clean up the mess.

The road manager's face burned crimson and clover, then turned a whiter shade of pale as he got down on his hands and knees and began scooping up slices of cold cuts and mustard-sodden bread.

"Hey, Artie, be sure and hold the mayo," Danny Darwin said. He and his brother sputtered with laughter.

Back at our end of the room, Kid Lee was still working on his sandwich. "I guess Chip and Danny are really mad at those guys, huh?" he said.

"Yeah, I guess so," Jack the Knife replied.

As Marcy and I turned to leave, Artie Crosby called out, "Hey, you two. That's enough. Stop hassling the band and get going."

"Is he talking to us?" Marcy asked.

Indeed he was. When the master kicks the dog, the dog has to find someone to bark at.

"We're on our way out," I assured him. As we passed, we both handed him our drink glasses.

"What am I, the busboy?" he muttered.

Danny Darwin was still convulsed with laughter when we left the room with Tommy Ventura, the burly roadie, and made our way out to the front of the concert hall.

"The boys put on a pretty good show, didn't they?" I said.

Tommy shook his head. "Man, that's nothing compared to when I was traveling with Ted Nugent."

The house was packed and the audience was beginning to get restless. When Tommy went onstage to check the equipment one final time, the crowd sent up a roar of premature anticipation. I figured he had plenty of experience fooling audiences who mistook him for a member of a band.

Tommy stepped up to one of the mikes and said, "Cool your jets, gang, it's only me." The crowd booed in response and Tommy grinned.

Marcy and I hung around in the corner off the first row. She was planning to stay down in front and snap photos. I could've gone upstairs to Chuck Darwin's private box, but I wasn't in any hurry to get there.

"It's too bad you didn't get any pictures backstage," I said.

Marcy shot me a sly smile. "Who says I didn't?"

"You're kidding. How did you manage that?"

"High-speed film, long shutter time. To pull it off, you've got to have a steady hand." She held hers out to demonstrate. It was steady, all right, but it was something else that attracted my interest. Marcy wasn't wearing her wedding band. I didn't comment on it, but you can be sure I made a note of it.

Just then the lights went down, and the crowd let out another deafening cheer. This time it wasn't Tommy Ventura fooling them. A few seconds later, a spotlight came on. It focused on the left side of the stage, and the audience began stamping their feet. A minute later, Danny Darwin appeared from behind a curtain and walked out onstage toward the mike.

Danny stumbled, and I thought he was having trouble finding his way in the glare of the lights. It's a strange sensation being onstage, because you can't see the audience at first. It's even difficult to hear the music. That explains why rock bands have more technicians working on the sound panels than NASA puts on the control board during space flights. But as Danny Darwin began speaking, I realized he was having other problems.

Danny raised his arms to silence the crowd, waiting a few moments for the din to subside. "Man, oh, man, it's great to be here in Minneapolis tonight," he said. "What you're about to hear is the ultimate, you know, the realization of . . ." His voice trailed off as he groped for the right words. Even though he was shouting, you could detect a slur in his speech.

"Of a dream, man," he continued, finally finishing the sentence after a long pause. "Yeah, man, that's what it is—a *dream.*"

The crowd applauded again, and Danny giggled. When they quieted down, he said, "Wow, man, do I feel *good* tonight." The audience cheered some more, but this time it wasn't a full house of applause. Danny stared blankly ahead, not saying anything for at least half a minute. When you're speaking onstage, that seems like a lifetime's worth of silence.

Danny continued with a rambling speech, marked by long pauses and liberal use of "wow" and "yeah." Sections of the audience laughed occasionally, and the cheering had all but stopped. Danny started to explain the history of Roots, but kept stammering and stopping in mid-sentence until he lost his train of thought completely.

The halting speech reminded me of a live album from the early Seventies by Mike Bloomfield, the blues guitar player, and Al Kooper of Blood, Sweat and Tears. Their first album together,

Super Session, had been a big hit with the underground crowd, but the next one, *The Live Adventures of Mike Bloomfield and Al Kooper*, was a bomb. It was a live jam session that they had planned for months, but during Bloomfield's introduction, it was clear that he was almost too burned out to speak, no less play. It was a double-album set, but Bloomfield only played on one of the discs. They had to bring in guest guitarists to finish off the two-day concert. It was a damn shame to see all that talent go to waste.

At first I thought Danny Darwin was drunk, but after a few moments I realized that it had taken something far more potent to turn his brain into that kind of mush. I had plenty of experience from my glory days to draw on to make this diagnosis. Just thinking back on it made me start to shiver, and I was beginning to get a queasy feeling in my stomach.

Luckily for Danny, there was help waiting in the wings. As he stood gazing silently into the dark mass of the crowd, a vacant smile spreading across his face, Artie Crosby came out onstage to lead him off. He refused Artie's assistance, flailing his arms, and Artie wheeled frantically in search of more help. It came in the form of Tommy Ventura.

The roadie put one of his stovepipe-sized arms around Danny Darwin's shoulders and hustled him off. The baffled crowd began hooting and cheering wildly as Danny freed one of his arms from Tommy's grasp and waved to them.

Artie Crosby stepped to the mike and said, "Ladies and gentlemen, Evolution Records is proud to present the best damn rock 'n' roll band you'll ever hear. From this very town of Minneapolis, please welcome—*ROOTS!*"

At long last, the concert of the year was about to begin.

6

A thunderous round of applause shook the Guthrie Theater as the members of Roots bounded onstage. I could make out their outlines taking position at their instruments while the din of cheers continued for at least another minute. When the hoots and wolf whistles finally faded away, a single spotlight focused on Chip Darwin.

"Are you ready to boogie?" he asked the crowd.

"Yeah," they yelled.

"Are you feeling funky?"

"Yeah."

"Are you ready to rock 'n' roll?"

"*Yeah.*"

Another spotlight went on, this one illuminating Kid Lee, who was bent over his guitar. As he lifted his head, Chip Darwin played a chord. Kid answered with a slick guitar lick. Chip strummed another chord, and Kid answered with a longer lick. Chip strummed two more chords, then Kid answered with a single note, which he held until it reverberated throughout the hall.

Then Kid Lee began to play.

Kid's fingers danced up and down the full length of the fretboard, and the notes ricocheted off the walls like machine-gun fire. It took me a few moments to realize that he was playing the intro to "Johnny B. Goode." I take a backseat to no man in my appreciation of Chuck Berry, but Kid Lee's opening riff was much better than the original. It was as if he had taken a '57 Chevy and polished it into a shiny new Corvette.

Although all the material on the Roots album was original, Chuck Darwin had told us that they planned to play plenty of "cover" songs in concert. He said the band was so versatile that planned "sets" were not required, and the concerts would go according to the band's whims on a particular night.

The list of songs that Roots would cover was an eclectic mix from the late Fifties and early Sixties that would showcase the talents of the individual band members. Chip might do songs by Buddy Holly and Elvis Presley, while Tina would cover Patsy Cline's "I Fall to Pieces" and a medley of such girl-group hits as "He's a Rebel" by the Crystals, "Be My Baby" by the Ronettes, and "He's So Fine" by the Chiffons. Jack Mitchell could do an updated drum solo of Sandy Nelson's "Teen Beat," and he would sing a couple of numbers, including "Quarter to Three" by Gary U.S. Bonds and "Chantilly Lace" by the Big Bopper. Kid Lee was capable of dressing up any song with hot guitar licks, and the band even had a version of one of Bobby Darin's big hits, with the name changed slightly to "*Jack* the Knife."

At the end of the intro, Kid fingered the last notes with only his left hand, bowing and waving to the crowd with his right. At that moment all the lights went up, and the rest of the band joined in. Tina Darling danced over to Kid, then twirled and joined Chip Darwin at the mike for the vocals. By the time they got to the chorus, everybody in the house was singing "Go, Johnny, go." Any anxiety that Danny Darwin had caused was all but forgotten.

The crowd went crazy at the end of the song, but Roots wasn't done yet. Kid held the last note for about four measures, then switched gears and went into "Maybellene," driving the audience back into a frenzy. Chip and Tina alternated lines on the vocal and did a duet on the chorus. Meanwhile, Kid, who had barely moved a muscle during the first part of the medley, strutted back to the drums, where he and Jack the Knife took turns producing car-engine sounds. At one point, Jack tossed his blades in the air like a juggler, all the while working the bass drum and high hat with his feet and knocking the cymbals with his elbows. It was then that I realized what made Jack the Knife and Kid Lee so special. They weren't merely accomplished musicians—they were show-men.

Roots capped off the Berry medley with "Nadine." When the crowd noise finally died down enough for Chip Darwin to be heard, he said, with perfect understatement, "Now we're going to play a fast one."

Chip wasn't joking. Kid put his guitar into overdrive and they went into "Fast Talker," an original number that featured Kid on slide guitar.

You can't judge a band by only a song or two, but I could tell by the end of Roots' second number that Tina Darling was a good rock vocalist, even if she wasn't the reincarnation of Janis Joplin. Kid Lee definitely lived up to his advance billing. His fingers were so nimble as they darted over the frets that the notes he played seemed to melt together, all the while enabling you to hear each one as an individual sound. Jack the Knife's switchblades gave the drums an interesting dimension of sound, and Chip Darwin, despite his limitations, was quite capable of strumming the right chords. The overall result was a fresh, tight sound, the kind of music you could get up and dance to or sit back and marvel at.

After the band went into the third number, I waved good-bye to Marcy and made my way upstairs to the box where Chuck Darwin and Max were seated. When I had glanced up there during the opening song I could tell that Darwin wasn't enjoying the show. He wasn't seeing Kid Lee for the first time, and he must have been either annoyed or upset by his son Danny's wacked-out intro. You could be sure Danny would get an earful from his father when he made it upstairs—if he made it upstairs. Chances were good that he was already sacked out backstage, wishing he had refrained from ingesting any foreign substances.

Chip Darwin was introducing the next song and the band members by the time I reached my seat. Chuck Darwin was watching so intently that he barely noticed me sit down. When Chip was finished speaking and the band resumed playing, Darwin said, "At least *he's* not drunk."

"I don't mean to meddle into your personal affairs, Mr. Darwin, but I don't think Danny was drunk," I said. "I think he must have taken something that he couldn't handle."

"You mean drugs?" There was anger in Chuck Darwin's voice.

I nodded.

"Well, you're wrong. Danny doesn't take drugs."

I was surprised by his reaction, considering that he had been tooting up himself only a few hours before. But I realized that could have been one of the reasons for his denial.

"But you're right about one thing," Darwin added. "It *isn't* any of your business."

Max and I exchanged looks. It seemed like he was always getting caught in the middle of something. He had told me previously that he didn't like either of Chuck Darwin's kids— even if they had called him Uncle Max at one point in time. I could have challenged Darwin, but I let the subject drop for Max's sake.

During the instrumental break in the fifth song, Kid Lee dropped to his knees and played a guitar solo that was sheer magic. It seemed all the more masterful because he appeared so out of place onstage with a rock band. He looked like he should be home eating milk and cookies and doing his homework. At the end of the number, the fans went wild and Kid took a sweeping bow. Tina danced over to him and planted a kiss on his cheek. Whether I liked Chuck Darwin or not, I had to admit that the band was every bit as good as he said it was.

All of a sudden, Kid walked to the front of the stage and held out his hand to a woman in the front row. She took it and he helped her up onstage. She was a tall woman and she was wearing a flowing Indian-print robe, sandals, and large, droopy earrings. She looked like a gypsy.

"Hey, what's going on?" Chuck Darwin said, as much to himself as to Max or me. "What's he doing?"

It was as if the woman had materialized from thin air.

Down onstage, Chip Darwin was gazing up at his father, arms extended in a posture of bafflement. Chuck waved his hands in response, trying to direct him. "Get her off there," he shouted. But, of course, his son could not hear him.

Kid Lee led the gypsy woman to the microphone. "This is my *mama*," he said, holding her hand in the air.

The crowd let out a howl of whistles and appreciative hoots, and some people in the audience started to hold their lighters in the air, a new trend at concerts.

Kid's mother leaned forward and said, "I'm Grace Lee and I just wanted to thank you all for being so nice to my son, Kid. He's the baddest guitar player in the whole wild world!"

I doubt there's ever been more noise in the Guthrie Theater than there was at that moment. A large part of it was coming from the mouth of Chuck Darwin, who had gotten to his feet and looked like he was contemplating a suicide leap through the glass to the floor below.

"Where the hell did she come from?" he demanded. "This is the first time I've even *heard* about this woman!"

"Hey, hey, calm down, Chuck," Max said. "The show's a smash. The Kid's a hit. What more can you ask for?"

"Kid's job is to play guitar. Chip's the leader of the band. That's how it works."

Max shot me a sidelong grin. I was doing my best to suppress mine. I kept my attention focused down on the stage, where Chip Darwin had come over to have a word with Kid Lee. Kid nodded, shrugged, turned, then launched into an up-tempo guitar riff and duck-walked back across the stage à la Chuck Berry. It took me a minute to realize it was a cover of "Blue Suede Shoes" by Carl Perkins.

Back upstairs in our box, Chuck Darwin was still fuming. "What's going on here? Where's Danny? Where's Artie? Why aren't they here yet?"

A moment later, he got the answer to three of his questions. Tommy Ventura arrived at the box, red-faced and puffing. "Mr. Darwin, there's trouble backstage," he said, taking in gulps of air between each word. "Danny collapsed. Artie's down there with him. He's in bad shape, Mr. Darwin. We called an ambulance.

It's a bad scene. One of the Larsen sisters is down there right now giving him mouth-to-mouth."

Chuck Darwin listened to Tommy's report without asking any questions, then rushed out of the box. Max got up to follow. I asked if he wanted me to come with him. I didn't see that I could be of any help, and the last thing in the world I wanted to see was somebody on a drug overdose. I think Max must have realized that.

"No, that's okay," he said. "You stay here."

Tommy Ventura lagged behind, still trying to catch his breath.

"What do you think he took?" I asked.

"Beats me. Danny doesn't do drugs. I mean, he doesn't even like to smoke a joint usually. He just drinks. Tina and Chip, man, now they're a different story. They're eating crank all the time."

Crank, I knew from my own experience, was another name for speed. It could kill you no matter what you called it. Recalling the scene Marcy and I had observed backstage, I asked, "What's the story with Tina and Chip? Are they an item?"

"Oh, that's all messed up, man. They were together, up until a couple days ago. But then Tina got all pissed off, so now she's with Danny."

"What was she pissed off about?"

"Man, she caught Chip messing around with the Larsen sisters."

"Who are they?"

"Groupies!" Tommy cleared his throat and spat, as if saying the word left a sour taste in his mouth. "Take it from me, man. Don't mess around with groupies. You don't know what you might catch."

I thanked Tommy for the advice, then suggested that he better get back downstairs before he caught hell from Chuck Darwin.

"Yeah, you're right," he said. "I just can't stand the thought of anybody actually dying, you know? Are you coming, too?"

"No, I think I'll stay right here where I am."

"Yeah, I don't blame you, man. It's a good show, isn't it?"

It was a great show, and it just kept getting better. I left the box and joined Marcy downstairs before the first encore. The fans called Roots out for three more. They finally finished the night with "Runaway" by Del Shannon. It was a smart pick because Bonnie Raitt, another local favorite, had done a cover of it on one of her recent albums.

It was a perfect pick for my mood, too. With all that had happened, I almost felt like running away myself.

7

The spectacular debut of Chuck Darwin's brainchild was overshadowed by the death of his younger son. The announcement that Danny Darwin had died from an apparent overdose of barbiturates—in drug vernacular, reds—was the lead story on the morning news at the start of a dreary day when, as the old blues song goes, "the sky was crying" over the Darwins' hometown.

Against Max's advice, Chuck had done a live TV interview that morning. Despite overwhelming evidence to the contrary, Darwin insisted that his son did not take drugs. He suspected that someone must have put something into Danny's drink without his knowledge, and he demanded a thorough police investigation. I figured this was probably a chilling thought to the band members and their entourage. If there's one enduring truism in the music industry, it's that cops and rockers don't mix.

While Chuck Darwin's comments were easily understood as the product of emotional distress, he made another statement that could not be easily dismissed. Without directly accusing his ex-business partner and friend of being responsible for his son's death, he did say that Gerry Stillman and Gerry Jr. "had some explaining to do."

It was a ridiculous thing to imply, especially for a person of Darwin's stature, who was usually slick and poised when dealing with the media. But some people handle grief by lashing out and blaming others. This is familiar terrain for me, because I almost destroyed my life blaming myself. The debut of Roots was one of the most important events in Chuck Darwin's professional life. In a matter of hours, he had gone from the peak of anticipation to the depths of despair. I knew exactly what he was going through. But I had a feeling Gerry Stillman might not be so understanding.

Later in the morning, while his father was sedated and resting, Chip Darwin took it upon himself to issue a public apology on Chuck's behalf and correct the impression that his brother's death was anything other than an unfortunate accident.

It may have only been my natural journalistic skepticism, but I had some lingering doubts about Danny Darwin's death myself. Unlike his father, I wasn't harboring suspicions of foul play. But Marcy and I had talked further with Tommy Ventura after the concert the night before, and he had repeated his belief that Danny Darwin steered clear of drugs. There was even a joke going around the Roots entourage that if Danny died young, it would be as a result of a motorcycle accident, not a drug overdose. He owned three bikes and had totaled two of them. Miraculously, on both occasions, he had walked away without breaking any bones.

Fueled by a rapid succession of half-quart beers, the roadie also filled us in on the relationship between Danny and Chip. He said the brothers were very competitive and had a rivalry going for their father's attention. It was common knowledge that Danny, the businessman, was Chuck's favorite. The rivalry had become even more heated of late when Tina Darling dumped Chip in favor of his younger brother.

"It was Chip's own fault," Tommy said. "He didn't treat Tina with any respect. He should've known better than to start messing around with a pair of groupies. But he's the kind of guy that just does whatever he feels like, no matter who gets hurt. Tina didn't even like Danny that much. She just did it to make Chip jealous."

The dispute reached a peak a few days before, when Danny and Chip got into an argument during a rehearsal. Tommy hadn't been there, but he'd heard about it from Tina. They'd squared off and were ready to mix it up, but Jack Mitchell stepped in to separate them.

"I'm the kind of guy that, if somebody wants to go at it, I don't back down from anyone," Tommy said. "But I sure wouldn't want to mess with Jack the Knife."

"That makes two of us," I told him.

On our way back to the hotel, Marcy told me she thought Tommy Ventura had a terrible crush on Tina Darling.

"What makes you say that?"

"Didn't you notice the way his face lit up every time he mentioned her name?"

I told her I hadn't, and she said it was because I was lacking in female intuition. That was part of it for sure, but there was another reason for my inattention. I was somewhat distracted wondering if Chip Darwin disliked his brother enough to try to kill him. Probably not, but there was some precedent to consider, starting all the way back with Cain and Abel.

I thought it more likely that Tina had given something to Danny and he had taken it willingly. One of the most prevalent misconceptions about drugs is that they can't hurt you the first time you take them. That's like saying you can't get pregnant if you do it with the lights out. From what I had heard about Danny Darwin's reckless motorcycle rides, I figured he was the sort of guy who never does anything in moderation. It sounded as if he had enjoyed looking death in the face. This time, on Friday the 13th, death winked and his luck ran out.

When I mentioned my suspicions about Chip to Max on Saturday afternoon, he raised a cautioning finger. We were on our way to the airport to pick up Chuck Darwin's wife, Sylvia. I thought it was strange that Darwin wasn't meeting her himself, but Max had offered to do it so that Chuck could get some rest. He invited me along to have someone to drink with while waiting for her flight to arrive. I agreed, on the condition that we didn't have to go in a limo.

"For all I know, you may be right about Chip," Max said. "But I don't want you going around asking a bunch of questions about it. Chuck's got enough problems as it is. The last thing he needs is for you to start suggesting that one of his sons killed the other on account of some rivalry. I want you to stay as far away from all this as possible. The sooner we can put it behind us, the

better off everybody will be. I want you to spend your time
thinking up a positive angle for the story. If you want to be
Woodward and Bernstein—"

"I know, I know. I should go to *The New York Times*."

"*Washington Post*," he corrected, forcing a smile. "Sorry I
got hot at you."

"Don't worry about it. I know this hasn't been easy on you."

"It's been a goddamn nightmare," he said, shaking his head.

We had plenty of time to spare, so I took the long way out
Cedar Avenue. As we passed a record store on the West Bank
near the University, I saw some material for the positive side of
my story. Despite the drizzle, there was a line of people outside
the store. There was no doubt about what they were waiting for.
Every radio station in the city had been playing *Rock For Real*,
and last night's concert was the talk of the airwaves. While
Danny Darwin's death was a tragedy for his family, it had only
served to heighten the public's interest in the band.

I let Max off at the terminal, and by the time I had parked the
car and joined him in the cocktail lounge, he was working on his
second martini. He suggested I have one for my nerves, and I told
him someone had to be sober enough to drive. I settled for a
ginger ale and gave him my cherry.

I didn't know what Sylvia Darwin looked like, but I had no
trouble picking her out of the line of people coming off the flight
from New York. She was the one wearing sunglasses. Sylvia was
probably fifty, but she wore her years well. She was tall, thin, and
well tanned, but her skin didn't have the leatherlike quality that
usually afflicts sun worshippers. She had light blond hair that
hung loose to her shoulders, and there was no evidence of
bleaching. When she took off her shades, despite the lingering
redness that made it obvious she had been doing a lot of crying
recently, her soft green eyes had a radiant sparkle. Not so long
ago, Sylvia had been a strikingly beautiful woman.

The tears started flowing freely when she and Max embraced,
and I began wishing that I had taken Max up on his martini offer.

"Oh, Max, what would I do without you?" she sobbed.

Max led Sylvia down the corridor with his arm around her

while I followed a step behind them with her carry-on bag. She had calmed down by the time I brought the car around, and it soon became clear that Sylvia Darwin was the sort of person who can hold up well under pressure.

"When the kids were little, I always used to worry about them," she said. "You always have it in the back of your mind that something bad might happen. Finally, when they get older, you stop worrying. You realize that you can't protect them anymore—even if you wanted to. You think they don't need protecting. Then the next thing you know . . . I guess when God's ready to take them he just—"

Sylvia's voice began to crack, but she was fighting it.

"It's okay, Syl," Max said. "Go ahead and have yourself a good cry."

I watched in the rearview mirror as Max took her hand and squeezed it. "I'm so glad you're here, Max," she said. "It's so comforting to know that no matter what happens, I can always count on you. I don't know what Chuck and I would do without you."

We drove in silence for a few minutes until Max said, "Did Chuck mention anything to you about Gerry Stillman?"

"Yes, that's one of the other terrible things about all this. I just hate the idea of Gerry and Chuck feuding. I can't understand it." Sylvia Darwin raised her voice. She was talking to me now.

"You know when Max and Gerry and Chuck were younger, they were such good friends. They were practically like the Three Musketeers. They did everything together. They were so competitive with each other, but they respected each other, too. They used to go off to all these little towns in the South on talent trips. At least that's what they called them—talent trips.

"Normal men go away on fishing trips. These guys went off to catch musicians. I thought it was just an excuse to go on vacation and leave the girls behind. But I've got to admit, they used to find people. That's how Chuck got his start."

"Is that when you were working for Chess?" I asked Max.

"Yeah, but even before that, we used to do it."

"I remember one time," said Sylvia, "when Chuck discovered

some band and signed them to a contract and then Max got so mad at him, they didn't even *talk* to each other for six months!" I watched in the mirror as she turned to Max. "What was all that about, Max? You remember."

"It's a long story," Max said. "It happened a long time ago. You don't want me to go into it."

"Well, the good thing is that you patched up your differences. Not like Chuck and Gerry. It all started when they tried to put Chip and Gerry Junior in the same band. They didn't understand that you can't force your children to continue the friendships you established. I tried to explain that to Chuck, but he refused to listen. I have a feeling that this one isn't ever going to get straightened out."

Sylvia directed her thoughts at me again. "That's the difference between Chuck's friendship with Max and his friendship with Gerry. They're both so stubborn, but Max isn't the type to let things simmer. That's why I know that he and Chuck will always be friends. You don't realize how lucky you are to know this guy."

"Oh, yes I do." For the rest of the ride I told Sylvia Darwin *my* history with Max. When I finished, I said, "That's why I'm so sorry about your son's death, Mrs. Darwin. It's too bad somebody like Max wasn't around to save him."

"Please call me Sylvia," she said. "I feel enough like an old lady as it is."

When we pulled up to the Darwin house across from Lake of the Isles, a police car was parked in the driveway.

"That's strange. I wonder what the cops are doing here," Max said.

We found out as soon as we got inside. Chuck Darwin, his son, and Artie Crosby were sitting in the living room talking to a pair of detectives. Chuck rose from the sofa and hurried over to where we were standing. I expected him to embrace his wife, but instead he went right to Max and showed him a note he was holding in his hand.

"Look at this," he said, thrusting the paper in Max's face. "Artie found it in the mailbox."

I read the note over Max's shoulder. It was written in crayon. It didn't take long to read. There were only five words: ONE DOWN, TWO TO GO.

"Doesn't this prove Danny was killed?" Darwin said. He still hadn't acknowledged his wife.

I knew the note didn't prove anything, but I thought it was a better idea to let the cops clue him in. I just stood there in silence, wishing I was somewhere else.

8

A huge, dark cloud still hovered over the Twin Cities when Sunday morning arrived like a wet slap in the face. As I sipped room-service coffee and read the paper, I couldn't shake the feeling that the cloud wouldn't be going away until Roots left Minneapolis. Even worse, I had a feeling it would be following the band out of town.

Exactly when they would be leaving and where they would be going was still up in the air. I had spoken to Max when I got up, and he said Chuck Darwin was considering canceling the tour.

"What would that accomplish?" I asked.

"Nothing. I think Sylvia and I managed to talk him out of it. He's just been too upset to make much sense. He'll be seeing things a lot clearer after a good night's sleep. He might have to cancel Milwaukee, but things should be okay for Madison on Tuesday. Meanwhile, Artie Crosby's going nuts waiting for Chuck's decision."

"He's always a little nuts, isn't he?"

"Yeah, but this time he's finally got a reason."

"How's Sylvia holding up?"

"Like the Rock of Gibraltar. She's one great piece of work."

"I noticed. Though it seemed to me that Chuck wasn't exactly thrilled to see her."

"Oh, you noticed that too. Chuck's a great guy, believe me, but I don't think he appreciates how lucky he is to have her. I've told him that before. I've told Sylvia, too. He just gets distracted, I guess."

That didn't seem like much of an excuse to me, but I didn't say anything. Max could already tell that I didn't share his affection for Chuck Darwin, and I didn't want to put him in the position of defending his friend any more than he had to.

"What's going on with the police?" I asked.

"Oh yeah, that. They're going to question everyone who was backstage before the concert. That includes you. And I think we'd all be better off if you kept your speculation about Danny and Chip to yourself. That'll only stir up trouble."

"What about the note?"

"The chief of detectives doesn't seem to think there's much to it. Like any successful guy, Chuck's got his share of enemies. With all the publicity surrounding Danny's death, he thinks it could be some nut playing a practical joke."

"Sounds like a guy with a great sense of humor. What did Chuck say about the cop's theory?"

"You kidding? He practically went through the roof. He threatened to have the guy's job if he didn't investigate. Sylvia finally pulled him aside and told him to cool it."

"Well, you can't blame him for being worried."

"No, I'm not saying that. It's just that, even if somebody did kill Danny, how would they ever be able to prove it? You couldn't prove it in a million years unless somebody actually saw somebody forcing the pills down his throat. And the chances of that are slim to none. Far as I'm concerned, the only thing to do is beef up security. I'll feel a whole lot better once the funeral's over and we can get out of town."

"That makes two of us." And there are probably a few more, I figured.

"So how did it go last night?" Max asked.

At his suggestion, Marcy and I had gone to see a concert by a local kid at a club. His name was Prince, and Max had heard about him from Gerry Stillman. Stillman and Darwin had both been thinking about signing him, but somebody from Warner Brothers had apparently beaten them to it.

"The guy definitely has a distinctive sound, kind of a cross between disco and rock. I think he's going to be a winner."

"I don't care about that. How did it go with Marcy?"

In fact, it had gone rather well, but I was paying for it in a big way the morning after. When the concert was over, we had gone to a bar on the East Bank near the University, where Donna Summer and Blondie were pounding out of the jukebox. I had consumed more than my share of bourbon and Marcy had matched me drink for drink. With our defenses down from the alcohol, we had done some badly needed soul-searching together. I was a little foggy on the details, but I could clearly recall Marcy playing "I Will Survive" by Gloria Gaynor and telling me it had been her anthem of late. When we got back to the door of her room, I gave her a good-night kiss that probably lasted a little longer than it should have. But she didn't seem to have any objections, and I was hoping she wouldn't come up with any retroactively when the reality of daylight began playing its inevitable drum solo in her head.

In answer to Max's question I said, "Wouldn't you like to know."

"Yeah, I would, smartass," he replied. "When you get to be my age, kicks just keep getting harder to find. You have to get them vicariously."

"Age has nothing to do with it, Max."

"It doesn't?" he said hopefully.

"No. In your case, it's more a question of weight."

Max laughed. "Oh, I see. So you think maybe I need to put on a few pounds?"

"As long as you put it on in the right places—like on top of your head."

I rang off before he could formulate a response, then dialed Marcy's room. "How's your head?" I asked when she answered on the fourth ring.

"Which one?"

"That bad, huh?"

"Actually, I don't mind. It's one of those sweet hangovers," she said, paraphrasing Diana Ross.

"I know exactly the kind. But if it gets to be too much, the

Mayo Clinic's only an hour away. I'll gladly ride in the back of the ambulance with you."

"No, that won't be necessary. I've got my own method of treatment—two aspirin every hour and a hot shower every half hour."

I didn't tell her about my treatment, the one that involved suffering through without pharmaceutical support. I was afraid she might think I was perverse.

"You know what else will straighten you right out," she said. "Being questioned by a cop."

"Oh, so you had your visit already. Did he come on the hour or the half hour?"

"The half hour. I was dripping wet when I answered the door. It was kind of creepy. I felt like the guy was undressing me with his eyes."

"If you don't mind my saying so, it sounds like the natural reaction of a red-blooded American boy."

"I guess I should take that as a compliment. Thanks, but I get a little nervous when somebody's wearing a gun."

"That sounds like a natural reaction, too. How long was he there?"

"Only a few minutes. Del, I think I might have made a mistake. I didn't mention anything about Tina and Chip. Do you think I should have?"

"I don't know. I've been trying to decide that myself. Max says we should leave well enough alone. It makes sense not to say anything, I suppose."

But when a six-foot five-inch cop named Sven Peterson came knocking at my door shortly after noon, I decided to go against Max's advice. I told Peterson about seeing Chip Darwin pass something to Tina and then watching Tina put it in her mouth. I told him what I had heard about Chip and Danny feuding and about Danny Darwin chewing out Artie Crosby after knocking over the tray of sandwiches.

Peterson took it all down on a small notepad, nodding occasionally as if to let me know he was still awake. He seemed bored by the whole affair, bored by everything. When I asked him about the note, he shrugged and said, "Who knows? You can never tell. Probably a crank. But maybe someone has an ax to grind. Proving it will be next to impossible."

As he turned to leave, he asked me if I would be traveling with the band. I nodded and he smiled. "You must know Miss Hopkins then," he said.

"Sure."

"I'd like a piece of that."

"I'll pass along the message," I said, opening the door.

"You will?"

"Yeah, I will. She'll probably leave town and never come back."

Sven got a baffled look on his face, but he didn't ask me to explain. I don't think he picked up on my sarcasm. I had a feeling he wouldn't be solving any murder—if there was a murder to be solved. But after he left, another thought crossed my mind regarding the crayoned note.

On the surface it appeared that there were two possible explanations. Either it was a crank playing a practical joke or someone was actually carrying out a vendetta against the Darwin family. But if, as I suspected, Danny Darwin had gotten the drugs that killed him from his brother, perhaps Chip had written the note in an effort to deflect any possible suspicion that might be cast at him.

After a moment of deliberation, I concluded that that scenario was pretty farfetched. I decided to stop playing detective and leave that to the professionals—like Sven. Instead, I took a hot shower and thought about Marcy.

9

If Danny Darwin's funeral on Monday morning had been a rock concert, it would have been a huge success. It certainly looked more like a rock concert than a funeral outside the white wood-frame church on Lyndale Avenue, where swarms of teenagers had been gathering for hours in advance, huddled in the light drizzle that continued to fall. It had been the same story the night before at the wake, when visitation hours had been extended to accommodate the overflow crowds.

The Darwin family had received hundreds of telegrams from people in the music industry and enough flowers to start their own conservatory. Despite his suspicions to the contrary, Chuck Darwin had reluctantly accepted the police's finding that his son's death had been accidental. The overwhelming public response had convinced him to continue the Roots tour, dedicating it to Danny's memory. Monday night's gig in Milwaukee had been canceled, but Roots was scheduled to play in Madison on Tuesday and Chicago on Friday.

I was inclined to suspect, as Tommy Ventura had pointed out the night before, that the large turnout probably had more to do with people's hope of glimpsing rock celebrities than with their sense of loss over the passing of Danny Darwin. A couple of radio stations had reported on rumors that the Bee Gees and the Doobie Brothers might be coming, and there was also talk around town that Donna Summer was a distant cousin of Kid Lee and might show up to play with him at the funeral. This probably explained why more kids had gone to the airport than to the funeral home the night before, and why, when we arrived at the church, many of them were holding stacks of record albums and had their pens poised.

Nonetheless, the publicity surrounding the Roots debut and Danny Darwin's death had caused a considerable stir around the country. The album had already sold out in the Twin Cities, and Artie Crosby was feverishly trying to get more copies shipped in from the distributor. Throughout the rest of the country sales were said to be brisk, despite the fact that radio stations had only been playing the record for a couple of days.

As Marcy and I made our way up the walkway to the church, it was also clear from the buzzing in the crowd that those people who had come out to see Roots were most interested in catching a glimpse of the young, diminutive guitar player Kid Lee and his mysterious mother, whom local deejays had taken to referring to as Amazing Grace. When they got there with Jack the Knife a minute or so after we did, a cheer went up outside the church.

It was a lucky thing, Marcy pointed out, that they arrived before the Darwins, who had remained back at the funeral home for a private moment before driving to the church.

"You're right about that," I said, recalling Chuck Darwin's blow-up at the concert Friday night when Kid Lee had brought his mother up onstage. It was one thing for Kid to steal the show at the concert, but it would be quite another to occupy center stage at Danny's funeral. As far as I knew, in the aftermath of Danny's death, the issue had not been discussed. But I had a feeling it was sure to come up again.

Kid signed autographs, engulfed by the waiting throng of predominantly teenaged girls. Jack Mitchell maintained his customary dour expression, but he obligingly carved his nickname, Knife, into album jackets with one of his switchblades. Meanwhile, Marcy and I stood with Grace Lee on the church steps under cover from the rain.

It was my first chance to get a look at Kid's mother close up. From my distant vantage at the concert, she had appeared to be overweight and I had guessed her age to be at least fifty. Standing on the church steps, I could see that it was the flowing dress she had worn that added a few pounds. Today she had on a black dress in the same style, but the outline of her shoulders was visible beneath it, making it clear that she was actually just a big-boned woman. She had large brown eyes set back into her face, giving the impression of lingering sadness and a dimension of experience that usually comes with advancing age. The creases around her eyes were wide and had already started turning into wrinkles. The overall effect was to make her appear a few years older than she probably was. If, as Chuck Darwin had said, Kid Lee could be thought of as a sorcerer, his mother could pass for a high priestess.

"You must be proud of your son," Marcy told her.

"Oh, yes I am. He's got so much talent and he's such a good boy."

"Where did he learn to play guitar so well?" I asked.

"Oh, he's got music in his blood, passed on by his daddy. He started him playing when he was such a little boy." She grinned, revealing a row of teeth crumbling from neglect. "He started him playing before he could rightly *walk* almost."

I had the impression that Kid's father was long gone. Details on Kid's background had been sketchy, as evidenced by the fact that nobody seemed to realize until the concert that he even had a mother.

"His father was a musician? What instrument did he play?" I asked.

"Oh, he played guitar and banjo and violin. Practically anything that had strings on it, he could play."

"Where did Kid grow up?"

"Oh, he was raised up outside of Memphis in a little town called Olive Grove. That's over the border in Mississippi. Then after Bumble died—"

"Pardon me. Bumble?"

"That's right. That was my husband's name, Bumble. Short for Bumblebee, which was his nickname on account of people said when he played he buzzed just like a bee. He really did, too. That was no joke. His real name was Lee, just like Kid and me, but everybody called him Bumble. Anyways, we moved on when

Bumble passed away. Kid was only six then and we went on down to Mobile, being I had kin there. Then a few years ago—I really don't remember exactly how long it was—we moved over to Athens in Georgia, which is where I got a sister living, and that's when Kid begun to play professional."

"What's Kid's real name?" Marcy asked.

Grace Lee answered with an uncomprehending look, then said, "Why, his name's Kid, of course."

Marcy shot me an embarrassed glance. I returned a smile. I was about to ask Grace Lee how Kid and Jack had found their way to Chuck Darwin's office in Manhattan, but just then she turned and called to her son, who was about twenty feet away, still surrounded by fans. All the while she had been talking to us, she seemed to be keeping one eye on her son.

"Kid," she said, "we best be going inside the church now."

"Okay, Mama," her son replied. A squeal of protest went up as he pulled away from the group of admirers.

Grace Lee stepped forward and addressed the crowd, her soft-spoken voice giving way to surprising volume. "You let Kid go inside now, folks. This is a time for praying, not for having a party. Be mindful that we all got to pay our respects to the dead."

The crowd parted politely, and the Roots guitar player and drummer made their way up the steps. When Kid got to his mother, she put her arm around her son and shouted to the crowd, "Ain't he bad?" The cheers and laughter left no doubt that they all agreed.

"Not a moment too soon," Marcy said, touching my shoulder.

I looked down to the street in time to see a black limousine pulling up to the curb. Out stepped Chuck Darwin and his wife, along with Max, Tina, and Chip. Behind them was a hearse. All of a sudden I got a queasy feeling in my stomach and I began to break out into a sweat. I didn't have any feelings of closeness for Danny Darwin, and the idea of attending his funeral now seemed inappropriate. More than that, I was reminded of another funeral ten years ago, one that I had been expected to attend but didn't.

I must have turned pale, because Marcy grabbed hold of my arm and asked, "Are you all right, Del?"

"It's nothing," I replied. "It'll pass." As she studied my expression with a probing gaze, I was tempted to tell her what was going on inside my head. But I knew I wouldn't be able to put it into words. I had tried numerous times before—on paper— but it never seemed to come out right.

I was still feeling weak and my hands were shaking when Chip Darwin, Artie Crosby, Tommy Ventura, and a guy I didn't recognize walked slowly down the aisle carrying the casket with Chip's dead brother inside. When I had asked Max why Kid and Jack were not selected as pallbearers, he had said that Chuck Darwin asked them to be, but they didn't seem to want any part of it.

The minister gave a short sermon, which had a genuine ring of sincerity because he was a friend of the Darwin family. He invited the congregation to join him in prayer, then Chip Darwin walked to the podium with an acoustic guitar. He played Elton John's song "Daniel," which seemed almost as if it had been written for the occasion, then Tina joined him in leading the crowd in "Let It Be." When they returned to their seats, the minister directed everyone to their hymnals for the words to "Rock of Ages."

Despite my agitated state, the spiritual had a calming effect almost as soon as the organist started to play. The blend of voices in the church made for a sweet harmony as the pallbearers picked up the casket and carried it out. Over the sound of my own singing, I could hear one voice ringing out, rising steadily above all the others.

It was a powerful voice, strong but soothing, steady but unwavering, with a rich texture that seemed almost to emit warmth on the low notes and chills on the highs. I wasn't the only one who was aware of it, because I could detect a few voices dropping off around me. I stopping singing, preferring to close my eyes and listen as the other voices dropped off one by one until finally, as we neared the last verse, only the one voice remained. I opened my eyes and watched the stunned expressions on the faces of those around me turn to peacefulness as we all listened to the powerful strains of Grace Lee's booming tenor vocal.

On the final verse, even the organist stopped playing, and the only sound that could be heard was the haunting voice of Kid's mother echoing through the church until it seemed that even the old wooden rafters were shuddering in astonishment. In the eerie silence that followed, it seemed like everyone in attendance had been touched deep inside. As the people filed out of their pews, some now weeping, it was clear to all that we had witnessed something very special. Danny Darwin had been sent off to his final resting place with the magical energy of music carrying him on his way.

It was such a moving experience that no one spoke of it again, as if to do so would tarnish its significance. After the burial, there was a small gathering back at the Darwin home. I didn't feel like attending, but Max had insisted that it would be the respectful thing to do. He turned out to be wrong.

I've never understood why people feel compelled to have parties after funerals. I suppose it's their way of saying farewell to remorse and welcoming the return of normal life. It makes sense in a way, but it's just not my style. Marcy and I were chatting on the front porch, watching the sun starting to peer through the clouds and finally chase the drizzle away.

Max came out to see us, accompanied by the two young girls who had been hanging on to Chip Darwin backstage before the first Roots concert. I knew from my conversation with Tommy Ventura that these were the dreaded Larsen sisters, but I didn't know their first names.

"Here he is," Max said, pointing at me with the hand that wasn't holding the martini.

The Larsen sisters came right up to me, elbowing their way past Marcy. They had changed from their funeral garb into their party clothes—tight faded jeans and T-shirts. Each of them was wearing a ROCK FOR REAL button. Tommy Ventura's advice about staying away from groupies probably made good sense, but I had to admit the Larsen sisters were cuter than a pair of puppies.

"Hi," the taller one with brown hair said, extending her hand. "My name's Vicki Larsen." She let out a giggle. "And this is my younger sister."

"I'm Suzi," the blond one said, "but you spell it S–U–Z–I." "My name ends in I, too," Vicki added.

As I took their hands, Marcy stepped forward and offered hers. "I'm Marcy—with a Y."

"Max said you used to be a rock star, too," Vicki said.

I nodded in response and shot a silent snarl at my friend Mr. Horton. If looks could kill, there would have been another funeral to plan.

"Yeah, he told us all about the plane crash," Suzi added. She wrinkled her nose. "That just sounds so *icky.*"

"It was," I assured her, as Marcy leaned in and said to me, "I think that's I–C–K–Y, but it rhymes with Vicki."

Had it been anyone else but the Larsen sisters, I probably would have been offended by Marcy's rudeness. But the girls were too busy giggling and maybe too stoned to be insulted. And I enjoyed the notion that Marcy, in addition to being offended in principle by the Larsen sisters, might have been a trifle jealous as well.

I smiled at Marcy and spoke to Max. "I think you should check on the age of consent in this state before you do anything foolish."

"Me? You kidding? I'm too old for that stuff."

"Well, it sure is exciting meeting you," Vicki Larsen said to me. "Maybe you'll give us a private concert some time." She looked at her sister and they giggled in unison.

I took a step back and replied, "Sorry, I don't play anymore."

"You don't? Why not?" Suzi asked.

"I just don't—that's all."

"It's because he's too busy being a *fink.*" I looked up to see Chip Darwin step out onto the porch behind Max. Tina Darling was trailing behind him.

I had the distinct impression that Chip Darwin didn't like me. I didn't particularly care, because the feeling was mutual. But as he moved past Max and drew a bead on me, I was worried that he might start some trouble that I wouldn't be able to get out of gracefully.

"You've got a big mouth, Barnes," Chip said, pointing his finger at me.

"Hey, what's this all about?" Max asked.

"He was telling lies about us to the cops. Wasn't he, Tina?"

"Yeah, that's right." Tina didn't sound very sure of herself.

"Come on, there must be some kind of misunderstanding here," Max said.

"There's a misunderstanding, all right. And I'm about to straighten it out."

I wasn't scared of Chip Darwin, but the last thing I wanted to do was get in a fight with him. I had done my share of fighting back in my dark days, and most of the time I had ended up on the seat of my pants. On those occasions when I hadn't, I felt like a fool afterward anyway. As Chip started with the preliminaries of trying to stare me down, I took another step back, and felt the railing of the porch behind me. There wasn't much room to maneuver.

"Cut the crap, Chip," a voice said off to my right. The voice had a ring of authority to it. In focusing my attention on Chip Darwin, I hadn't noticed Tommy Ventura come out onto the porch.

Chip turned, gave Tommy Ventura a long look, then sneered. "Since when do *you* tell *me* what to do? You're just a flunky around here, pal."

Tommy swaggered forward. It was obvious that he wasn't feeling like a flunky. "You wanna piece of him, Chip, you're gonna have to fight me first."

As Chip Darwin sized Tommy Ventura up, I could see the Adam's apple constricting in his throat. The sound of the gulp it made was clearly audible. Fear is very democratic. It doesn't make a distinction between flunkies and superstars.

"Don't do it, Tommy," I said. "He's not worth it." With that, I moved with Marcy along the railing. Tommy held out the palm of his hand, and I slapped it on my way past him. "Thanks, I owe you one," I said.

"Don't mention it," he replied. I had a feeling Tommy had been wanting to set Chip straight for a while now.

"Why don't you guys both shake hands," Max suggested.

I shook my head and kept going down the steps. Out of the corner of my eye, I caught sight of Jack the Knife standing in the doorway. For the first time since I had met him, he actually had a smile on his face.

Part II:

Second City on the Tour

10

Minnesota is known as the land of 10,000 lakes, but its neighboring state Wisconsin has plenty of water, too. There are 8,500 lakes in Wisconsin, three of which are in Madison, the state capital. The downtown section of the city is only about twelve blocks wide, a narrow wisp of land nestled between the glistening waters of Lake Mendota and Lake Monona. The old white-marble capitol building is set on a hill at the center of the city, visible from almost any vantage on the streets that branch out from it like spokes on a wheel. For my money, Madison is the prettiest city in the Midwest.

Although it's less than half the size of Minneapolis, Madison has a big enough population to support a thriving music scene. That's because it has the right kind of population. More than a quarter of the 150,000 people who live there are college students. A friend of mine who attended school there once told me that Madison led the country in two demographic categories: most beer consumed and most books read per capita. I doubted that anyone actually bothered to keep those kind of statistics, but one look at the bookstores and bars along State Street told me that it wasn't worth disputing the point.

Most college towns empty out during July and August, but many of the students at the University of Wisconsin preferred to stay in Madison. It's a great place for the young at heart during the summer, but not for the faint of heart during the winter.

The sun was shining and the lakes were dotted with sailboats when we pulled into town shortly after noon. While the flight out from New York had helped alleviate my fear of flying, I didn't see any reason to try my luck again until it was absolutely necessary. I opted to make the five-hour drive in a rental car, following Tommy Ventura in the equipment truck. By evening, when Marcy and I arrived at the Civic Center, a sinister line of storm clouds was getting ready to dampen the city's spirit. I didn't need Creedence Clearwater to tell me there was a bad moon rising.

It was madness again outside the concert hall. The show was sold out, and kids who didn't have tickets were offering to pay double to kids who did, but they weren't finding many takers. A pair of luckless guys in Foreigner T-shirts got so "Hot Blooded" about being shut out that they had to be handcuffed and hauled away by a squadron of police.

No matter how ugly the mood was outside the arena, it was nothing compared to the demeanor inside, or more specifically, backstage. As Marcy and I tried to enter the room, Artie Crosby put his arm across the entrance to block our way.

"Sorry," he said, "new security measures. Only authorized personnel permitted backstage."

From my vantage, I could see the Larsen sisters seated on either side of Chip Darwin, who was lounging on a couch and drinking a can of beer. Marcy must have seen them, too.

"If that's so, what are the Bobbsey Twins doing in there?" she asked.

"Friends of the band." Artie was looking right past us.

Recalling the scene backstage at the first Roots concert, I didn't really have much desire to go into the room. But I had a job to do, and doing it well involved getting a sense of the atmosphere before the concert.

"I think we qualify as authorized personnel, Artie," I said.

"How do I know that? If I make an exception for one person, I've got to make an exception for everybody."

"We're doing an article on the band. We've got Chuck Darwin's permission."

"How do I know that? Do you have a note?"

Marcy and I looked at each other in disbelief. "Do you have a list?" she asked.

He did, but our names weren't on it. There was a good chance that Artie had put together the list in the first place.

"Do you know where Chuck Darwin is?" I asked.

"I got no idea. Maybe he's upstairs in his box. I got enough things to do without having to keep track of everybody."

There was no disputing that Artie Crosby was being pulled in a dozen directions at once, but it was getting a bit tiresome having to listen to him complain about what a tough job he had. Just then Tommy Ventura sauntered up behind us.

"What're you guys doing hanging outside here in the hallway?" Tommy asked. "Why don't you come inside and have a brewsky?"

"Maybe we can go in as friends of the roadie," Marcy said to me.

Tommy looked puzzled. "Hey, what's the matter? C'mon, Artie, these guys are okay."

"Who says so? Are you in charge of the door now?"

"Mr. Darwin says so." I barely caught sight of Tommy giving Marcy a wink. "I just talked to him a minute ago."

Artie Cosby frowned, then let out a disgusted sigh. "Well, okay," he said at last. "But if there's any trouble on account of them, it's your ass, not mine."

"Sure, that's cool."

As we stepped past Artie ahead of our musclebound guardian angel, Artie called after Tommy, "You shouldn't be back here, either. You should be out front watching the equipment."

"I'm just going to get a screwdriver, okay? Tina asked me to tighten her guitar strap."

I wondered if Artie Crosby's comments about security were a cover for hostility directed at me. After my encounter with Chip Darwin after the funeral, it figured that I might be persona non grata. But I gave him the benefit of the doubt anyway, thinking his attitude could be symptomatic of his general state of paranoia. Whatever his motivation, there definitely was a smaller crowd backstage in Madison than there had been at the concert in Minneapolis. I counted a dozen people in all, band members included.

Chip Darwin saw us enter but pretended he didn't, even after I gave him a neutral nod. One of the Larsen sisters—to be honest, I couldn't remember their names—waved to me and I waved back. Afterward, Chip whispered something in her ear, and they both broke into laughter.

"What's so funny?" her sister squealed.

Chip leaned over and clued her in, for which he got the identical response. I tried to ignore them, but Marcy whispered, "I think they're having a laugh at your expense."

"The best things in life are free," I replied. But I was going to be earning my money when it came time to interview Chip Darwin. I had taken lots of notes, but I had decided to wait until after the second gig before doing any formal interviews. But there probably wouldn't be a good time to talk to Chip.

In the far corner of the room, Kid Lee and Jack the Knife were talking to a guy with a ponytail who was writing notes on a steno pad. I assumed the guy was a writer for one of the many underground newspapers in town, but he might have worked for the mainstream press. Ten years after Woodstock, Madison still was a haven for hippies.

Kid was pretty much blocked from view, but I could see one of his hands. It was holding a sandwich. At least it was a sandwich to Kid. To anyone else, it would have been a salad bar. Jack was directly in my angle of vision. When I waved, he answered with a barely perceptible nod. When Marcy waved, he almost managed a smile.

Tina Darling was just finishing an interview with another reporter along the wall across from where Chip Darwin and the Larsen sisters were slouched. She came over and stood next to us and Tommy. He had gotten his screwdriver but was pausing to chug down a can of beer.

"Tina, I'm just about to go out and tighten that strap for you," Tommy said, holding up the screwdriver.

"Thanks, Tommy, you're a lifesaver," she replied. "I don't know where this band would be without you."

"It's nothing. You know I'd do anything for you." Tommy wiped his mouth with his hand and grinned. "And I do mean *anything*."

"Oh, Tommy," Tina said in a deep, dreamy voice. "I just love it when you talk dirty to me." She put her hand on the roadie's bicep. "*Feel* the muscle on this guy," she said to Marcy.

Marcy grinned sheepishly but followed Tina's instruction. Tommy's face turned beet red under the attention, but he managed to boast, "I can handle two chicks. No problem. What do you think, Del?"

"Tommy, I think even you might have your hands full with these two."

He grinned, then finished off the beer. "I might die trying, but it would be worth it."

Just then, another volley of laughter went up across the room, where Chip Darwin and the Larsen sisters were having their photo taken. Chip was mugging for the camera, opening his mouth and roaring like a lion as he pretended to bite off the blond Larsen sister's ear.

"I gotta go get some air," Tina said. As she turned and walked from the room, she clicked her heels loudly. This was obviously intended to catch Chip Darwin's attention, but it didn't work. He was busy holding his hand a few inches in front of Vicki's—or was it Suzi's?—chest. The optical illusion in the photo would look like he was getting to second base.

"The atmosphere seems a little thick in here tonight, Tommy," I said.

"This is nothing compared to what happened at the sound check this afternoon," he replied, lowering his voice. "Chip was treating Tina like garbage. Man, I was this close"—he held an inch-thick thumb and forefinger a millimeter apart—"to going up there and slugging the jerk. I mean, man, I don't need this job, you know? There's a thousand bands out there I could work for. Chip was flirting around with the groupies, you know, just screwing off, wasting time. Meanwhile we're trying to get the sound right. I mean, the acoustics in this place aren't that good, man. Finally, Jack the Knife lets him have it. He got him good, man."

"What happened?" Marcy asked. "Did he hit him?"

"No, nothing like that. But Chip's over goofing around with

the Larsen sisters and Jack says—I mean, he was *shouting,* man. He says, 'Boy, get your white ass over here right now and start playing that ax or I'm gonna break it over your head.'"

"Then what happened?"

"You kidding? What would you do if Jack the Knife was yelling at you? He went right over there and started playing, man. No more screwing around." Tommy laughed and shook his head. "Well, I gotta go out front and see if I can find Tina. Catch you later, man."

We watched Tommy leave, then the guy with the ponytail walked over and put out his hand. "You're Del Barnes, aren't you?" he asked.

"Yeah, that's right." I shook his hand.

"Mitch Beswick," he said. "I'm the music writer for the *Journal.*"

I introduced him to Marcy, who then took her leave to go take some photos of Kid and Jack.

"I saw your last concert in Chicago," Mitch Beswick told me. "You guys were great. I'm really sorry about what happened."

I offered Mitch a cigarette, then lit one for myself. We chatted about the old days for a few minutes until Tina and Tommy returned to the room. Artie Crosby announced that it was time for everybody to clear out.

As Marcy and I were about to leave, Chip Darwin called out, "Hey, Kid, I've got to talk to you about something." Chip was tapping his fingers on the arm of the couch, and I got the impression he was expecting Kid to come to him.

The request didn't seem to register with the Roots guitar wiz, who had his hands and mouth full working on another salad bar. Kid just sat there gazing at Chip, waiting to hear what he had to say.

Chip got out of his chair slowly, then ambled across the room. "I just wanted to remind you that tonight, I do the talking. Okay? It's nothing against you personally, but I just don't think it's a good idea, you know what I mean?"

Kid stared at Chip Darwin blankly. It was clear that he had

heard Chip, but he continued eating without giving any indication that the directive had struck a chord.

Chip tried again. There was a trace of frustration creeping into his voice. "What I mean is . . . what I'm saying is, I don't want you bringing your mother up onstage tonight. Do you understand?"

Kid finished chewing and swallowed deliberately before saying, in a barely audible voice, "Why?"

"Because it's not the right way to do things."

"Why?"

"Because it's just not a good idea."

"Why?"

Chip Darwin looked like he was ready to knock over a tray of food again. "Because I said so, Kid, that's why. Do you understand?"

"Uh-uh, Chip. I sure don't."

Chip Darwin let out a sigh, then pointed his finger at Kid Lee. His hand was shaking, and his voice was trembling as he cranked up the volume. "Your mother's not coming up onstage. You *got* it?"

It was only then that Jack the Knife rose slowly to his feet and entered the conversation. "If the boy wants to bring his mama up onstage, the boy brings his mama up onstage. *You* got it?"

Chip Darwin stared at the large man towering over him. Maybe it hadn't been such a good idea to start a band with a guy who played drums with switchblades after all.

In Max's absence, the role of peacemaker fell on the broad shoulders of Artie Crosby. "You know, Chip, I think it's kind of a good idea," Artie said. "I think it really works."

Chip Darwin wheeled and stared down the manager. "I think it doesn't matter what you think."

Marcy leaned in close to me and whispered, "What do you think?"

"I think it's time to go find our seats."

She smiled. "Great minds think alike. Let's go."

11

Out in the packed arena, the audience was getting restless. The mood changed as soon as the members of Roots came onstage and took their positions under the enormous banner that said: IN MEMORY OF DANNY DARWIN. They wasted no time going into "Lie to Me," the first cut off their album, which was being considered for release as a single. They went right into another tune from the album, then followed it with Tina belting out Del Shannon's "Runaway." Whatever problems the band had offstage, they left them behind when they got out in front of the lights.

Chip Darwin introduced the band, then wandered to the rear of the stage to get another guitar. Most guitarists like to have at least two. They'll tell you that different instruments give them distinctive sounds appropriate to certain songs, but it's mostly a matter of ego. I know. I used to play four of them.

I wasn't paying close attention to Chip, so I didn't really see what happened until a few seconds after it happened. From my vantage near the far end of the stage from where Chip had been playing, I could hear his scream penetrate the noise of the crowd. By the time I looked up to see why Chip had screamed, he was already flat on his back. The guitar was on top of him, and he was gripping it. It was as if the guitar had attacked him and he couldn't let go. In fact, there was no way he could have pried his hands loose from the guitar. Not with a six-hundred-pound amplifier on his chest.

It was a small amp compared with some I've seen, but it was

heavy enough to break your foot if it tipped over on you. The amp had been stacked atop another that was about six feet tall. From that height, it could crush a person to death.

The crowd gasped in horror, the loudest collective gasp I've ever heard. Marcy yelled in my ear, "What the hell happened?" but before I could answer she moved closer along the stage and began clicking pictures frantically. I suppose I should have been worrying about Chip Darwin, but the only thought going through my mind at that moment was that this might be Marcy's chance to shoot an award-winning photo.

Up onstage, the members of the band rushed to Chip Darwin's side. Artie Crosby and Tommy Ventura appeared out of nowhere, charging out from behind the curtain on the side of the stage. Tina, on her knees, looked out into the crowd and screamed. Her voice was a strangled sob amidst the noise in the arena, but I could make out her words: "Help! Somebody, help!"

I looked up toward the box where Max and Chuck Darwin were sitting. It was empty. The gasping in the crowd had given way to a steady murmur of whispers. Taken together, the whispers comprised a pounding din.

Tommy Ventura, Artie Crosby, and Jack the Knife tried to lift the dead weight of the amplifier off Chip Darwin's chest, but it wouldn't budge. Then the roadie and the drummer braced their shoulders against it and pushed with all their strength. This time the amp gave way, and they succeeded in tipping it over on its side. As Artie Crosby lifted the guitar off Chip, I could see that the fretboard had snapped and the frame was wet with blood. Apparently the sharp edge of the fretboard had punctured Chip's skin. Exactly where and how deeply, I couldn't tell.

Tommy and Jack lifted Chip Darwin and carried him offstage by the side exit. Tina was still on her knees weeping. Kid Lee stood over her, shaking his head in disbelief.

Even though I hadn't seen the accident, I knew full well what had happened. Somehow the patch cord to Chip Darwin's guitar had gotten caught around the amp. When he encountered resistance as he stepped back from the amplifier, he must have tugged hard. With gravity and leverage working together, it

wouldn't have taken that much effort to pull the amp down—
especially if someone had set it up in a precarious position.

I could see when Jack and Tommy lifted him that Chip had
been knocked unconscious. If he was lucky, the guitar had
cushioned some of the impact and he might only be in a state of
shock. But he'd have to be awfully damn lucky. The way things
had been going on the Roots tour so far, I didn't think that was
too likely. I figured Chip Darwin was as good as dead.

It only took the crowd a few minutes to turn fickle. Some
people were holding their lighters aloft, others were beginning to
chant the band's name, still others were starting to jeer and boo.
They had paid good money to see the show, and they expected to
see the show. It was a cynical thought, but I wondered if some of
them were disappointed that they hadn't actually seen Chip
Darwin pull the amplifier down on top of himself.

My better judgment told me to stay right where I was, but my
journalistic curiosity got the best of me. I ran down the hallway
leading to the room backstage. The paramedics, who had been
standing by as a precaution, were putting Chip on a stretcher. The
Larsen sisters were weeping piteously as Chip was carried out the
back door to the ambulance. Chuck Darwin was shaking his
head. Max had his arm around Darwin's shoulders, holding him
steady.

"He's not breathing, Max!" Darwin said.

"Hold on there, Charlie, they're doing everything they can,"
Max replied. As he caught my attention, Max rolled his eyes, as
if to say, "Another one bites the dust."

There probably wasn't a good moment to do it, but Artie
Crosby picked a bad one to ask, "Mr. Darwin, what do we do
about the concert?"

"Screw the concert! I don't care about the damn concert!"
Darwin shouted. As he and Max went out the back door,
followed by the Larsen sisters, Darwin turned on a police officer
who was holding the door. "I repeat what I said before. This was
no accident. Somebody tried to kill my son. I expect a complete
investigation."

"Yes, sir, we'll see to that," the cop assured him. But when he closed the door, the cop asked, "Who is that guy, anyway?"

"That's Chuck Darwin," Artie Crosby said. "He's the president of Evolution Records."

"He acts like he's the damn President of the United States," the cop replied.

Chuck Darwin's lack of interest in the concert was understandable, but he wasn't the person who had to go onstage and announce that it was being canceled. After conferring with the band members, Artie Crosby announced that the show would go on. While the crowd cheered the announcement, Tommy Ventura and the road crew checked all the other equipment. There had only been one booby trap, and now it was too late to do anything about it.

Less than half an hour after the incident, Roots was rocking and rolling again, minus the leader of the band. I expected the songs to sound a little thin due to Chip Darwin's absence, but I turned out to be wrong. That was because I underestimated Kid Lee's guitar prowess. I'll never make that mistake again.

Kid took over Chip's rhythm parts and had no trouble filling in the leads. If anything, both parts were more complete now that Kid had the freedom to do what he wanted and didn't have to defer to Chip. Except for Tina singing Chip's vocals, it was the same great sound—but better.

I didn't know how the argument backstage about Grace Lee had been settled, but the question was academic with Chip out of the picture. Not only did Kid invite his mother onstage, but she joined with Tina for a duet on her girl-group medley. Her son put on an incredible show, playing guitar blindfolded, behind his back, with his teeth. I once saw a guy in a band called the Nighthawks play a perfect twelve-bar blues with his teeth, and I had seen some of Jimi Hendrix's legendary guitar tricks, but they were nothing compared with the dazzling display put on by the little guy with glasses.

The crowd went wild after the last song, and it took five encores before the band could finally stop. Though it hardly seemed possible, by the end of the concert, Jack, Kid, and Tina had almost managed to make everybody forget that the band had started out the evening as a foursome.

There were exceptions, of course, and one of them was Tommy Ventura. I talked with him backstage before the first encore. His head was hanging as if he were carrying the proverbial weight of the world on his shoulders. In a sense, he was. It was his job to make sure all the equipment was working properly. One oversight, and now he had Chip Darwin's life weighing on his conscience.

The roadie was sucking down a beer like it was mother's milk. His eyes were red and watery. If his mother had been there, he probably would have tried to crawl up on her lap. But she wasn't and he was a big boy, so he leaned back against the wall and lit a joint. I was tempted to tell him that might not be the smartest thing to do, but I restrained myself. The last thing he needed right then was a lecture from his dad.

Tommy inhaled deeply, then offered the joint to me. I shook my head.

"You don't do drugs, do you?" he said.

"No, I don't."

"But you used to take drugs, didn't you?"

"Yeah, for a while. Then drugs took me."

Tommy nodded. Then, almost by way of apology, he said, "You don't know how terrible I feel, man. The whole thing—it's all my fault. I should have spotted it, man."

I told him I did know how he felt and it wouldn't do any good to blame himself. I also knew that my telling him wouldn't make his guilt go away. Some burdens you can help people carry, but guilt isn't one of them.

But in this case I wasn't so sure Tommy Ventura had anything to feel guilty about. I wasn't as certain as he seemed to be that the accident had been his fault. It might have only been a series of coincidences, but after Danny Darwin's death and the note his father had received, I wasn't convinced the incident on stage *had* been an accident.

I took a deep breath and mentioned my suspicions to Tommy Ventura. Then I asked him what he thought.

"They don't pay me to think, Del. They just pay me to set up the equipment."

"You want to make a guess?"

Tommy sighed. "No, I don't."

"The cops are going to be asking. So's Chuck Darwin."

"Hey, lay off, man. Don't you think I know that?"

"I'm sorry, Tommy. I wasn't trying to pressure you."

"That's okay, man. Don't worry about it. I just don't feel like thinking about it right now."

Maybe not, but he continued to talk, as much to himself as to me. "The cord must've been wrapped around the amp. Man, can you imagine how awful that must've been, just for a second, to see that thing come crashing down on top of you?" Tommy closed his eyes.

"But you checked it before the band went on."

"Yeah, I did. At least I thought I did. I guess maybe I could've missed it."

"Somehow I don't think that's too likely."

"No, you're right, man, it's not."

"So maybe somebody set it up like that after you did your check."

Tommy shook his head. "Thanks, Del. I know you're trying to help get me off the hook, but I just don't buy it. If anybody did that, they'd have to know they could kill him. But who'd want to kill Chip?"

I shrugged. "I can think of a few possibilities."

"Like who?"

"Well, Tina was pretty mad when she—"

"No way, man. Now you're talking trash." Tommy pointed his finger at me. "Tina would never—"

"Okay, okay," I said, putting up my hands. "I'm just trying to point out that Chip wasn't exactly a beloved character around here. What about Artie? Chip's always pushing him around. What about Jack? You said they had an argument this afternoon. What about *me*, for that matter?"

"*You?*" Tommy held the joint up in the air. "Are you sure *you* haven't been smoking any of this stuff?"

I laughed. It was nice to see the roadie smiling again, if only for a moment.

"I can tell you right off that I didn't try to kill Chip," I explained to Tommy. "But not everybody's as nice as you and me. I had a dispute with Chip the other day. For some people, that would have been reason enough to try and get back at him."

Tommy shook his head. "I don't buy it, man. I think I just blew it."

"Hold on a second," I said. "Maybe somebody was just trying to scare Chip. Maybe somebody tucked the cord under the amp, thinking it might tip over but it wouldn't fall on him."

Tommy shook his head again. "I don't know. It's pretty obvious to me—"

"To you, yeah. But you lift this stuff all the time. You understand about leverage. Not everybody's as smart as you are."

Tommy laughed. "Man, I barely graduated from high school. That's the first time anybody ever called me smart."

"But you are smart about this stuff. You know what you're doing."

"Maybe so. But who'd be dumb enough to go out there and tamper with the equipment with five thousand people watching them do it?"

"Nobody in the crowd would've given it a second thought," I said. "Besides, that stuff was hidden behind the curtain, wasn't it?"

"Yeah, you're right, it *was* behind the curtain." Tommy slapped his palm against his forehead. "How could I be so dumb? I was standing out there watching it."

"So who went onstage after you did your final check?"

"Let's see. Artie went up there, and Chip, and me, and Jack. That's it."

"What about Tina? Remember she left the room when we were talking?"

"No, not Tina. She was just out in the hallway, man. She didn't go up onstage. She was just standing out there crying. You're right. Chip was a jerk."

"Is," I corrected.

"Yeah, for the time being. But you didn't see him close up like I did. It'll be a miracle if he makes it."

"Anybody else?"

"Nope, that was it. I don't know, Del. I know you're trying to make me feel better, but I think I just blew it."

"Tommy, I'm not so sure you'd feel better if you thought somebody tried to kill Chip."

"Yeah, well, you know what I mean." Tommy snapped his fingers. "Hey, wait a minute. Kid's mother. I forgot about Kid's mother."

"Grace Lee went onstage?"

"Yeah, she said she wanted to go up there and kiss Kid's guitar for good luck. What do you think of that?"

"I think it's too bad she didn't kiss Chip's guitar while she was at it."

12

Marcy, the three remaining members of Roots, and I must have constituted a pretty glum group while waiting for the midnight hour back at the hotel suite. One of the hardest parts about touring in a band is figuring out how to fill the time between gigs. One minute you're performing onstage before thousands of people, and your adrenaline is pumping like a geyser. The next, you're holed up in some hotel room or bar, fighting a losing battle to preserve that emotional high. Small wonder that so many rock musicians turn to drugs to keep them going. They just can't face getting off the roller coaster. They'll do anything to keep it going.

Normally, after a performance like Roots had just turned in, it wouldn't have taken much for the band to stay "up" all night. But the reality of Chip Darwin's accident had sent the roller coaster screeching to a halt. Onstage, when they could forget everything but the music, the band members were fine. After the concert, there was nothing else to keep their minds occupied. They were merely killing time until they could get onstage again. It was a chilling thought when you considered how precious that time must have been to Chip Darwin.

Max had called me from the hospital when I got back to the hotel. Chip was still alive, but the doctors thought his chances of making it through the night were slim to none. No matter how grim it was to be keeping a vigil in the suite, I thought it was a lot better than sitting around the hospital with Max, Chuck Darwin, Artie Crosby, and the Larsen sisters.

Kid was reclining on a lounger in the corner of the suite, softly playing an acoustic guitar. Marcy and I were on one couch, and Jack and Tina were across from us on another.

"How can you just sit there playing guitar at a time like this?" Tina asked. "I mean, Chip could be dying this second, and you're just picking away like everything was normal."

Kid shrugged and continued playing while he answered. "I don't know. It makes me feel better. Playing guitar always makes me feel better."

As I watched his fingers glide over the strings, I knew exactly what Kid was talking about. I remembered how nice it used to feel to lock myself away and play when I got depressed. Music was good therapy. I began to wonder why I had stopped playing. The answer, of course, was obvious. I had wanted to punish myself. For some reason, that explanation didn't seem to make much sense anymore. I was getting tired of doing penance.

"I know what I'd like to do right now," Tina said. "I wish we had some toot."

Jack the Knife reached into his pocket and pulled out a small vial of white powder. He held it up for Tina to see.

"Wow, man, where did you get that?"

"Found it on Chip," Jack answered. "I figured he wouldn't want them finding it at the hospital." Jack held out a little spoon of the cocaine for Tina to snort.

"Wow, I don't know," she said. "I mean, it doesn't seem right to be using up Chip's stash."

"Suit yourself," the drummer replied. Then he sniffed Tina's serving into his nose.

"Well, okay," Tina said, "you twisted my arm. Chip probably would've wanted us to do it."

Jack looked at me, then held out a spoonful of the powder. "Want a little blow, bro?"

"No thanks."

"Chip wouldn't mind," Tina assured me.

I assured her that had nothing to do with it. Jack then held out the coke for Marcy. She looked at me uncertainly and asked, "Do you mind if I do?"

"Not at all," I lied. I didn't know what I objected to more—
her taking the drugs or her asking for my permission. I knew she
was trying to be sensitive, but all she accomplished was making
me feel more uncomfortable for being the odd man out.

For a fleeting moment I was tempted to change my mind, to
see how it would feel again. A voice inside me said, "Go ahead,
one hit won't hurt." But another voice, the smarter voice, was
louder. It said, "Yeah, but it'll only make you feel worse."

I got up off the couch and walked to the window. Marcy looked
at me as if she thought I was mad at her. I think she was right. I
probably was. But the wave of nausea spreading over me had
nothing to do with her, and I knew it. It had to do with feeling
trapped. It was a feeling I knew well, like an old friend, only it
wasn't a friendly feeling. It was a feeling I couldn't explain. I had
learned to live with it, but that didn't make it go away. It would
always be with me, and I would always be learning to live with it.

I looked out the hotel window and stared at the capitol
building. It was a pretty sight, and I tried to make myself
concentrate on that thought. The voice inside me commanded,
"Think nice thoughts."

Across the room, I could hear Jack and Tina chatting away
above the sound of Kid's guitar. It was the most I had ever heard
the drummer talk, but I wasn't listening to what he was saying.
Instead, I tuned in to the guitar and concentrated on how nice it
sounded. When Jack had passed the vial around, he didn't offer
any to Kid. It was understood that Kid did not take drugs. So I
wasn't alone after all. Tina might not understand, but I figured
there were a lot of things that didn't make sense to Tina. I had a
feeling Tina didn't do a whole lot of thinking. I sure didn't when I
was her age, and I had the benefit of a college education.

Just then, I felt Marcy's hand on my shoulder. "Are you all
right, Del?"

"Much better." It was hard to pinpoint, but there was
something I liked about the way Marcy said my name. There was
a tone of familiarity to it, and that gave me a sense of security.

"I hope you're not mad at me."

"Absolutely not." This time I meant it.

"I don't do this all the time," she said, a tone of apology in her voice.

"It's okay," I said. "People have to figure out what they can handle. I had to learn the hard way."

"It's still hard, isn't it?"

"Sometimes." I gave her a kiss, and she embraced me. "It's easier when you have some help."

As we pulled apart, Tina got up and walked over toward Kid. "How old are you anyway, Kid?"

Kid answered with his usual shrug, still running his fingers over the strings of the guitar. "I don't know."

"Oh, come on. What year were you born?"

"Fifties," Kid said. "I was born in the Fifties."

"Yeah, but what *year*?"

This time Kid answered with a blank stare. As with Chip Darwin earlier in the evening, I couldn't determine if Kid understood the question but wasn't acknowledging it or if he simply wasn't listening.

"The *year*," Tina said. "You know, like fifty-two, fifty-three." She counted on her fingers for effect.

"Yeah," Kid said.

"Yeah, *what*?" Tina shrieked. "That's the question I'm asking."

"Fifty-two, fifty-three," Kid replied, all the while playing soft licks on the guitar. He grinned widely, flashing his teeth.

Tina began to laugh. Marcy and I did too. After a minute, even Jack the Knife joined in. That proved there was a first time for everything.

Tina turned and looked at Jack. "Does Prince Charming have any of his magic powder left?"

"Anything for Snow White." Jack pulled out the vial and they each snorted some more. Marcy took a pass, I hoped not in deference to me, but I wasn't about to persuade her to partake.

Tina spoke to the room. "I don't wanna say anything or nothing, but what about the band?"

"The band?" Kid asked. "What about the band?" He was running his fingers silently over the guitar strings as he spoke.

"I mean the *band*," Tina said. "I mean, what's gonna happen to us? You know, because of Chip."

"Oh, yeah," Kid said. "Maybe we should make up some new songs, on account of Chip being dead and all."

"Don't say that!" Tina said. "You'll jinx him."

Kid shrugged. "Sorry. I forgot we don't know if he's dead yet."

"He's dead all right," Jack said. "Count on it."

"God, it was so awful. You know, we're lucky it wasn't one of us. It could've been us. I don't wanna say anything or nothing, but Tommy should've checked everything better."

"Tommy *did* check," I said. It annoyed me that Tina was so quick to blame the roadie, especially since Tommy couldn't say a bad word about her.

"Well, if that's true, then why did the accident happen in the first place?"

"Chip's father doesn't think it was an accident," I replied.

"Chip's father is crazy," Tina said. "He's one of those people that thinks everybody's out to get them."

"A paranoid," Marcy said.

"Yeah, that's it. Chip even told me so. Danny, too. I just feel sorry for Sylvia. She's such a nice lady."

"Yeah, she is a nice lady," Kid said.

"Chuck Darwin may be paranoid," I said, "but it is kind of strange that both his sons get killed in the same week. It's more strange when you consider the note."

"I don't know about the note," Tina replied. "But Danny just OD'd, that's all. It was Chip that gave him the reds in the first place. I gave him some because he said he wanted to try it. But he already went and got some off Chip. I didn't know he already took some. He just did too much, that's all."

"Oh, so that's all." I shot a glance of horror at Marcy, and she returned it. "Did you mention any of this to Chuck Darwin?" I asked.

"Are you kidding? And get Chip and me in trouble? What's that supposed to accomplish?"

Within the framework of Tina's convenient logic, her question almost made sense. I didn't bother to answer it. I just stared at her and wondered what it would take to pack some real sense into her head before she went the way of Danny Darwin.

"I'm getting antsy," Tina said. "Does anybody wanna go downstairs to the bar?"

Nobody responded to the invitation until Jack the Knife finally shrugged and said, "Why not?"

As soon as they left the room, Marcy said, "It's a good thing Tina found a career in rock music, because she's dumber than a box of rocks."

"You don't like Tina, do you, Marcy?" Kid asked.

"She'll set the women's movement back ten years all by herself," Marcy replied.

Kid answered with a puzzled expression. I was pretty certain he had no idea what Marcy was talking about. "Yeah," he said, "she's a crazy little lady, all right."

With that, Kid began playing and singing a song called "Crazy Little Lady," which was a big hit back in 1958. It had been done by a one-hit wonder named Richie Randall, whose career ended almost as soon as it began. Randall had been killed in a car accident.

"Hey, Kid, that's not bad," I said. "I always liked that song."

Kid smiled and nodded. When he reached the instrumental break, he said, "My daddy wrote that song."

"No, I don't think so."

"Yeah, he did, Del." Kid continued playing the song until the end, adding a slick series of licks before strumming it to a close.

"You say your father wrote that?" I asked.

"That's right. My daddy wrote a whole bunch of songs. Mama says we were supposed to get rich off them, but some man from a record company stole them all."

I was well aware that it had been a common practice for unscrupulous talent agents to rip off songs back in the Forties and Fifties, but I was a bit dubious about Kid's story nonetheless. It was equally common for musicians to claim they had been ripped off. I tried to picture the single of "Crazy Little Lady" back home in my collection of 45s, but I couldn't remember what label it had come out on.

"Do you know the name of the guy?" I asked.

"Uh-uh. Even Mama didn't know. She said Daddy kept it a secret. He was going to surprise her with the money. That was his favorite song, on account of he wrote it about her. That's what he used to call Mama—crazy little lady."

Kid rested the guitar on his lap. "Do any of you know what time it is? I got to be back in my room by twelve-thirty, on account of that's when the room service closes. I want to get me a sandwich."

Marcy looked at her watch. "Quarter to twelve, Kid. You've still got forty-five minutes." To me, she said, "Quarter to one back in New York. Too late to call Gary." Gary was the name of her husband. "I guess I've failed in my wifely duties again."

"Hey, Del," Kid said, "you want to play the guitar?" He was holding it out to me.

"No thanks, Kid. I don't play anymore."

"You used to play guitar but now you don't. Why not?"

"It's a long story, Kid."

Kid grinned as he walked over toward us, then sat on the couch where Jack and Tina had been. "How long is it? I still got forty-five minutes."

I gave it to him in fifteen. At the conclusion he said, "That's why you stopped playing? On account of those people dying?"

I nodded. "I stopped playing guitar and I stopped taking drugs."

"I understand why you stopped taking drugs. But why did you stop playing music?"

"He's got a point there." Marcy smiled and squeezed my arm.

"I don't know," I said. "It just seemed like the right thing to do."

Kid shook his head in disbelief. "That doesn't make any sense, Del. If it was me, I would've played more than ever. You know, try and make myself feel better."

"Me, too," Marcy said.

Kid got up and grabbed the guitar. "Come on, Del," he said,

handing it to me. "It won't bite you. Marcy and me, we're your friends. There's no reason to be afraid."

I took the guitar from Kid, then took a deep breath. I played a few chords. It felt awkward and unfamiliar. My fingertips got sore just from pressing the strings down for a few moments. I handed the guitar to Kid, but he wouldn't take it back.

"Come on, Del, play that ax," he said.

"I'd really like to hear you play," Marcy added.

"You wouldn't want to turn down a nice lady like Marcy now, would you?" Kid was grinning from ear to ear.

My hands were shaking as I put my head down and addressed the strings. I began playing, but I didn't look up at Marcy or Kid. My fingers hurt, but it was the right kind of hurt. It was the way they used to feel when I first learned to play. My fingers would throb until I thought they'd fall off, but I'd keep on playing anyway, for an hour, sometimes two hours, without stopping. My mother would tell me to stop and go to bed, but I'd keep playing—quietly, so she wouldn't hear me. One time I stayed up all night playing and didn't fall asleep until it was almost time to get up for school. My mother came into my bedroom and found me asleep in a chair with the guitar on my lap. She let me stay home from school that day.

After a few minutes, my fingers were running fluidly over the strings. I was rusty, but it didn't sound as bad as I expected. All of a sudden, I wondered what had been holding me back. Why had it taken me so long to get up the courage to try playing again? I didn't know the answer. It was buried somewhere too deep to call up.

"There, you see?" Kid said. "Your fingertips got their own memory built right in. It's like riding a bike. Once you learn, you never forget how to do it."

I looked up and nodded. Kid and Marcy were smiling. So was I. "Come on, Del," Kid said, "play that song."

"Which one?"

"Just how many *hit* songs did you have?" he asked.

I put my head down again and started playing the intro. When I got to the opening verse, Kid began singing. I couldn't believe he knew the words, couldn't believe I remembered them. But I did. Of course I did. We were singing the chorus one last time when Tommy Ventura poked his head into the suite.

"Hey, Del, that's great to see you playing again," Tommy said when the song was over.

"Thanks, Tommy." I could feel the blood surging to my head. There was no reason to be embarrassed, but I was.

"He's good, ain't he?" Kid asked as I put the guitar down next to him on the couch. "Promise me you'll play again tomorrow. We'll play together, okay?"

"I don't know."

"Promise," Kid said. He put out his hand for a shake.

"All right, we'll play tomorrow."

"Any word on Chip yet?" Tommy asked.

No sooner had he posed the question than the phone began to ring. It was Max. Chip Darwin had passed away a few minutes before. Massive internal injuries, the doctors said. Chuck Darwin was certain that his son had been murdered. He was talking about canceling the tour. Max said he was about to take Chuck out for a drink. I told him Darwin needed more than a drink. He needed a long vacation.

"So he's dead, huh?" Tommy asked when I hung up the phone.

"Yeah, he's dead." I didn't feel any loss for Chip Darwin, but I was concerned about the roadie. "It's not your fault, Tommy."

Tommy Ventura buried his head in his hands for a minute. "Did he say anything about what's gonna happen with the tour?" he asked.

"Max said Darwin's thinking about canceling it."

"He can't do that," Kid said.

"Oh yes he can," Tommy replied.

"Don't worry," Marcy told Kid. "Max will talk him out of it."

"What makes you so sure?" I asked.

"Darwin listens to Max. Besides, Max owns a piece of the band."

"*What*? Are you sure?"

"I'm positive. You didn't know that? I figured Max probably told you about it."

"No, I had no idea. How did you find out about it?"

"I overheard him talking on the phone in the office one night when I was working late. Surprised?"

"Yeah, very."

"So was I."

Kid got up from the couch. "Well, I better be going. I'm sorry about Chip, but I'm sure glad it was him and not somebody else."

Tommy stayed at the doorway after Kid left the room. "He's right, you know. If it had to happen, I'm glad it was Chip."

"You want to come in and sit down, maybe talk about it for a while?" Marcy suggested.

"No, I gotta go find Tina. Have you guys seen her?"

"She went downstairs to the bar with Jack," I said.

"With Jack, huh?" Tommy gazed at me with a dazed look in his eyes. He shook his head. "Man, it's been a hard day's night."

Yes, it sure had been. For some people more than others. I was one of the lucky ones. I had played guitar again for the first time in ten years. Despite everything that had happened, I actually felt pretty good. I felt even better when I walked Marcy back to her room.

"I don't know exactly how to say this, but would you like to come in?" she asked.

"Are you sure you want me to?"

"How can I be sure?" Marcy sang, mimicking the Young Rascals song.

I smiled. "Yeah, yeah, I know. In a world that's constantly changing . . . I guess that was a dumb question."

"It's okay. You're just trying to be sensitive. That's nice."

"Glad you think so. Now, would it be _in_sensitive of me to say yes?"

"Not at all," she said.

13

We awoke to a gloomy, overcast day, the kind that's custom made for hiding under the covers, when you never seem to wake up, no matter how much coffee you pour down. In another place, at another time, it would have been a perfect opportunity for Marcy and me to get to know each other better. We needed that, although we had done a pretty good job of getting acquainted the night before.

There were other factors to consider, however, the first one being the phone call that stirred us from our slumber a few minutes before eight o'clock. Even if I hadn't known the name of Marcy's husband, I would have been able to tell he was the one calling from the tone in her voice.

"Oh, hello, Gary," she said. There was a long pause while she listened to him. I could tell he was giving her an earful. "I know, I know, I got your message. I got both of them. I'm sorry, but it was too late to call." Another pause. "I said I'm sorry. What else do you want me to say?"

It was at that point that Bobby Vee's song "The Night Has a Thousand Eyes" began echoing in my head. I got out of bed and went to the bathroom to wash my face and see how much I had aged during the night. In fact I felt much younger. Falling in love will do that to you. The mirror, of course, didn't have any way of knowing that, so it was the same old face staring back at me.

I tried not to listen to Marcy's end of the phone conversation, but it was impossible not to hear her. They were arguing now, and she was on the defensive. When I stepped back into the main room, I could see that she was starting to cry. I walked over to her and planted a soft kiss on her forehead. She shook her head sadly and tried to fight back the tears. I could tell it was going to be a losing battle. I thought about leaving a note, but the smartest thing would be to get out of there right away. That's what I did.

I went downstairs to the lobby and ordered Marcy some coffee and orange juice from room service. Then I strolled outside to air out my head. The rain had stopped, but judging by the storm clouds hanging low over the city, it would be coming back with a vengeance any minute. I picked up a copy of the *Wisconsin State Journal* at a newsstand down the block, then parked myself at the counter of a greasy spoon and ordered breakfast.

Mitch Beswick's story on the Roots concert was on the front page. I figured that was a first for him. Even in a hip town like Madison, it would take something extraordinary for a music writer to make page one. Chip Darwin's death definitely fell into that category. Mitch's account was a bit rambling and confused, but that was to be expected. The whole event had been confusing, and the editors had no doubt held the page open until Chip Darwin was declared dead. There was no mention of the possibility of foul play, but there was one line certain to put Chuck Darwin in a foul mood.

Mitch had gotten to Kid Lee after the concert and asked him how Chip Darwin's death—if he died—would affect the status of the tour.

"We can still play," Kid was quoted as saying. "We can play just as good without Chip."

In a sidebar review running next to the story on an inside page, Mitch Beswick said pretty much the same thing himself. "Not only did Roots live up to its advance billing," he wrote, "but the band actually got better *after* Chip Darwin left the stage."

I personally agreed with him, but then I wasn't Chip's father. I hoped, for Kid Lee's sake, that Chuck Darwin didn't read the story. After the stink he had raised about Kid's mother coming onstage, there was no telling how angrily he'd react to seeing something like this in print. It was the sort of comment that, taken out of context, might be the straw that broke the camel's back when Darwin decided whether or not to cancel the tour.

As I made my way up State Street past a place called Ella's Deli, I heard somebody rapping on the window. I turned to see Mitch Beswick. He was eating breakfast with a bearded guy who looked familiar to me, but I couldn't place him because he was at a bad angle. Mitch waved for me to come inside and join them. When I reached their table and got a good look at Mitch's dining partner, I didn't have any trouble matching the name with the face. I wondered what Gerry Stillman Jr. was doing in Madison.

"Do you guys know each other?" Mitch asked.

Gerry Jr. shook his head, then opened his eyes wide when I replied, "We almost met last week backstage at the Roots concert in Minneapolis."

"You were there?" Stillman asked. He tugged at his beard and some stray pieces of scrambled egg fell onto the table.

"Yeah," Mitch answered for me. "Del's doing a story on Roots for *Rock of Ages*."

"Oh, that's Max's magazine."

"That's right," I replied.

"When're you gonna do a story on me?" Gerry Jr. asked.

"You might make the one I'm working on," I said.

Gerry Stillman eyed me warily. "Whaddaya mean?"

"I just meant because of your little scene backstage."

"You write about that and I'll sue your ass."

"Just joking," I said. It was apparent that Gerry Stillman Jr. didn't have much of a sense of humor.

"Del used to play in Meet the Press," Mitch said. "You remember them."

Gerry Stillman nodded and began shoveling eggs into his mouth.

To me, Mitch said, "Gerry's got a solo gig in a club here tonight and tomorrow. You ought to come and see him."

"I don't know," I replied. "Things are a little up in the air after what happened." Then, to Gerry Stillman, I said, "Were you at the Roots concert last night?"

"No," he answered, face down to meet his fork halfway. "But I'm sorry I missed it."

"It was a great concert," Mitch said.

"That's not what I meant." Gerry Stillman looked up now and wiped his hand on his sleeve. "I wish I could've been there to see that amp fall on top of Chip Darwin."

Mitch Beswick and I exchanged looks. While there had been no love lost between me and Chip Darwin, I had a feeling I might have liked Gerry Stillman Jr. even less.

"So I guess you're really upset about the news?" I said.

"Yeah," Gerry replied. "I'm heartbroken, man."

Suddenly it occurred to me that rock musicians had gotten progressively dumber since the days when I played in the band. I knew I had behaved stupidly, but at least I wasn't indifferent to death. Based on Gerry Stillman's comment about Chip and the remark that Tina Darling had made about Danny the night before, it seemed like they looked upon dying as if it meant nothing more than moving to another town or switching to another band. Maybe I'd get a chance to discuss the point with Mitch Beswick, sometime when Gerry Stillman Jr. wasn't around.

"Do you want to pull up a chair?" Mitch asked. I had a feeling he really wanted me to.

"No, thanks, I've got to get back to the hotel."

"Did you read my story?" Mitch pointed at the paper.

"Yeah, I did, first thing this morning."

"I was up half the night working on it. What'd you think?"

"I thought your analysis was right on target. I'm a little sorry that you used that quote from Kid Lee, though."

"Yeah, I know, that struck me, too. But that's exactly what he said. It's a direct quote."

"Oh, I don't doubt that it's accurate. I just hope Chuck Darwin doesn't believe it."

"Oh, yeah, I see what you mean. Jeez, I sure hope I don't get Kid in trouble. Would you tell him I'm sorry? You know, so he doesn't take it the wrong way?"

"Don't worry, Mitch, it won't bother Kid at all. If Darwin does say something, Kid probably won't even understand why it bothers him."

"Yeah, he's off in his own world, isn't he? But he's a helluva guitar player."

"He's the best I've ever seen."

"Yeah, I think maybe you're right."

As I started to leave, Mitch asked me what the status of the Roots tour was.

"Your guess is as good as mine."

"Well, if you hear anything, would you let me know? I mean, as long as it doesn't interfere with your story."

"Sure," I said.

"Hey, try and stop by and catch the gig," Gerry Stillman called to me as I left. "Tell Max to come, too."

That request I wasn't so sure about. On my way back to the hotel, I stopped at a florist and bought some red anemones for a blue friend. I thought about dropping them off myself, but I decided to let the bellhop take care of it. Marcy probably needed a little time alone.

When I got to Max's room, it looked like he wanted some time alone, too. The DO NOT DISTURB sign was hanging on the doorknob. I ignored it and started to knock, but the door came ajar. I figured Max was drunk when he got back, no doubt at an ungodly hour. It was just like him to remember to hang the sign up but to forget about closing the door.

As I pushed it open, I could see that Max had opted for breakfast in bed, but I was mistaken about his wanting to be alone. He was sitting upright with a pillow supporting his back. There was a tray on his lap and a Larsen sister on either side of him.

"Hey, hey, can't you read the sign?" Max said as I stepped into the room.

"The door was open," I replied. I looked at the Larsen sisters, who were busy pulling up the sheet. They were giggling. Max was red-faced. "What are you having for breakfast, Max?" I asked. "Two over easy?"

"Hey, come on, get the hell out of here," he replied. "I haven't even been to sleep yet."

"I'm sure it wasn't for lack of trying."

"No, I mean it. I was up all night with Chuck. I'll talk to you later."

"I want to talk to you now, Max."

"You sound serious."

"I am serious, Max."

The blond Larsen sister made room for Max to crawl out from under the covers. He was wearing white boxer shorts. I suggested that he get some with red polka dots.

"What a comedian," he muttered as he led me into the adjoining room of the suite. "Be back in a minute, girls."

"Okay, Max," they answered in unison. They sounded like David Seville doing the Chipmunks.

"I thought you said you were too old for that stuff," I commented when we got into the next room.

"Well, I guess I was wrong." Max grinned. "What can I say?" He lit a cigarette. "So what's so important that you've got to talk to me right now?"

"I have it on good authority that you own a piece of Roots."

Max frowned, then choked on his cigarette smoke.

"You ought to lay off the butts," I said.

He ignored my comment. "Who told you that?" he demanded.

"A good journalist never reveals his sources."

"Who says you're a good journalist?" Max chuckled nervously, but I wasn't laughing.

"What's the story, Max? Is it true?"

"Yeah, okay, it's true. So what's the big deal?"

"Isn't that a conflict of interest? You're publishing a magazine with glowing stories about a band that you own."

"Yeah, I guess you're right," he said. "But, come on, it's only rock 'n' roll."

I stared at Max long and hard.

"Hey, it's a sleazy business, what can I say?"

"I thought you were one of the few clean guys in it."

"Yeah, well, you were wrong. I'm sorry to destroy your fantasy. So what now? Do you want out?"

I thought it over for a moment. I didn't know what I wanted. I just knew that I was going up and down on the roller coaster again—happy one minute, depressed the next, angry the next.

"No, Max, I don't want out," I said finally. "I just want you to start leveling with me."

"Okay, I am leveling with you. I own a third of the band, that's all."

"I take it you're going to use your third to convince Chuck Darwin to continue with the tour."

"You kidding? Damn straight I am. This is the hottest band to come along in years."

"What does Darwin say about the tour?"

"Chuck, he'd like to shitcan the whole thing. But he won't. I'll talk him out of it. He's just got this crazy notion that somebody killed Danny and Chip."

"What's so crazy about it? I think he could be right. At least about Chip. Tina says Danny OD'd because Chip gave him the stuff."

"She's probably right."

"Did you mention anything about that to Chuck?"

"No, of course not. Chuck doesn't want to hear that stuff. He wants to believe Danny didn't take drugs."

"What about Chip?"

"Chip's a whole 'nother matter. Anybody could tell Chip was on something just by looking at him. Even Chuck knew that. I think he was high as a kite when he pulled the damn amp over. That's why he died. It was just an accident."

"I'm not so sure."

"What makes you say that?"

"Any number of reasons. Here's one: Gerry Stillman Junior is in Madison."

Max's jaw dropped about half a foot. "You're kidding." When he could see that I wasn't, he said, "Are you sure?"

"I'm positive. I talked to him half an hour ago."

"Was he at the concert last night?"

"He says he wasn't."

"That doesn't mean squat."

"Exactly."

"Chrissakes. I better tell Chuck right away."

"What about your breakfast?" I asked, nodding toward the other room from which the Larsen sisters could be heard giggling. "Aren't you going to finish it?"

Max smiled sheepishly. "You're right. Chuck's probably trying to get some sleep. I'll talk to him *after* breakfast."

14

I was getting ready to take a stroll in the rain with Marcy when the knock came on the door to my room at quarter to three. It was Detective Helga Schmitz of the Madison police. She was about six feet tall, weighed at least one seventy-five, and had a voice like a foghorn. Needless to say, she was all business. I soon found out that she had come to give me the business.

We started with the usual preliminaries—my name, address, occupation, reason for traveling with the band. Then she hit me with a sneak attack. I had mentioned to Tommy Ventura that I might technically be considered a suspect, but it hadn't actually crossed my mind that I would be under suspicion from the police.

"I understand you had an altercation with the deceased at Mr. Darwin's house on Monday afternoon."

"Well, yes, I guess you could say that, but I didn't regard it as such."

"How exactly did you regard it, Mr. Barnes?"

"You can call me Del," I said.

"Just answer the question, Mr. Barnes."

"It was only a brief argument, and it was Chip Darwin who started it," I said. "He was upset because he found out I told the Minneapolis police that I thought he might have passed some pills to his brother shortly before Danny died. I figured he was upset about his brother's death, so I left. That was the end of it."

"I see." Detective Schmitz scrawled some notes on a pad. "What were you doing onstage before the concert last night?"

"I beg your pardon?"

"What were you doing onstage before the concert last night?"

"There must be some mistake. I didn't go onstage before the concert. I went backstage, but I didn't go onstage. Who told you that?"

Detective Schmitz ignored my question and asked one of her own. "Can you account for your whereabouts between six-thirty and seven-thirty last night?"

"What is this? Am I a suspect?" I sat down on the bed and lit a cigarette. I could feel my hands shaking, and I'm sure she could see them shaking. All of a sudden, I felt like a character in a Hitchcock movie. Only it wasn't a movie.

"Just answer the question please, Mr. Barnes."

"I was with Marcy Hopkins—she's a photographer for *Rock of Ages*. We had dinner, then we went to the concert. We went backstage and stayed there until a little while before the band started playing."

"Funny. I spoke to Ms. Hopkins and she didn't mention anything about it."

"Did you ask her, goddamnit?" My voice was trembling with anger. It wasn't smart to lose my cool, but now I didn't care. I realized I didn't have anything to worry about. Marcy would confirm my story.

"No, but you can be sure we will." Detective Schmitz simpered, as if to say she had me right where she wanted me. "There's no need to get defensive, Mr. Barnes. We're just following up on all the leads we have. When somebody thinks they saw you up onstage, we consider that a lead."

I nodded. I knew she was only doing her job, but I didn't especially like the way she was doing it. "Would you mind telling me just who that person was?" I asked.

"Sorry, that I can't do. You understand, I'm sure."

I understood, all right. If Sven Peterson, the Minneapolis cop, had been as protective of his sources as his Madison counterpart, I wouldn't have had the argument with Chip Darwin in the first place. It was a catch-22 situation, only I seemed to be catching it from all sides. I didn't think I would gain anything by pointing that out to Helga Schmitz. I suspected she would be a little short on sympathy.

"Well, I think it would also be a good idea to check back with the person who told you I was onstage," I said. "Because whoever it was, he was lying."

"Do you think someone has a grudge against you?"

"You tell me." Without thinking, I lit another cigarette. "But it stands to reason that the person who told you might be pointing the finger at me to keep suspicion away from himself."

She nodded. "You think like a cop."

"Is that a compliment?"

"Take it any way you want. But there's a good chance she—I mean the person who thought you were onstage—was simply mistaken. We're not even sure that the whole thing wasn't an accident. The autopsy showed that Chip Darwin was loaded up on amphetamines. That could explain why he was able to pull the amplifier down on top of himself in the first place."

"Well, I still think you should talk to *her*, just the same," I said.

"Or him."

"You slipped. You said it was a she."

Detective Schmitz smiled. "Who knows? I could've said that just to fool you."

"Yeah, you could have," I said. Based on what I had seen so far, I wouldn't have put anything past Helga Schmitz. But I didn't think she was crafty enough to plan the slip. "Did anybody mention anything to you about Gerry Stillman?" I asked.

"No, who's that?"

"He used to play with Chip Darwin in another band. They had a feud going on between them."

"Oh, yeah. Their fathers are at each other's throats, too, right?"

"That's right. And I happen to know for a fact that Gerry Stillman Junior is in Madison."

"Really." She paused to underline Gerry Stillman's name on her pad. "And did you see him at the concert?"

"No. I don't know if he was even there." I smiled. "And I certainly don't know if he went onstage."

"Thanks," she said. "You've actually been a big help."

"Does that mean I'm not under suspicion?"

She shrugged. "I'm sure we'll clear that up when we talk to Ms. Hopkins. By the way, are you and she intimately involved?"

"Do you expect me to answer that?"

She put out her hand. "No, Mr. Barnes, I think you just did."

As I shook Detective Schmitz's hand, I noticed a wedding band on her finger. I felt a little sorry for the guy who had bought it for her.

"Just one more thing, Mr. Barnes," she said as I let her out the door.

"What's that?"

"You smoke too much."

The smoke was coming out my ears by the time she reached the elevator. Despite my suspicions that somebody had killed Chip Darwin, I had resolved to sit back and let the police handle it, just like Max would want. But now that somebody had implicated me, even by mistake, I couldn't do that. I got on the phone and rang Marcy's room.

"Hi, I was beginning to wonder what happened to you," she said. "Did you fall asleep?"

"Afraid not. I was run over by a dump truck wearing a police badge."

"Oh, you mean Detective Schmitz? I thought she was kind of nice."

"Indeed?"

"At least compared to that goof up in Minneapolis. He gave me the creeps."

"Well, now I know exactly how you felt."

"What happened?"

"Someone told her that I was onstage before the concert."

"You're kidding. That's ridiculous."

"Thank you. I'd appreciate your telling her that when she comes back to see you."

"Why is she coming back?"

"To confirm my alibi."

"God, I don't believe it."

But I'm sure she started to when she heard a knock at the door to her room. I suggested that we put off our walk until after dinner. Then I strolled out to find Tommy Ventura.

He wasn't in his room, but I located him in the suite, where he, Kid, Tina, and Artie Crosby were having a meeting. I didn't know it was a meeting until Artie told me so.

"You're not allowed in here, Barnes," the band manager said. "This is private. We're having a band meeting."

I understood that Artie was rattled. He had good reason to be. But I was in no mood to play the role of dog just because he felt like kicking somebody. "I just want to talk to Tommy for a minute," I said. "Besides, how can you be having a band meeting if Jack the Knife's not here?"

"That's our problem, not yours," Artie retorted. He turned to Kid, who was leaning back and playing his guitar. "Where is Jack, anyway?"

Kid shrugged, playing the intro to "Layla" as if it were as easy as a C-scale. For him, it was. Move over, Eric Clapton.

I ignored Artie and motioned to Tommy to step outside. He ignored Artie, too, even though the band manager was telling him to stay put.

"Hey, here's an idea," Kid said, still playing his ax. "Why don't we get Del to play with us?"

"Huh?" Artie said.

"If you think we got to have another guitar player, maybe Del could play with us," Kid repeated.

"Are you crazy?" Artie said. For the first time, I agreed with something that came out of Artie Crosby's mouth.

"He plays good," Kid said. "Better than Chip."

"No, Kid, I don't think so," I said.

"Why not?"

"I don't know. I couldn't handle the pressure."

"Pressure?" Kid's fingers glided down the length of the fretboard, underscoring his point.

"I just couldn't do it, Kid. But I appreciate your thinking of me."

Kid looked at me uncomprehendingly, then shrugged. "Okay, Del, whatever you say."

"I don't think it's such a bad idea," Tommy told me as we stepped out into the hall. "You sounded pretty good last night."

I shook my head. "It wouldn't work for a million reasons, Tommy."

"Sure, man. What did you want to talk to me about?"

"A little while ago, a cop stopped by my room to talk to me."

"Me too, man. Did you have this big broad that looked like she was in the roller derby?"

"That's the one."

"Man, she talked to me for like an *hour,* giving me the third degree and all." He shook his head. "Can you imagine what it would be like waking up next to her in the morning? She reminded me of my drill sergeant from boot camp."

"Perish the thought," I replied. I lit a cigarette, and Detective Schmitz's comment about smoking lingered in my ears. "Anyway, she says somebody told her that I went onstage before the concert."

"You? Why would anybody say that? You were nowhere near the stage, man." Tommy lowered his voice to a whisper. "I told her just like I told you. The only people who went up onstage were me, Artie, Chip, Jack, and Kid's mother. Man, that's weird, Del, that anybody would've told her that."

"That's what I thought. I just wanted to make sure—"

Just then, something even more weird happened. At the far end of the hallway, around the corner, we heard someone let out a scream, followed by someone yelling.

"Hey, that's Jack the Knife," Tommy said.

The roadie sprinted down the hall, with me right behind him. As we got closer, I could hear the unmistakable voice of Jack Mitchell. He was more talkative and animated than any time since I'd met him.

"Hold it right there, white boy, or I'll slice you up like a hunk of cheese. What the hell do you think you're doing here?"

As we rounded the corner, we almost stumbled into the drummer. He was standing outside Chuck Darwin's suite, holding one of his switchblades at arm's length from a skinny guy with black hair and a beard. The guy had his arms up for protection and was cowering against the wall.

"Jesus Christ!" Tommy said. "It's Gerry Junior!"

"I caught him slipping something under Old Man Darwin's door," Jack said.

Just then, the door to Chuck Darwin's room opened, and the head of Evolution Records peered out through the crack. "What's going on out here?" he said. Judging from the glaze over his eyes and the lines on his face, Chuck Darwin had been taking a nap. But it didn't take him long to figure out the answer to his own question.

Darwin leaned over and picked up a slip of paper off the floor. There was a short note on it, written in crayon. He read it aloud: "'Two down, one to go.'"

Chuck Darwin glared at Gerry Stillman Jr. "You little bastard!" he screamed. "I'll kill you!"

He damn near did. Gerry Jr. put his arms over his head and slid down the wall as his father's ex-partner began pummeling him with his fists. Tommy Ventura pulled Chuck Darwin off him, with an assist from me. Darwin flailed his arms in an attempt to wriggle free, but even Houdini couldn't have escaped the roadie's grasp.

"Calm down, Mr. Darwin. Calm down, please," Tommy pleaded. "I'm scared I might hurt you."

Chuck Darwin nodded, sobbing and shaking. He didn't take his eyes off Gerry Stillman Jr.

"Somebody call the police," Chuck Darwin ordered. By that time I was already pushing the buttons on the phone in his room. But I didn't call the police. I tried Marcy's room.

"Is Give 'Em Helga Schmitz still there?" I asked when she picked up the phone. I was a bit surprised at my ability to wisecrack at such a serious moment, but I guess that proves what a little cognitive dissonance can do for the imagination.

"Yes, she is."

"She's been seeing an awful lot of you lately. I think maybe she has a crush on you."

"I think you might be right. You want to talk to her?"

"No, that's okay. Just tell her when she's done checking out my alibi, she might want to come upstairs to Chuck Darwin's room. We're holding a murder suspect for her."

"What? Who?"

"Gerry Stillman Junior."

"I don't believe it."

After I hung up, I called the *Wisconsin State Journal* and asked for Mitch Beswick. When his voice came on the line, I said, "Mitch, you want to make the front page again tomorrow?"

"You kidding? Of course I do."

"Then get over to the Best Western right now. Oh, and by the way, you might want to change your plans for this evening. Something tells me Gerry Stillman's not going to make it to his gig tonight."

15

By the time I got back out to the hallway, Kid, Tina, and Artie Crosby had joined the huddle around Gerry Stillman Jr. It wasn't long before we heard Detective Schmitz's foghorn voice bellowing from around the corner near the elevator. Marcy was with her, and somewhere along the way they had picked up Max. A few minutes later a pair of uniformed cops arrived, with Mitch Beswick right on their heels.

While one of the cops was putting the cuffs on Gerry Jr. and Detective Schmitz was reading him his rights, the phone rang in Chuck Darwin's room. I was the closest one to the doorway, so I went inside and answered it.

"Hello, Chuck, is that you?" a woman's voice asked. The voice was soft and weary. "I'm sorry, I must have the wrong—"

"Mrs. Darwin, this is Del Barnes."

"Oh, yes, Del, how are you?"

"I'm fine, Mrs. Darwin, considering the circumstances. I guess I'm much better off than you. I'm so sorry, I . . ." What do you say to a woman who's lost both of her children in less than a week? I couldn't take much solace in knowing that she probably felt more awkward than I did. "I'm sorry about Chip," I said.

"Yes, I know, Del, thank you. It's just terrible. Is my husband there? I've been trying to reach him, but he hasn't called me back. Is he okay?"

"He's right outside the room, Mrs. Darwin." I wasn't about to tell her why. Basically, I just wanted to get off the phone. "I'll get him for you right away."

I went to the hall and told Chuck Darwin he had a call.

"Take a message, will you?" he said.

"It's your wife," I replied.

"Tell her I'll call her back."

I understood that Chuck Darwin was upset, but nonetheless I didn't enjoy playing the role of personal secretary. "I think she'd like to talk to you," I said.

"And I told you, I'll call her *back.*"

It took every ounce of restraint I had not to let Chuck Darwin have it right there. Whatever he was going through, his wife was going through worse. She was hanging on by her wits, without a clue as to what was going on, and he was content to leave her hanging on the end of a telephone.

"I'll talk to her, Del," Max said. He went inside the room and slammed the door behind him. Apparently, I wasn't the only one who was annoyed at Chuck Darwin.

"I want this man charged with murder," Darwin demanded.

"First things first," Detective Schmitz replied, raising her hands in a plea for reason. "We're taking him down to the station for questioning."

"I didn't do shit," Gerry Jr. snarled. "This guy"—he pointed at Darwin—"attacked me. He's the one you should be arresting. Not me. I was just joking."

"Yeah, funny, real funny, Gerry," Artie Crosby said.

"Shut up," Gerry retorted.

"How *did* this man's face get all bruised?" Detective Schmitz asked.

No one answered at first, then Jack the Knife spoke up. "I guess he must've fallen down."

"That figures." She motioned to one of the cops. "Let's get him out of here."

As they began to lead Gerry Jr. away, Mitch Beswick asked, "Gerry, do you want me to call someone for you?"

"Yeah, call my old man," he replied. "Tell him to get his ass down here and bail me out right away."

"I already called your old man, Gerry." Max stepped out from Chuck Darwin's room and glared at Stillman. "He's on his way."

"Thanks, Max," Gerry Jr. said.

"Don't mention it. I told him if I were your father, I'd take my sweet time getting here, Gerry."

Stillman glowered at Max, then let loose with a verbal blast at Chuck Darwin. "We're gonna sue your ass, Darwin."

"Get him *out* of here," Helga Schmitz barked. "These kids don't have any damn manners anymore."

"Chuck, call Sylvia," Max said.

"Yeah, in a minute."

"*Now,* dammit," Max said.

It was nice to see my boss finally lose his patience with Chuck Darwin. I was so pleased with him, in fact, that when he looked at his watch and announced "Happy Hour," I accepted his invitation to stop by the cocktail lounge for a martini. I would have joined him even if Marcy hadn't agreed to come along.

Luckily, Max had a plane to catch in a few hours, so it didn't turn into a drinking marathon. At Sylvia Darwin's request, Chip's funeral was to be a small, family-only ceremony. Max was considered family, so he would be making the trip back to Minneapolis with Chuck. Tina Darling's nose got a little out of joint from what she perceived as a snub, but she came to accept the plan graciously when Max explained to her that Sylvia wanted it that way. It probably didn't hurt that he also told her the Larsen sisters hadn't even made the standby list.

With Gerry Stillman Jr. locked away for the time being, Chuck Darwin gave his approval for Roots to continue the tour in Chicago on Friday night. The decision was a big relief, particularly for Artie Crosby, whose job it was to make all the booking arrangements. Artie was so relieved by the news that he became almost sentimental. I'm sure the liquor had something to do with it, but while Sister Sledge's "We Are Family" was blaring out of the jukebox in the lounge, Artie even put his arms around Marcy and me and apologized for being so rude.

"The thing you've got to learn about me," he explained, "is never to take anything I say personally. When you've been in this business as long as I have, you just get to be a cranky old fart. Isn't that right, Tommy?"

"Yeah, you're okay, Artie," the roadie replied. "I mean, for an S.O.B."

Artie laughed and took a friendly jab at Tommy. "This guy's my protégé," he told us. "I started in the business as a roadie myself. Worked my way up the ladder. That's why I'm grooming Tommy. He's like a son to me."

Tommy smiled and gave us a mocking nod.

"No, I'm serious," Artie said, "serious as a heart attack. Tommy's as good a roadie as you'll find anywhere in the business today. And he's getting better all the time. There's nothing I want more than to see him get to the top. I know I yell at him all the time, but that's just my way. Believe me, there's nothing I wouldn't do for this kid. *Nothing.*"

"If that's so, why don't you buy me another beer," Tommy joked.

"Beer," Artie snorted. "That's kid stuff. What we need is some *tequila.*"

"Now you're talking," Tommy said as Artie started to hum the song by the Champs.

"Now I'm *walking,*" I said.

"Me too, while I still can," Marcy added.

Despite the relative calm that fell over the Roots entourage, there was still a storm to come that evening. Chuck Darwin started the thunder and lightning by taping an interview for the ten o'clock news before he and Max left town. He accused Gerry Stillman Jr. of killing Chip and announced that he was calling on the Minneapolis police to reopen their investigation into Danny's death. Gerry Stillman Sr. arrived in Madison just in time to issue a live response in which he maintained his son's innocence and announced that he would be filing a slander suit against Darwin at his earliest convenience.

That moment came the next day, shortly after Gerry Jr. was released from jail and shortly before Chip Darwin was buried. Young Stillman was charged with criminal trespass for leaving the note under Chuck Darwin's door, but the police hadn't been able to come up with any witnesses to place him at the concert, much less onstage. That was because Gerry Jr. was having dinner with three friends in a restaurant on State Street when the incident occurred. While it was conceivable that Gerry's friends might have been lying to protect him, the waitress who served them hadn't forgotten Gerry and his party. They'd run up a hundred-dollar tab and stiffed her on the tip.

Although the investigation was still technically continuing, even the suspicious Detective Schmitz was leaning toward the belief that Chip Darwin's death was another accident. I thought she was wrong. When I talked with Max on the phone Thursday afternoon, he told me to forget it and just write my story.

"Doesn't it bother you that somebody in the band might be a murderer?" I asked.

"That's not my problem, and it's not yours either. It's better just to let sleeping dogs lie."

That was easy for Max to say, but it wasn't easy for me to accept. Someone in the entourage had made an accusation against me and I was determined to find out who and why. But I had spoken to everyone I could think of, and no one admitted giving my name to Schmitz. That meant somebody was lying. Maybe the person had lied to me to cover up for an honest mistake. But I didn't think so. I figured the person was lying to cover up a murder.

I called Detective Schmitz. "As long as the investigation is at a stalemate, I thought you might be willing to tell me who it was that said I went onstage."

"You thought wrong, Mr. Barnes." I could almost hear Helga Schmitz smiling at the other end of the phone. "And we're not at a stalemate. We've just suffered a setback, that's all. We've still got a few suspects."

"Am I one of them?"

"Let's just say you're on the list, but there are a couple others ahead of you. But one wrong move and you could get to the top of it."

"Number three with a bullet," I muttered.

"What?"

"Nothing. Just a music business term."

"Why are you so insistent on trying to find this out?" she asked. "Are you paranoid or something?"

"Maybe so. But just because I'm paranoid doesn't mean they're not out to get me."

Detective Schmitz let out a laugh that shook the phone. "Don't you have anything better to do?"

"What would you do if somebody implicated you and you knew it wasn't true?"

"I'd find out who it was and whip their ass."

"Is that why you won't tell me? You're afraid I'll go do that?"

"You? I don't think so, Mr. Barnes. You strike me as kind of a wimp."

"You're right. I'm scared of the dark. I just want to know to satisfy my curiosity."

"Curiosity killed the cat, Mr. Barnes. If you want me to satisfy yours, you're barking up the wrong tree."

"And you're mixing your metaphors."

Detective Schmitz laughed again. "I don't know what it is, but there's something I like about you, Mr. Barnes."

"You've got a certain charm yourself."

"Tell you what I'm going to do. If you promise me you won't do anything stupid, I'll give you a little hint."

"What is it?"

"You promise?"

"Cross my heart and hope to die."

"Okay. The person who said they thought you went onstage is a woman."

"I think I already knew that."

"Well, now you know for sure. That's all for today. But if you keep snooping around, like I think you're going to, let me know if you come up with anything."

"I'll think about it."

"You damn well better."

16

I sat down and made a list of the names of the women traveling with Roots. I put Tina at the top, then the Larsen sisters, then Grace Lee. I added Marcy, then crossed her name off immediately. Detective Schmitz was right: I *was* getting paranoid.

I wanted to do something constructive, something that would take my mind off Chip Darwin's death. I had a story to write and God only knew how I was going to start it. Writing a puff piece on a rock 'n' roll tour should have been a piece of cake. But so far this had not been an ordinary tour. The cake had a bomb ticking inside it. After kicking around a few ideas in my head, I finally decided to focus on Kid Lee, to chart his rise from nowhere to the center of the rock music scene.

I called Marty Goldberg, an old friend from my own music days. When I met Marty, he was a booking agent for a club in upstate New York. But a few years back, he bought a roadhouse outside of Athens, Georgia, and turned it into a music club. Although I had never been there, I knew that Athens had a pretty big music scene. But I figured it was a small enough town that Marty must have crossed paths with Kid Lee.

"Oh, yeah, Del, how are you? What's up? Are you finally getting off your ass and coming down here for a visit?"

Marty's a friendly guy, the sort who would talk your ear off if you gave him the chance. But there was no b.s. about his schtick. Next to Max Horton, Marty was the most trustworthy guy I'd ever met in the music business.

"One of these days, Marty," I replied. I felt kind of guilty that I hadn't been down there to see him, because I promised to do so every time we talked, about once a year. But Marty knew about my demons, knew how scared I was to fly.

"Well, what are you doing with your life nowadays?"

I told Marty about signing on with Max Horton. "You know Max, don't you?"

"Funny thing. I've heard a lot about him. We used to work a similar circuit. But I've never actually met him."

"He's a straight shooter, Marty."

"Yeah, that's what I've heard. So what's the magazine called?"

"Rock of Ages."

"Yeah that's right, I've been meaning to get a copy. It's hard to find around here."

"It won't be for long. I'll put one in the mail to you today. But that's not what I'm calling about. I wanted to talk to you about Kid Lee. Have you ever heard of him?"

"You kidding? Kid Lee, Jack the Knife Mitchell. We used to have those guys here all the time. They're outasight!"

"I know. I've been traveling with them."

"You are? That's great, Del. You're finally back on the road again. It won't be long before you've got your own band."

"No, Marty, that's a long ways off. I don't think that'll ever happen."

"So you're covering their tour, huh? What's it like?"

"So far it's been pretty weird."

"Oh, that's right," he said. "I just read something about that in the paper. What's it, like, two of the guys have been killed or something? The Darwin brothers?"

"Yeah," I said. "One of them OD'd and then the other was killed onstage. Believe me, it's been pretty strange."

"I believe it. Just being with Kid and Jack would be strange enough. They're like from another planet or something, aren't they? And the best part is Kid's mom. Have you met her? Amazing Grace?"

"Indeed I have."

"She's a trip, isn't she?"

"Indeed she is."

"You know, she's like a legend down here, Del. I mean, she used to drive those two around in this old VW van, you know, with all their equipment and stuff. She was like their road manager. She used to come in here, hauling stuff around. She used to set up the equipment for them. She knew how everything worked—the amps, the sound system. It was amazing.

"Kid would invite her up onstage, and she'd get up there and sing with them. We used to pack the house when they played down here. It was just the two of them—guitar and drums, strange combination. Real minimalist sound. Sometimes they'd have a singer or some of the locals would jam with them. You know, it was real loose. But the weird thing is, the rumor around here was that Kid and his mother used to sleep together. And you know what? I believe it. But you can't print that."

"Don't worry, Marty. I'm not with the *National Enquirer*."

Marty laughed. "Yeah, okay, I hear you. Now what about— I read in the paper that they thought that guy Gerry Stillman might've killed one of the Darwins."

"They thought so, but it turns out he didn't. He and Chip Darwin had a feud going because they used to be in the same band but they split up."

"Oh, yeah, I know about that. Band called Survive. I saw them play once. They stunk. You know, I don't spend much time reading the trades anymore, but I did hear about that big split-up between their fathers, you know, with Chuck Darwin starting his own label and that squabble they had over at American Records. In fact, that kind of surprised me when I heard Kid and Jack signed with Darwin's label."

"What surprised you?"

"Well, it was real strange, you know. They were here one day, gone the next, same way they came into town. Next thing I knew, I heard they were in this band. But I figured they would have signed with Gerry Stillman at American."

"Why's that?"

"Because Stillman was down here scouting them."

"He was? When?"

"A few months ago. I could find out exactly if you want to know, but I remember that it was about a month before I found out Kid and Jack had a major contract. I didn't really think anything of it, you know, I was just happy for them. They deserved to be discovered. Most of the scouts who came through here didn't think they were polished enough. That's the big word, you know—*polished*. I think it means they didn't sound enough like disco."

"Are you sure it was Gerry Stillman?"

"Yeah, I'm positive, I talked to the guy for a while. The funny thing was, is that he watched Kid and Jack play and then he left without even bothering to introduce himself."

"Maybe he didn't like them."

"No, I don't think so. He told me he thought they were great. Now, he may have just been saying that, but why would he be handing me a line of bull? It's no skin off my nose if he liked them or if he didn't."

"You're right, that is strange."

"Yeah, I thought so, too. But it's a strange business. You know that. You can't trust anybody."

"How well I know that. Do you know anything about Kid and Jack before they got to Athens?"

"Not really. They just showed up one day out of the blue. Grace had a sister or a cousin or something, and they lived out with her near Eastville on Highway 53. I think they came from Alabama or Mississippi. Originally, I think they came from Memphis."

"What about Kid's father? Do you know anything about him?"

"I guess I should, but I don't. He had some crazy name like Butterfly or something like that."

"Bumblebee," I said.

"Yeah, that's right, Bumblebee. You know, if you want to find

out more, I know a guy you should call. His name's Elmore
Jackson. He lives near Memphis. He's about ninety years old, or
at least he looks like he's ninety, and he used to own a race club in
Memphis, you know, one of those blacks-only clubs they used to
have."

"Oh, I remember. The ones where the white kids used to hop
the ropes and dance with the blacks."

"That's right. It was bad enough that the kids were dancing to
rock 'n' roll to start with. But doing it with blacks, that was
unconscionable. It's hard to believe how much things have
changed, Del."

"We're just getting old, Marty."

"Tell me about it. Anyway, if you need to find the answer to
any question about the roots music scene, Elmore Jackson's the
guy you should talk to. He's a walking encyclopedia, only he can
barely walk. Tell him I told you to call. He should remember
me."

"Thanks, Marty, I'll do that."

"Let me look up the number."

"Do you still have that old address book?" Marty used to carry
around a tattered bundle of loose paper scraps that he tied with a
rubber band. He called it his hobodex.

"Nah," he said, "I left it at a girlfriend's house once. We went
on the rocks and I never had the balls to go back and get it. Some
guy moved in with her who was like seven feet tall and didn't like
Jews." Marty laughed. "I wonder how long it took him to figure
out that she was Jewish. He wasn't real swift."

"They don't have to be when they're seven feet tall."

Marty gave me the number. "Okay now, Del, if you're flying
again, there's no excuse why you can't come down here and visit.
I'll take you out for barbecue, it'll be the best chow you ever ate.
And send me a copy of the mag."

"You're on, Marty," I said. And I meant it. I put a copy of
Rock of Ages in an envelope, then took it down to the desk and
asked them to send it out the fastest way it could go. I had a weird

feeling inside, a feeling I wanted to shake but couldn't. Something Marty said had set an alarm off inside my head. Then I went back upstairs to call Elmore Jackson. There was something I wanted him to look up in that enyclopedia he carried on his shoulders.

17

The phone number that Marty Goldberg gave me for Elmore Jackson had been disconnected. I forged on in the spirit of Chuck Berry, singing "Long-distance information, give me Memphis, Tennessee . . ." while waiting for the operator to answer. I had a little more luck finding a listing for Elmore Jackson than Chuck Berry did with his Marie, but there was no answer when I called. I tried again an hour later and got a little luckier.

A woman answered and told me that I did indeed have the right number, but Elmore was out for the evening and wouldn't be back until after eleven o'clock. For a guy who was pushing ninety years old, it sounded like Elmore Jackson still knew how to have fun.

"Would it be too late for me to call him back then?" I asked.

"Oh, no, not Elmore," the woman replied. "He's a real night owl. You just don't want to talk to him before noon. He's meaner than a grizzly bear in the morning."

I killed some time by going out to dinner with Marcy, but she could tell there was something on my mind. It's amazing how quickly people can get to know each other's moods.

"What's troubling you, Del?" she asked.

"Nothing," I lied. "I'm just thinking about my story."

"You expect me to believe that?"

"No, I don't. You're right. There is something bothering me, but I'd prefer not to talk about it."

"It might make you feel better if you do."

"Not this time, Marcy. I just need a while to think something through."

"Is it about us? Are you having second thoughts?"

"No, of course not. Are you kidding?"

"Good." She smiled and reached across the table to take my hand. "I think things have reached the point of no return with Gary," she said. "As soon as I get back, I think I'm going to move out for a while. How do you feel about that?"

"Me? I think you should do whatever you feel you need to do."

"Is that all? I was hoping for a little moral support."

I didn't like the direction our conversation was taking. I was too distracted to focus on the subject Marcy wanted to talk about. I get that way sometimes—inattentive and distant. I didn't want her to see me like that. I was afraid we'd get into an argument. That was exactly what I didn't need. I'm sure she didn't either.

"I'm sorry, Marcy," I said finally. "I'm just not all here right now. You'll have to bear with me. Please?"

"Okay," she said at last. "But does this have something to do with Chip Darwin's death?"

"Yeah, I think it might."

"Max told me he wanted you to stop playing detective."

"I know. He told me the same thing."

"I think he's right. Why don't you just leave it to the police?"

I shook my head. "I don't know. I guess I can't."

"Why not?"

"Somebody implicated me in this thing, and I guess I take that as a personal challenge. I've got a hunch about something, and I don't want to talk to the cops until I find out if I'm right. Until then, I'm not sure they'd believe me anyway."

"Well, at least tell me about it."

"Not now. I don't want to get you all caught up in it. I'll know more when I'm finished talking to Elmore Jackson."

"Who's that?"

"He's an old guy in Memphis. I think he probably knew Kid Lee's father."

"And what does that have to do with Chip Darwin?"

"I don't know. I hope nothing at all."

"That's kind of vague," she said.

"I know. I'm sorry. I get like this sometimes when I'm working on a story. I just don't want to talk about it."

"And I don't want to sit here playing Twenty Questions. If you need my help, you know where to find me."

"Are you mad at me?" I asked.

"No, I'm not," Marcy said.

But I could tell she was as we walked back to the hotel. I didn't blame her, but I didn't enjoy putting up with it, either. We walked in silence most of the way, and I finally tried a little small talk to lighten things up.

"Max tells me the Darwins are going to Chicago tomorrow," I said. "Sylvia convinced Chuck to take a long vacation, but he wants to stop in Chicago and see a couple of old friends before they go."

"I know. I talked to Max, too."

"I forgot." I tried to pretend I didn't notice that she was giving me the silent treatment. That probably only made her madder. "If I were Chuck Darwin, I wouldn't want to go anywhere near the next Roots concert," I said. In fact, I was already starting to feel squeamish about returning to Chicago myself. And getting the cold shoulder from Marcy wasn't making me feel any better about it.

"You want to come in?" she asked when we got to the door of her room. Her tone indicated that she didn't particularly care either way.

"I can't," I replied. "I've got to go make that phone call."

"Oh, that's right. Elmore James."

"Elmore *Jackson*," I corrected. "Elmore James was the father of rhythm and blues."

"And if you ask me, you could use a little more rhythm and a lot less blues."

I nodded. "I guess I haven't been very good company tonight."

"It's not entirely your fault," she said. "I was just hoping for a romantic evening."

"I'm sorry it didn't turn out the way you expected."

She forced a smile and intoned the Rolling Stones: "You can't always get what you want . . ."

I gave her a kiss. When we parted, she said, "The offer still stands of helping you any way I can."

"I might take you up on that very soon."

"The sooner the better."

I ordered up a beer from room service, then called Elmore Jackson. It was almost midnight. The woman answered again. "You're in luck," she said. "Dad just rolled in this minute."

"Yessir, what can I do you for?" Elmore Jackson said when he picked up the phone. His speech was slurred, indicating that he had spent the better part of the evening knocking back the better part of a bottle.

I told him who I was, then mentioned Marty Goldberg.

"Marty Goldberg," Jackson said. "That the skinny fella with the New York accent, always looks like he ain't had a bath for a month?"

"Yup, that's Marty, all right."

"Nice fella," Jackson said. "Kinda smelly, but a nice fella just the same."

"Marty thought you might be able to tell me something about Bumblebee Lee," I said.

"Bumblebee Lee? I don't know anybody by . . . oh, you must mean Bumblebee Mitchell!"

"No, I don't think so. The man—"

"That's right. You mean Bumblebee *Mitchell*. Lee was just his first name, you see. I know the fella you're talking about. Terrible story. Terrible, terrible, terrible."

"Mr. Jackson, I want to make sure we're talking about the same person. The man I'm asking about had a wife named Grace—"

"That's right, I know exactly the fella you're talking about. Amazing Grace Mitchell, that was his wife's name. Used to call her Amazing Grace. Nice lady. Real nice lady. And by the way, you can call me Elmore. Ain't nobody calls me Mr. Jackson 'cept the minister, and that's because he's being polite to try to get me to start going to church. Maybe if he called me Elmore I might go ahead and take him up on it. But it's probably too late to do any good anyhow. I'm seventy-five years old and raised too much hell to get back in the Lord's good graces. Yessir. Bumblebee Mitchell. He could play the guitar like nobody I ever seen before or since. Played the fiddle and the banjo, too. Had a younger brother that played the drums."

"That would be Jack," I said. "Jack the Knife." I was talking as much to myself as I was to Elmore Jackson.

"What'd you say?"

"Jack the Knife," I repeated. "That's his nickname, because he plays drums with a pair of switchblades."

"Ah go on," Elmore said. "You're pulling my leg."

"No, it's true."

"Well, I don't know anything about that. I just knew him as a young fella that could play the drums. He was much younger than Bumblebee. I don't know what exactly became of them all after the tragedy happened."

"That's what I'm calling about," I said. "What exactly did happen to him?"

"You don't know?"

"I haven't the slightest idea." Actually, I had an inkling of what Elmore Jackson was about to say.

"Bumblebee Mitchell killed himself. Walked right out in front of a freight train on a hot summer's day. Couple days before he done it, he bought himself a big insurance policy. Of course his wife, she wasn't able to collect on it, on account of his death being ruled suicide. You can't buy insurance, then kill yourself, then expect them to pay on it. But Bumblebee, you see, he wasn't too bright. He was what you call *naive*, if you know what I mean."

"Yes, Elmore, I know exactly what you mean." I thought of Kid and realized that he was probably the spitting image of his father. "Did he leave a note? Did anybody know why he did it?"

"No, no note. Bumblebee Mitchell, he couldn't read or write. But I can tell you exactly why he done it, if you got the time."

I told him I had all the time in the world.

"Okay, you just hang on there a second while I fix myself a drink if you don't mind."

"I've got no objections." Just then the room-service waiter arrived. I popped open my beer and had a long-distance drink with Elmore Jackson.

"What year did Bumblebee kill himself?" I asked.

"Let me think, it was back in fifty-eight, I think it was. That's right, fifity-eight. Did you ever hear a song called 'Crazy Little Lady'?"

"Yes, I know it well."

"Well, Bumblebee Mitchell wrote that song, you see, only he didn't get the credit for it. You know why? Because he got ripped off, that's why. It used to happen all the time back then, believe me. If I had a dime for every player I seen get ripped off, I'd be a rich man today.

"It must of been a year earlier, in fifty-seven, that some guys come down to my club and seen him play. Talent scouts. There was three of them. Two fat fellas and a skinny one. They was talking him up, you know, telling him how good he was, telling him how much money he could make if he signed a contract to make a recording. Well, I told him he better be careful, and I'm asking them fellas some questions, which they don't particularly care for, which is the tip-off right there, you know, that maybe they got something up their sleeve.

"Well, they left. Then what happens is a couple nights later, one of the fellas comes back, you see. And he's got the contract there with him, so I says to Bumblebee, 'Don't go acting like some dumb catfish jumping for the first worm you see.' I told him he's young, he's got plenty of time. But he wouldn't listen to me, you know, most of them never did. Then during the break Bumblebee goes outside with the man and goes ahead and signs his name on that dotted line. Now you know what happens next, don't you?"

"Bumblebee heard his song on the radio."

"That's right, that's exactly right. Heard it over and over and over again. Only it wasn't his song anymore, you see, on account of they stole it from him. And of course, before then he's going around bragging about how he's going to be a big star, which is the big mistake, you see. Because after that, not only did he get himself ripped off, but he lost face, too. And then I suppose it was just a couple weeks later that he went and walked out in front of that train. Dragged him half a mile down the track. There wasn't much left of him by the time that train finally stopped.

"I remember the funeral. It was so sad on account of he had a little son, couldn't of been more than six years old. And you know that little bugger, he already could play the guitar back then. Bumblebee showed him how. Sometimes I wonder what ever became of him."

"Kid," I said.

"Huh?"

"That's his name—Kid."

"That's right. You're exactly right. That's what they used to call him."

"He's doing fine, by the way," I said. "He's playing in a rock 'n' roll band called Roots. His uncle Jack's in the band, too."

"Is that so?" Elmore let out a soft whistle. "Well, I'll be damned. Are they any good?"

"They're great," I said.

"I figured as much. You could tell that little boy had the talent. He was a natural. It was in the genes, you see. Well, I sure would like to hear the two of them play sometime."

"I'll send you a copy of their album."

"You would? That would be awful nice."

"Do you remember the name of the man who ripped Bumblebee off?" I asked.

"Hmm, let's see. I should." I took a mouthful of beer while waiting for Elmore to remember. "No, I'm sorry, I don't. But I should. It's just I met so many people back in them days, and my memory for names ain't what it used to be. Is it important to you? I guess that's a silly question. If it wasn't important to you, why would you be calling in the first place? I bet if you give me a day or two to think it over, I might be able to dig around in my mind and dredge it up. But I should warn you, that might not help very much, on account of he probably used an alias. Most of them did, you know. But the funny thing is, I can almost picture his face."

"So you'd remember the man if you saw him."

"Oh, Lordie, yes, I sure would."

"Would you recognize a picture of him, do you think?"

"Sure I would. Well, at least I think I would. It's been a long time, you know. It probably depends on how recent a picture it was and all that."

I figured Elmore was probably right about the man's using an alias, but I decided to ask him anyway. "Could the guy's name have been Chuck Darwin?"

"Darwin, Darwin," he repeated softly. "That name sounds familiar, but it don't exactly ring a bell."

"Charles Darwin was the guy who came up with the theory of evolution," I said. "You might be thinking of him."

"Lordie, I think you're right," Elmore said. "You know we had that big monkey trial down here in Tennessee on account of him. That was back in 1925, I do believe. Over in Dayton. I think you're right. I must be thinking of him. But I know I must have that name written down on a slip of paper somewhere. I'll bet I could find it if I took the trouble and looked through some of my old boxes."

"I'd appreciate your doing that," I said. "What about Grace Lee?"

"Who?"

"I'm sorry. I mean Grace Mitchell. Did she know the name of the man who ripped off her husband?"

"No, she didn't. She didn't even meet the man. If she would've met him, Bumblebee never would've signed that piece of paper in the first place. You see, Grace was a sharp lady. But Bumblebee, he went ahead and signed the contract, thinking he would surprise her with the good news. And, of course, there wasn't any good news.

"I'll tell you one thing, though. I was standing right there beside her when Grace Mitchell swore she would get revenge on the man that killed her husband. You see, that's how she saw it. She figured Bumblebee never would've killed himself if it hadn't been for that man, and she was probably right. And I'll tell you another thing. If Amazing Grace say she's going to get her revenge, you best believe she meant it."

I had seen enough of Kid's mother that I didn't need Elmore Jackson to convince me she meant what she said. I had a sinking feeling in my gut as I drained the last of my beer. I had found out a lot from Elmore, almost more than I wanted to know. But I knew I had been taking that risk when I called him. I now had reason to suspect that Grace Lee might have killed Chip Darwin, but I didn't think it was reason enough to go to the police. Before that, I had to find out for sure that Chuck Darwin was the man who ripped off Kid Lee's father. If he was, I had a feeling he wouldn't be long for this world.

"Elmore, are you busy tomorrow?" I asked.

"Tomorrow? You mean do I have any plans?"

"That's right."

"I never got any plans. Not since I sold the club."

"Would it be okay if I came down to see you?"

"See me? When?"

"As soon as possible."

"You mean in the morning?" There was a tone approaching horror in Elmore Jackson's voice. I recalled what his daughter had said about Elmore being a night owl.

"How about afternoon?" I asked. "I mean, right after noon."

"This must be an awful important story you're writing."

"It is, Elmore. Very important."

"Okay, then, I'll be waiting here for you."

18

I called Marcy as soon as I was done talking to Elmore Jackson.

"Hello," she answered in a sleepy voice.

"I guess I woke you up."

"No, no, that's okay, Gary. I was just dozing off."

"This isn't Gary. It's Del."

"Oh damn, I'm sorry. I didn't—"

"No harm done," I assured her. "That just proves you must have been asleep."

Marcy yawned. It was a nice sound, like proverbial music to my ears. I could picture her tousled hair, her blue eyes peering out from behind heavy lids. All of a sudden, I missed her, as if we hadn't seen each other for a long time.

"I need your help now," I said. "I have to get some of your photos. The ones from backstage before the first concert, or maybe from Danny Darwin's funeral."

"Sure, but what do you need them for?"

"I have to show a couple of them to Elmore Jackson."

"Are you going to tell me what's going on?"

This time, there was no doubt in my mind. If I didn't share the information I had uncovered, my head was going to explode.

"Yes," I said, "I'll tell you everything, as soon as I get down there. Is it presumptuous of me to think that your invitation to come over still stands?"

"No, Del, it's a standing offer."

"Great. I'll be there as soon as I'm done making the plane reservations."

"Plane reservations? Where are you going?"

"Memphis, Tennessee."

Getting from one small city to another is a logistical nightmare, but anything is possible with modern technology and saintly patience. I arranged for a flight from Milwaukee to St. Louis at seven A.M. From there I'd have to switch planes for Memphis. If that wasn't sufficient to test my mettle, I could catch a puddle jumper from Madison to Milwaukee. But I thought two plane rides was plenty. I elected to drive to Milwaukee.

When I got to Marcy's room, I told her everything I had learned from Marty Goldberg and Elmore Jackson. Her notion that talking about it would make me feel better proved to be correct. But in the process, I made her feel bad.

"Do you really think Kid's mother killed Chip Darwin?" she asked. "I just can't believe that."

"I know. I guess the problem is that I *can* believe it. I just don't want to. One of the women traveling with the band told Detective Schmitz that I was onstage. I guess it must have been Grace."

"I think she likes you, though. I just can't imagine her implicating you."

"Neither can I. But people do get desperate when they do desperate things."

"I guess so. But what about Kid and Jack? Were they in on it, too?"

"I don't know. Probably Jack, at least. After all, he was onstage before the concert and I'm not sure Grace would have been strong enough to move the amplifier into a precarious position by herself. Also, he was Bumblebee's brother. It makes sense that Grace would have told him who Chuck Darwin was. But maybe not. She is, as the song goes, a crazy little lady."

"She sure is." Marcy shook her head sadly. She looked like she was about to cry. I took her hand.

"Maybe it's all a coincidence," I said. "Maybe Chuck Darwin wasn't the guy who ripped off Kid's father."

"You don't believe that."

"No, I don't. I'd like to, but I don't. I'll find out for sure when I see Elmore Jackson."

Marcy got off the bed and walked to the dressing table. She picked up one of my cigarettes and lit it. She looked unnatural with it. "The thing I don't understand is how Grace found out where Chuck Darwin was in the first place."

"That's the easy part," I told her. "Gerry Stillman was down in Athens, Georgia, at Marty Goldberg's club. Based on what Marty said, that was right after Stillman and Darwin had their falling-out. Stillman must have told Grace where to find Chuck Darwin."

"But Marty Goldberg told you that Stillman didn't even talk to her."

"Not that night," I said. "But he could have called her on the phone. Or sent her an anonymous note."

"But how did Gerry Stillman find them in the first place?"

"That's a good question. I don't have the answer." Sorting out all the details was a lot like writing a news story. You ask people questions to get answers, but the more answers you get, the more questions you seem to be left with.

Marcy looked at her cigarette and curled her nose in disgust. "How can you smoke these damn things?"

"They're an acquired taste. I'm also addicted to them."

"But if Gerry Stillman wanted to get even with Chuck Darwin, why didn't he just sign Kid and Jack to a contract himself? That would have been a much better way of getting back at Darwin."

"I agree with you," I replied. "But when people get revenge on their minds, there's no telling how they'll think or what they'll do."

"Revenge is sick," she said, crushing out the cigarette.

"I agree with that, too."

Marcy took my hand again and pulled me toward her. We embraced, for a long time. She felt so warm and soft against me that all I wanted to do was sit there hugging her forever. I wanted to forget about Kid Lee and Chip Darwin and rock music. Suddenly, Marcy pulled away, and I felt a chill, followed by a momentary surge of panic. The spell was broken and we were back to reality.

"Do you think Grace or Jack killed Danny Darwin, too?" she asked.

I shook my head. "I'm inclined to believe Tina's version of that. I think Danny probably got the drugs from Chip and just overdid it."

"That's a relief," she said softly.

"But not much of one."

"Are you going to call Max?" Marcy asked. "He's always good to talk to."

"Not this time. I'm afraid I know what he'd say."

"He'd tell you to leave it alone."

"He might. But he'd also realize that his friend Chuck Darwin could be next in line. I'm afraid he might want me to go to the police. I'm not ready for that yet. I have to find out for myself."

Marcy picked up her watch off the night table. "If you want to get a good night's sleep, you better get ready for bed," she said.

I had already given up hope of that, but getting into bed sounded wonderful just the same. Falling in love gives off its own special energy, the kind you'll never get from an eight-hour vacation in dreamland. By the time we finished getting to know each other better, the sun was beginning to make its presence known. I didn't want to leave, but I had to. Marcy felt the same way about my departure and insisted on driving me to the airport in Milwaukee. She said she would drive the car down to Chicago later in the day, and we could meet up there. At first I resisted the idea, but she insisted. As Kid had said, it's hard to turn down a nice lady like Marcy.

Her company kept my spirits up, and I didn't even start to feel anxious until she waved good-bye at the gate and I boarded the plane. But when it finally hit, it hit me all at once—the fear of flying, the worry about Grace Lee, the lack of sleep. I tried to dismiss the feeling as a bad case of the caffeine jitters, but it was far worse than that. I broke out into a cold sweat and my hands began shaking. I gripped the arms of my seat and wondered how the guy in the suit beside me could sit there calmly reading a newspaper. My stomach was growling like a mad dog. I wondered if he could hear it.

I closed my eyes and tried to think nice thoughts, the way my therapist had taught me to cope with anxiety attacks. I thought about Marcy, about her easy smile, her soft voice, her ocean-blue eyes peeking out through silky strands of jet-black hair, but my mind was blocked. No matter how hard I tried, I couldn't picture her face. I was all alone, locked up with my demons.

I started to feel a little better after takeoff, but it was still hard to imagine feeling any worse. Against my better judgment, I forced down the airline breakfast to fill the hole in my stomach. Afterward I used the Max Horton nerve cure: I drank two screwdrivers. It had been almost ten years since I had a drink before noon, and it would be at least ten more before I'd do it again. As a stop-gap measure, however, it seemed like a good idea.

The landing went smoothly, as landings go, but when we got to St. Louis, I began entertaining the thought of renting a car and doing the second leg of the trip on terra firma. Regardless of what they say about the odds, I'll take my chances driving over flying any day. But that notion got dispelled as soon as I looked at a road map and found out Memphis was three hundred miles away. I was finding out firsthand that it's a big country, almost too big. But it was still a small world. After my talk with Elmore Jackson the night before, I realized it was too small. And it was shrinking by the minute.

I went to the cocktail lounge and had another drink, then crossed my fingers and boarded another plane.

19

When we touched down at Memphis International Airport, I got a sudden burst of energy. Not only was I back on solid ground, but I was thrilled to be in a town that's a living monument to the roots of rock 'n' roll. I grew up on Elvis Presley, Chuck Berry, and Jerry Lee Lewis. In college, I discovered their blues predecessors—Robert Johnson, Furry Lewis, Sleepy John Estes. The Delta was where it all started, and Memphis was its capital. As I crossed mean old Highway 51, now known to locals as Elvis Presley Boulevard, I was tempted to make a quick swing by Graceland. But I had business to attend to, so I drove straight out Highway 61, contenting myself by singing Bob Dylan songs.

Elmore Jackson lived in an old farmhouse southwest of the city, the last house before you crossed the Mississippi line. Elmore proved true to his word. He was waiting for me on the front porch, lounging in a rocking chair that must have predated the Civil War. He had mentioned that he was seventy-five years old, but Marty Goldberg had been right about him looking ninety. His face was a mosaic of splotches and wrinkles, and his eyes were like slits trapped under lids that wanted to stay shut. He was a tall man, well over six feet, but as the old blues song goes, he was nothing but the skin and bones.

Elmore had a bottle of Pabst Blue Ribbon in his hand. On a rickety table beside him was a pint of Jim Beam and a pack of unfiltered Camel cigarettes. He put down the beer and held out a hand the texture of leather.

"Well, Mr. Barnes, right on time," he said. He grinned, revealing yellowing teeth, and winked. "Right on time for a drink, I mean." He picked up the bottle of bourbon and began pouring it into plastic tumblers on the table.

"No, please, not for me," I said. "I've been drinking vodka and orange juice all morning. And you can call me Del."

"That's right, we got a deal, don't we? I won't call you Mr. Barnes if you don't call me Mr. Jackson. But vodka and orange juice, that ain't a drink! Don't you want just a little nip, you know, to be polite?"

I stared at the bourbon and swallowed hard. The last thing I needed was more alcohol.

"It's my daughter, see," Elmore said. "She don't let me drink before five unless I got company. So this is kind of a special occasion for me."

"Well, in that case, okay," I said. "But please, just a little."

"Naturally," Elmore replied. But there turned out to be a big difference between his idea of a little and mine.

Elmore toasted with his glass, then gulped down his drink while I sipped mine. "Must be five o'clock some place in the world," he said as he poured himself another.

I smiled and nodded, then handed him the Roots album. He held it about two inches from his face and studied it for a few minutes, squinting to read the names of the songs, then staring at the pictures of the band members.

"Yessir, Bumblebee Mitchell. And this must be his brother and his son," he said, pointing at the photos of Jack and Kid. "And you say they're good?"

"Very good," I said. "They're going to be very successful. The record's selling well."

"Is that right?" Elmore nodded and lit a Camel.

Just then, a tall pretty woman in her thirties stepped out onto the porch. "Oh, your company's here. That's good. Lunch is almost ready. Do you want some lemonade?"

Elmore snorted. "Of course we don't want no lemonade." He tilted his head. "This is my daughter, Lucille."

"Del Barnes," I said, shaking hands with Lucille. Then, in a whisper, I added, "If it's not too much trouble, I could use a little lemonade."

"Of course," she said, smiling.

Elmore shot me a disapproving glance, but he refrained from chastising me. I sat down in the chair beside him and took out the photos Marcy had given me. I handed them to Elmore.

"Do any of these guys look familiar?" I felt a little silly asking the question, because I wasn't sure how much sight Elmore had left in his eyes.

He squinted at the photographs, then shouted, "Lucille, bring me my eyeglasses, honey."

Lucille appeared a moment later carrying Elmore's glasses, a pitcher of lemonade, and a tray with ham, beans, cole slaw, and freshly baked bread. "Why don't we move around the corner to the picnic table," she suggested.

"Not now, honey," Elmore replied. "Me and Del's talking *business.*"

Lucille poured me some lemonade, then handed the glasses to her father and disappeared around the corner with the tray.

Elmore looked at one of the photos that Marcy had snapped backstage before the first Roots concert. "Yessir, them's the three fellas I was telling you about, all right. And this one here, that's the fella that cheated Bumblebee Mitchell."

I leaned in to get a look at the person he was pointing at. "Are you sure?" I asked.

Elmore gave me a look that made me feel like I was about six inches tall. I had a feeling he had been giving people that look all his life, any time someone questioned something he said.

"Of course I'm sure. Elsewise, I wouldn't say so in the first place." He paused to let that sink in. "By the way, last night I did me some checking, like I told you I was planning on doing. And you want to know what? Turns out I was right about that name after all."

Elmore pulled a scrap of paper out of his shirt pocket and handed it to me. "You see, just like I told you. Just like you asked. The name of the fella that drove Bumblebee Mitchell out

into the path of that train was Charles Darwin. What do you think
of that?''

I didn't know what to think, never mind what to say. I grabbed
for the tumbler of bourbon and drank it down. It tasted strong,
too strong, and my mind was swirling. I chased the bourbon
down with the whole glass of lemonade, but my head was still
spinning. I had come to see Elmore Jackson to find out the ugly
truth, but now that I was face to face with it, I found out it was
uglier than I had imagined.

Just then, Lucille stepped around the corner. "You men finish
up with your business and come eat your lunch before it gets
cold."

"We was just about to do that," Elmore said. It was only when
he lifted himself out of the rocking chair that I noticed Elmore
Jackson's wooden leg. He noted my startled reaction, shrugged,
and said, "Had me a little accident way back when. Sure comes
in handy when you got to knock on wood. My grandkids, you
know, they sure used to get a kick out of it. I used to tell them
they got such a tough granddaddy that I got to hold my socks up
with thumbtacks!"

Elmore pulled up his pants leg to reveal an argyle sock with
two thumbtacks in it. He let out a laugh and I joined in. At
another time, I could have had a great time listening to his
stories. But not today. I walked to the table more unsteadily than
Elmore did and sat down. I was in a daze, but it wasn't from the
alcohol. There was something more powerful than that working
on me. I think it was fear. But I wasn't in any danger. I was
worried about Grace Lee and what she might do. Actually, I
knew what she was going to do. She was going to kill Chuck
Darwin as sure as the sun rose and set. I just didn't know when
she was going to do it.

I wanted to leave right away, but I realized that would be
impolite. I sat at the table with Lucille and Elmore, picking at the
food that I had no appetite for even though it was delicious, and
listened to the old man's stories about the good old days. They
were good stories, but I wasn't paying much attention to them. I
had more important things on my mind.

"Now later on, Del, how about you and me, we'll go clubbing," Elmore said.

"Clubbing?"

"You know, we'll go into town and hit all the clubs. Drink us some drinks, hear us some music."

"I'm sorry, Elmore. I've got to get back up to Chicago this afternoon."

"This afternoon! Why, you didn't arrive until just a few minutes ago in the first place."

"I think Del's got business to attend to," Lucille said.

Elmore snorted. "Business! Everybody got business to do. Nobody got time to have any *fun* anymore."

Lucille leaned over and touched my shoulder. "Don't mind him," she said. "He's just been in an *ornery* mood lately. You see, his dog died a couple weeks ago, and ever since he's been acting like it was his last friend on earth."

Elmore scowled at his daughter. "Horseshit! That dog was nothing but a damn nuisance. I don't miss him, not one bit."

I looked at the old man until our eyes locked. "I'd love to hang around here with you, Elmore," I said. It was the God's honest truth. Next to seeing Marcy, there was nothing I wanted to do more. "But I've got to do something really important."

"Important! What's so important?"

"Thanks to you, I think I might be able to stop a murder."

"Lordie, that is important. Who's murdering who?"

"I think Grace Mitchell is going to kill Chuck Darwin."

"Well, good for her then. If you ask me, that's exactly what he deserves after what he went and done to her husband."

"I agree with you, Elmore." That wasn't entirely true, but I didn't want to get into a philosophical discussion of when homicide was justifiable. "But unfortunately, it's not that simple."

"Why not?"

"It's too complicated to explain, but I'll come back and tell you about it sometime."

"And what exactly are you going to do about it? You ain't planning on turning Grace Mitchell over to the police, are you?"

"No, I'm not." In fact, I thought it might come to that, but I didn't feel like telling Elmore Jackson about the death of Chip Darwin. "I intend to try to talk her out of it."

Elmore shook his head. "Well, good luck to you, Del, and mark my words, you'll surely be needing it. If you succeed in doing that, you'll go down in history as the first person that ever talked Amazing Grace Mitchell out of anything."

I nodded and looked at my watch. "I'm sorry to be rude, but I've got to get going if I want to catch that plane."

"That's all right, we understand, Del," Lucille said.

Elmore was less understanding, but he did take the trouble of hobbling down the steps to the car with me. "When you talk to Grace, you be sure and tell her old Elmore Jackson got his mojo working overtime for her. I'd say her some prayers, 'cept I forgot how to pray a long, long time ago."

Even following the shortcut that Lucille had told me about, I barely made it to the airport in time for my flight. It was better to be in a rush, though, because I didn't have the luxury to sit around the terminal and worry about flying. I had more pressing matters to worry about anyway. As their weight grew heavy on my mind, I drifted off into an uneasy sleep.

I flashed on the photos that I had shown to Elmore Jackson, then more pictures began flipping across my field of vision, like pages turning in an old photo album. I saw my mother and father, then my brother and my aunt and uncle. I saw my first-grade teacher, then my classmates from elementary school. The pages began turning more rapidly, and soon I couldn't keep up with the pictures. I barely caught a glimpse of the band, the cover photo for our album. Then I saw the cover of the Roots album, with Chip Darwin's face covered over with a skull and crossbones.

I wanted to put my hand out and stop the pages from turning so fast, but I couldn't. I heard a voice inside my head—my voice— say, "This is your life passing before you. There's nothing you can do to stop it."

Then the dream came. It had been a long time, more than a year, since I'd had the dream. When it came, it was more vivid than ever. It was the same nightmare: I was on the airport runway, carrying my guitar, chasing the plane. I caught up with it and tried to climb aboard, but it was moving too fast and starting to lift off the ground. Karen was leaning out the window, waving frantically. She said something, but I couldn't hear her. Then I realized it wasn't Karen. It was Marcy.

The plane took off and I was left standing there all alone, cold and frightened. I knew it was going to blow up and I wanted to take my eyes off it, but instead I stood there and watched. I couldn't will myself to stop watching. When the plane exploded into flames, I let out a scream.

I woke up with a start and lurched forward, but the seat belt prevented me from hurtling out of my seat. I looked around quickly, feeling scattered, scarred, scared. In the row across from me, a lady and her young daughter were staring in horror at me. Luckily, there was no one sitting beside me. It was only me, beside myself.

I became aware that my shirt was drenched in sweat. My head was throbbing, and my body ached all over. The flight attendant, a pretty blond woman, appeared next to me and gripped my arm. In a Southern drawl, she asked, "Are you all right, sir?"

"Nothing," I blurted, "it's nothing. I was just having a bad dream."

"I'll say you were. Can I get you anything?"

"No, nothing. Yes, a glass of water."

"Sure thing."

As she turned away, another female voice came over the P.A. system: "Ladies and gentlemen, welcome to Chicago."

I looked out the window of the plane. We were back on solid ground. That should have made me feel better, but it didn't. As the Rolling Stones had sung on their last album before Brian Jones ended up in the bottom of a swimming pool, I felt like I was 2000 light years from home.

Part III:

Third City on the Tour

20

I was still groggy and disoriented as I made my way down the vast corridor at O'Hare Field in Chicago. I've heard that O'Hare is the busiest airport in the world. I don't know if that's true, but it certainly seemed like the biggest. The arrival gate must have been ten miles from the baggage claim. I was glad Marcy had taken my luggage by car, but that was only a small consolation, considering my frame of mind. I tried to reframe it with a cup of coffee from the snack bar, but it tasted like it had been brewed quite a while ago, probably some time before the Chicago Fire.

I picked up a copy of the *Sun-Times* to read in the taxi and was amazed to learn that Steve Dahl's disco demolition at Comiskey Park was still big news. It had happened a week before, but it seemed like a year to me. As we crawled into the city in an inexplicable mid-afternoon traffic jam, I couldn't help but think that the Roots concert that night would displace the disco riot as the year's most bizarre music news story—if I didn't get to Grace Lee beforehand.

I still didn't know exactly what I would say to Kid's mother, when I checked into the Drake Hotel at four P.M. I resisted the temptation to stop in the bar for a bracer and decided instead to talk things over with Marcy. I came away from her room humming "Where Were You When I Needed You." I figured she was out shopping or maybe just taking a walk. I couldn't blame her. It was a beautiful sunny day, although the wind was starting to swirl in off Lake Michigan.

The next stop on my itinerary was Max's room. I had some

questions for him, and I wanted some answers. But I didn't get them, because he wasn't in his room, either. For a moment, I felt all alone, as if everybody in the entourage was hiding from me. But that was just my paranoia rising to the surface.

On my way to the elevator, I bumped into the Larsen sisters. "Have you seen Max?" I asked.

Vicki provided the answer while Suzi provided backup giggles. This time, for some reason, I was able to get their names straight. Or at least I thought I had them straight.

"I think he's over at Chuck Darwin's hotel," she said. "That's where he said he was going."

I wasn't aware that Darwin was staying at a different hotel, but considering what I had learned from Elmore Jackson, I thought it was a good idea for him and his wife to stay as far away from the band as possible. Maybe it was dumb luck or maybe they had planned it that way. From what Max had told me, I had the impression that Sylvia Darwin didn't even want to be in Chicago. I felt exactly the same way, but of course I had my own set of reasons.

"How long ago was that?" I asked.

"Oh, I don't know," Vicki replied. She turned to face her sister. "How long would you say it was, Vicki?" Oops. I had gotten the Larsen sisters confused once again.

The real Vicki began giggling relentlessly. She was on something and I knew it, and she knew I knew. Her sister joined in, then Vicki got momentary control of herself and said, "An hour maybe. No, half an hour."

I gave them a look that would have frightened a lion, but they continued to laugh. "Do you know what hotel Darwin's staying at?" I asked.

"The White something," Suzi blurted out between giggles.

"No, no, I think it's the *Black* something," her sister said.

"No, it's the *White* something," Suzi repeated. "I'm *positive.*"

That counted for a whole lot. "Thanks," I said, "you've been a big help."

I went back to my room and started to call Artie Crosby. He

would know for sure where Chuck Darwin was staying. But before he could answer, I hung up. I figured Artie was at the sound check anyway, but even if he wasn't, I realized I couldn't handle one of his hyper moods. I picked up the Chicago Yellow Pages and checked under hotels. I found a listing for the Whitehall on Chestnut Street, a block south of the Drake. I also found a listing for the Blackstone, on South Michigan Avenue in the Loop.

I tried the Whitehall first. After all, Suzi Larsen had been positive Darwin was staying at "the White something."

Bingo. Something was finally going right. But as the phone in Darwin's room began to ring, I realized that I wanted to talk to Max in person, not on the telephone. And I certainly didn't want to speak to him with Chuck Darwin and his wife standing nearby. I hung up again.

I sat on the bed, dazed, and weighed the merits of ordering a bottle of bourbon from room service. I thought about it for two cigarettes, then concluded it was time to face the music. I made my way to Grace Lee's room.

I thought I could hear a man's voice inside as I knocked on the door. I had to knock a second time before Grace Lee asked, "Who is it?"

"It's Del Barnes," I said.

"Just a second, Del," she replied. But it was more like a minute before Kid's mother unfastened the chain lock and slowly opened the door. She was wearing an Indian print robe, the same one she had worn at the first Roots concert, when she had seemed to materialize from thin air. There was a smile on her face, but I sensed tension beneath it. Maybe it was just my anxiety coming through.

We stood there staring at each other awkwardly for a moment, then Grace asked, "Yes, what is it, Del?"

"I'd like to talk to you about something," I said.

"Why, yes, of course, come in." Grace peered at me as I stepped inside. "You look troubled, Del," she said.

"Yes, I am, Mrs. Lee."

She nodded, then walked to the TV set and turned down the

volume. That explained the man's voice I had heard while waiting outside.

"You don't have to call me Mrs. Lee, Del," she said. "You can call me Grace."

I nodded. I didn't know how I was going to work my way to the delicate subject I wanted to discuss, but I realized this was my shot. "Maybe I should call you Mrs. Mitchell," I said.

I figured that would trigger a reaction, but Grace was cooler than sherbet and just as smooth. She smiled, a forced smile, and said, "Now, why in the world would you want to do that?"

"I know who you are, Grace. I spoke to Elmore Jackson about you earlier today. He said to tell you he's got his mojo—"

"Elmore *who*?" she asked. This was one slick lady.

"You don't need to try to fool me," I said. "I know the whole story. Or at least I know most of it. I know all about your husband and the man from the record company who ripped him off. I know—"

There was something I didn't know, something I should have known. I stopped speaking the instant I noticed Grace recoil slightly. She was looking over my shoulder toward the bathroom. Before I could turn to see what had distracted her, I realized that the man's voice on the TV was not the voice I heard while knocking at the door. The voice was live, not Memorex, but it sure fooled me. It was one of the most foolish mistakes I've ever made, and I've made plenty.

I realized a lot of things in that momentary flash of time. I realized that the sound check was over. Otherwise, Jack the Knife wouldn't have been in the room. I realized that Tommy Ventura had been right about it not being a good idea to cross the man who played drums with switchblades. I realized that I should have spoken to Marcy or somebody, *anybody*, before going into that room by myself. But as Johnny Mathis and Deniece Williams had sung in their duet the year before, it was all "Too Much, Too Little, Too Late."

As I turned and caught a glimpse of Jack Mitchell bearing down on me from behind, I heard his sister-in-law Grace say,

"No, no, don't hit him." But Jack the Knife was obviously the sort of guy who doesn't listen to advice from his relatives.

He hit me, all right. Hit the one-hit wonder with a blow that made me wonder what the hell he hit me with. It was a big hit, a smash. Any thoughts I had of making a comeback were over. He hit me so hard, he knocked me right off the charts.

21

It was a pleasant surprise to wake up, but only because I hadn't counted on ever waking up again. Practically everything else about the experience was unpleasant, starting with the dog that was licking my face like it was a beef-flavored lollipop. I tried to look on the bright side of things. I was lucky the dog was licking instead of biting. For that matter, I was lucky just to be alive.

He was a scrawny brown mutt, a mix of every breed that had ever walked on God's earth, with a touch of cyclops thrown in. He had started out with two eyes, but somebody or something had poked out the left one. He was a sorry sight, but no sorrier than the guy he was crawling on.

As I pushed him away with my arm, I became aware of another unpleasant sensation. My head was throbbing like someone had been doing street repairs on it. There was no doubt that Jack the Knife had drilled me good. I felt the back of my head and discovered a lump the size of an orange. It must have been a blood orange, because when I looked at my hand there was blood all over it. There also was a sour taste in my mouth.

I sat up and tried to get my bearings. I was in an abandoned lot that was overgrown with weeds and littered with every brand of beer can and soda pop bottle you could imagine. Plus there was garbage, all kinds of garbage. Directly above me was a crumbling concrete structure, an elevated highway of some sort. I later found out it was a street called Ogden Avenue. A car rumbled overhead, and I felt like somebody was knocking me on the head again.

I was about fifty yards in from the corner of two wide streets. Across one of them, I could see a row of red-brick high-rise buildings. Something told me the buildings weren't luxury apartments. Maybe it was the clusters of black kids hanging around outside, maybe it was the piles of trash all around them, maybe it was the graffiti on the buildings. Whatever it was, I knew I was on the poor side of town.

I looked at my watch. Seven o'clock. That meant I had probably been out for an hour. Despite the pain in my head, I felt surprisingly alert for some reason. For a moment, I thought maybe I had been out for thirteen hours and it was already the next morning. The thought gave me a momentary spasm of panic, as I remembered how I had gotten into this mess to begin with and wondered whether Chuck Darwin was still alive. But even in my disoriented state, I realized that couldn't be possible. The realization gave me even more cause for panic, and this time the spasms lasted longer than a moment. I suddenly knew why I felt so alert, and the thought of it made me shudder all over.

There was a familiar sensation running through my body, and to be honest it was kind of a pleasant sensation. I felt strong, energetic, almost euphoric. That's not a natural way to feel after you've been clobbered on the head. But there was nothing natural about the sensation. It was chemically induced. Jack Mitchell had slipped something into me after he knocked me out. I was speeding my brains out.

My heart was pounding as I felt it slide up to my throat. It was like a clock ticking off the seconds until the bomb goes off. And I was the bomb.

I ran to the intersection and looked at the street signs. I was at the corner of Division and Halsted. I didn't know my way around Chicago, but I was pretty sure Division Street was on the North Side. The evening sun was hiding behind storm clouds that had blown in off the lake. I told myself I wanted to head east toward the Lake. It took me a few moments to figure out which direction I had to go based on where the sun was setting. That's how wacked out I was. I still wasn't even sure if I was going the right way until I got out from under the overpass and saw the John Hancock Center on Michigan Avenue. It didn't look very far away. In fact, it looked so close it seemed like I could reach out and touch it. But I realized that was just the drugs working on me.

I took off sprinting along Division Street. I felt like I could run all day. I felt like I could fly, for that matter. I had to get to a hospital fast.

I slowed to a walk as I approached a pair of black guys standing on the next corner. One of them was short and fat, and he was holding a radio the size of a washing machine on his shoulder. I recognized a song by Kool and the Gang blasting out of it. The other was tall and wiry, and he was dressed to the nines in white patent-leather shoes, red pants, a shiny black shirt, and a Panama hat. They didn't look threatening, but what did I know in my state of mind? I thought about crossing the street to avoid them just to be safe, but that would have put me on the side near the housing project where a gang of a dozen kids was playing baseball. Or at least a few of them were holding baseball bats. I didn't actually see a ball.

The black guys were laughing above the roar of the radio, so I decided to take my chances on asking for directions. As I stopped, I realized they were laughing at me.

"Hey, dude," the guy in the hat said, "you're in the *wrong* part of town."

"You're telling me," I managed to blurt out while catching my breath. "I'm lost."

"I'll say he's lost," the radio guy said. "He's as lost as you can get."

They both broke up with laughter again. I forced a smile and tried to tell myself not to show fear.

"You got any spare change, dude?" the hat asked.

"Sure, sure." It was only when I began to reach into my pockets that I realized Jack the Knife had lifted my wallet. As I looked at their expectant faces, I felt terrified. I remembered that I had stuffed a ten-dollar bill into the small niche at the top of my jeans pocket when I was at the airport. It was still there, but I wasn't about to part with it—not until it was absolutely necessary. I had a feeling that moment might be coming very soon.

"I'm sorry," I said, "I was robbed."

The radio guy elbowed his friend. "He was robbed," he said. They broke into laughter again.

"Ain't that a tragedy."

"Oh yeah, tragic."

"I got clobbered on the head and dumped in that lot back there." I pointed toward the lot, as if that would help my case. I looked up the street and thought about running away.

The guy with the hat walked behind me. "Ooh, lookee here, Slim," he said to the fat guy. "The boy *did* get hit."

Slim took a look and started to laugh. "Man, oh man! Look at the size of that lump."

"Dude, looks like somebody been playing drums on the back of your head."

I didn't see any gain in telling him that the guy who hit me actually *was* a drummer. I simply said, "I've got to get to a hospital. Can you tell me where the nearest hospital is?"

"Hospital," Slim said. "The boy needs to find a hospital. You know where there's a hospital around here? Must be one right in this neighborhood, wouldn't you think?"

The guy with the hat laughed. "Dude, you come around here and you don't have any spare change and you expect me to tell you how to get to the nearest hospital?"

I didn't think he was really expecting an answer, and I was too paralyzed with fear to give him one.

"When one of us goes to the hospital, we go to Cook County Hospital," Slim said.

"Where's that?" I asked.

"Oh, you don't want to go there, dude. That's a long walk. Real long walk. They put it far away, see, on account of they're hoping maybe we'll die on our way there in the ambulance."

Slim began laughing so hard at his friend's joke that he almost dropped his radio. I was about to give up and begin running when the guy with the hat put out his hand to shake. I put mine out tentatively, bracing myself for the possibility that he might try to flip me.

He didn't. "Tell you what you do, dude," he said. "You keep going along this street here for a while until you get to Clark Street. On Clark Street, you turn right. Then you go three blocks down and you'll see a hospital. It's called Henrotin Hospital. It's a nice hospital. Pretty nurses, the works. You go there and you tell 'em I sent you. Okay?"

"Sure, okay." All of a sudden, I realized that they posed no threat. They were just a pair of guys who lived in a bad neighborhood. They were probably scared to be there, too, only they didn't have any choice.

"Thanks a lot," I said. "I mean it." I started to walk off, then turned back. "What's your name?" I asked.

"Huh? My name?"

"Yeah, for when I tell them who sent me."

They both convulsed with laughter. Slim slapped his leg while balancing the radio. "This boy's got a sense of humor on him, don't he?"

His friend nodded. "He sure does. The name's Julius," he told me. "Julius Johnson."

"Julius, did you ever hear of a band called Roots?"

"Yeah, I've heard of them."

"Do you want to go to their concert tonight? It's at the Park West. Do you know where that is?"

"Yeah, I know where it is. I never actually been in there, but I know where it is."

"Go to the box office right now and tell them your name's Del Barnes. They'll let you in."

"Del Barnes. That's your name?"

I nodded.

"And all I got to do is say I'm you and they'll let me in?"

"That's right."

"You're kidding me, man."

"No, I'm not."

Julius shook his head. "Damn, I might just do that."

"What about me?" Slim said.

"You tell them your name's Max Horton."

"Max Horton." Slim turned to Julius. "I think I like this dude, man."

"Yeah, so do I. He kinda *grows* on you."

Slim put out his hand. "Take good care, my man."

As I turned and began walking away, Julius called after me. "Hey, Del, don't stop and talk to anybody else now. Some of the brothers around here, they're kinda mean. They're not all nice like us."

I broke into a trot, making sure to stay right near the street, as far away from doorways as possible. I tried to look over my shoulder for a taxi, but the few I saw were occupied. It was highly unlikely that a cabbie would be cruising in that neighborhood for fares. My head ached with each footstep against the pavement, and my heart was pounding even faster now. I knew I had to get medical attention soon. But getting through the encounter with Slim and Julius had strengthened my resolve. The tune to Gloria Gaynor's "I Will Survive" was warming the inside of my head, and I thought about Marcy saying it had been her theme song. I thought about how much I wanted to see Marcy again. I tried to cling to that thought. It lifted my spirit, and all of a sudden I was positive that somehow, someway, I was going to make it out of this one alive.

My confidence got all shook up when I came to within a block of the El tracks. Up ahead I could see four black guys loitering under the tracks. I could tell that they saw me. Something told me these guys weren't going to be as friendly as Slim and Julius. And I hadn't really been convinced that Slim and Julius were such friendly guys in the first place.

I came to a stop and pondered what I should do. All the while the guys under the tracks were watching, waiting to see what my next move would be. Maybe I was being paranoid. Maybe it was just the drugs making my head spin like a pinwheel. Maybe I could just stroll right past them, nod my head, and go about my business. Then again, maybe not.

I decided to try it anyway. I didn't really have any choice. If I backtracked, I'd be losing precious time. I'd have to find another way out. All streets led through hell in this part of town, anyway. Boy, do I hate Chicago.

Casually, ever so casually, I began to angle across Division Street. Of course, there was nothing casual about it. I was flat-out petrified. As soon as I started off the curb, two of the guys from the tracks sauntered across the street. Now, there was no doubt they were waiting for me.

I turned and began walking in the opposite direction, back the way I had come. I looked back over my shoulder and saw that all four of them were beginning to follow. I began to run, and I heard their footsteps keeping pace. Suddenly, there were no cars on the street.

Or so it seemed. Just as I hit the first side street, a rusty Chevy Impala screeched to a halt at the corner. I stopped, glanced at the car, then started running across the street in front of it. The driver rolled down the window and yelled at me.

"Hey, dude, you're going the wrong way."

I wheeled around to see Julius grinning at me. From inside the car, I could hear K.C. and the Sunshine Band blaring "I'm Your Boogie Man" out of Slim's boom-box.

"Some guys are after me," I managed to blurt out between breaths. I pointed back down the block.

Julius opened the back door of the car. "Well, get in then, dude. What're you waiting for?"

22

Julius and Slim gave me door-to-door service, right to the emergency-room entrance via the AMBULANCES ONLY driveway. This was the first indiscretion that made me unpopular with hospital personnel. It earned us the wrath of a wheezing, obese security guard who was probably counting the days until early retirement. I left him to argue it out with them, figuring I had more urgent things to do. But as I opened the door, I heard them settle it quickly, by taking off with the accelerator pedal to the floor, burning rubber and kicking up loose gravel.

I was even less responsible for the second indiscretion, but I took all the blame anyway. I went to the desk, where a middle-aged lady with bifocals was sitting behind a glass divider. She wore a name tag that said Miss Fairchild.

"I need immediate attention," I said. "I've taken an overdose of amphetamines. Actually, I didn't take them. Somebody forced them down me. I need to be treated right away."

Miss Fairchild barely looked up. "Do you have an insurance card?" she asked.

"Yes. I mean no, not with me, but I do have insurance."

"I need to see your insurance card," she said.

"Look, I was robbed," I said. "Somebody stole my wallet."

Miss Fairchild shrugged and picked up a clipboard with a form attached to it. She pointed to a waiting area, where five or six people were sitting in orange and blue plastic chairs. None of them was bleeding or in severe pain that I could see, and they all looked perfectly content watching a TV sitcom.

"Fill this out and take a seat," she said, handing the clipboard and a pen to me under the glass. "Someone will be with you in a little while."

"Don't you understand? This is an emergency. A *real* emergency." I was shouting now, and I could feel waves of anger surging through me from the speed. It was an awful feeling but a familiar one. It reminded me of when I used to fight with Karen and the other members of the band. It was hard to control even when you wanted to, but now I didn't care.

"Listen, lady. I didn't risk my life roaming through the meanest streets in Chicago only to be jerked around over a piddling insurance card by some tight-ass bureaucrat." Maybe I didn't actually say that. The drugs were pumping through me so fast that everything was a blur, including my memory. But I do recall saying one thing for sure: "I want to see a doctor *now*."

I could feel the people in the waiting area watching me. This was much more exciting than a TV show. I turned to look at them. I felt an urge to scream at all of them. Speed can make you totally crazy.

"Take a seat," she repeated. "And my name isn't 'Lady.'"

"No, I won't. I want to see a doctor right now."

"Mr. Brady, I've got a problem here," she said.

Mr. Brady turned out to be a plainclothes police officer. He was about ten years older than I am and probably fifty pounds heavier. Even in my agitated state, I thought it was curious that he had been sitting with a bunch of people watching a program called "The Brady Bunch."

"Great," I said when he showed me his badge. "I've got to talk to you about something important."

"Drug overdose," Miss Fairchild said. "No insurance card. I wish they'd take these people to County."

Officer Brady took hold of my arm. "Come over here, buddy. I've got a few questions for you."

"Fine," I said, "I'll answer everything. But first I need to see a doctor."

Brady began to pull me toward the waiting area. I began

pulling in the opposite direction. "So what'd you take?" he asked, yanking at my sleeve.

"I don't know." I pulled away from his grasp. "And I didn't take anything. Somebody forced it down me."

"Oh, somebody *forced* you to take drugs." Brady chuckled. "That's a good one, buddy." He grabbed my sleeve again. "You know, that's the first time I've heard that one all day."

"I'm telling the truth!" I shouted. "I want to see a doctor right now." I shoved him, and he lost his balance, crashing into the window that separated Miss Fairchild from reality. That was the third time I was indiscreet, and it didn't exactly work like a charm.

Brady gave me a shot in the ribs that sent me sprawling to the floor. I felt a stab of pain as I pulled myself up to all-fours. He was walking toward me, a smirk on his face. I could have charged him and taken my chances. With the speed coursing through my veins, I was definitely tempted. But I realized that probably would have made his day. The beefy security guard was inside now, and he was standing beside Brady for backup.

Just then, a doctor appeared in the hallway. He was a young guy, about my age. I didn't know if he had seen or heard the commotion. I only know that I began grinning from ear to ear when he said the magic words: "Bring him in."

Officer Brady began to lift me to my feet, but a cute young black nurse appeared out of nowhere and took over for him. I wondered for a moment if Julius actually had been at this hospital before, but I didn't bother telling her that he had sent me. I had some difficulty walking as she led me down the hall, but it didn't have anything to do with the drugs. I was still reeling from my collision with Brady's fist.

The doctor's name was Joe Boyle. There was a calm, reasonable tone in his voice that I hadn't heard since God only knew when.

"What'd you take?" he asked, feeling my pulse and putting me up on a surgical table.

"Oh, he didn't take anything," Brady said sarcastically. "Not this guy. He wouldn't take drugs. He says somebody *forced* him to take them.''

The doctor seemed to ignore the cop. He looked directly at me.

"Amphetamines," I said. "It must've been. My heart's beating like crazy.''

"It sure is," he said, counting off the pulse rate. "What's your name?''

"Del Barnes.''

"Open your mouth, Del." He looked inside. "There's a real good chance he's telling the truth, Mr. Brady. A lot of the stuff dissolved on his tongue.''

"I swear, I haven't taken drugs in ten years.''

Dr. Boyle nodded as a nurse on my left began to approach with a clear plastic tube about two feet long. She was another cutey, but the tube detracted from the overall effect.

"Roll over on your side, Del," Dr. Boyle said. "How did you hurt your head?''

"A guy smashed me from behind.''

"I'll say he did." Dr. Boyle felt the bruise, then walked over to the black nurse, who was holding three white robes. He put them on, one after another. He smiled. "This is going to be a little sloppy," he said. "But you're going to be okay.''

As I started to roll over, Brady asked, "Did the guy hit you on the head *before* or *after* he forced you to take the stuff?''

"Before," I said. "*Obviously*." I could feel another wave of anger coming over me. This time, it wasn't so frenzied and uncontrollable. I realized that the worst was over. I was going to be all right, after all.

"You wouldn't happen to know the name of the guy who hit you?''

"Jack Mitchell," I said. "He plays drums in a rock band called Roots. They're playing a concert right now at the Park West. The reason he tried to kill me is he killed somebody from the band a few nights ago in Madison and I found out about it. He's also planning on killing another guy tonight.''

"And what's this other guy's name?''

I couldn't tell if Brady was still humoring me or if he was

starting to believe my story. "Chuck Darwin," I said. "He owns a record label. He's—"

Dr. Boyle leaned in and started to put the tube in my mouth. "Officer, why don't you wait outside. You can talk to him as soon as I'm finished. Del, this is going to feel like you swallowed a razor blade."

He was right. It did. And that was just giving me the anesthetic so that it *wouldn't* hurt. If you've never had your stomach pumped, you can take it from me: You're not missing anything.

He lowered the end of the tube into my mouth and began sliding it down my throat. "Swallow it," he said.

I swallowed it, all right, and the instant I did so, I began choking like I've never choked before. I convulsed and started to turn, but he held me down with one hand while pouring warm water down my throat with the other. I could tell that Dr. Boyle had performed the procedure many times before, because he continued talking calmly as I tremored and gagged. I could tell the nurses had some experience, too, because they were standing back at a safe distance to make sure they didn't get splattered.

"Del Barnes," Dr. Boyle said. "Are you the same guy that used to be in a rock band called Meet the Press?"

It was like being at the dentist, when he talks to you and you want to respond but can't because he has his hand and a drill and half a pound of cotton stuffed into your mouth. It was just like that—only a hundred times worse. I'd rather be drilled every day of my life than have my stomach pumped once. Nonetheless, I managed to nod in answer to the doctor's question.

"Yeah, I thought so," he said. "I have your album at home. It's a very good record. I also remember your tour, when you came to Chicago. I was doing my internship in emergency medicine then. The night of the plane crash, I was working out at O'Hare. I've seen a lot of terrible things, but that was the worst I've ever seen."

I tried to nod again, to show that I was listening, but I was out of control by then. Globs of white powder and black pieces were shooting up the tube like it was a geyser. Dr. Boyle stood there calmly holding the tube while the contents of my stomach splattered all over the front of his medical robe. It was no wonder that he put on three layers.

"Yup, here they come," he said. "Black beauties. He gave you an overdose, all right. There's enough speed coming up to get the whole city high. You're a lucky guy that you got here in time, Del."

I closed my eyes and tried to think nice thoughts, with very little success. The whole process probably only took five minutes, but it seemed like an eternity to me. I couldn't believe that anybody who went through this experience would even think about taking drugs again.

When it was finally over, when he pulled the tube out of my throat, I was completely exhausted. I had a terribly foul taste in my mouth, and I was drooling out the sides.

"You've lost your gag reflex," Dr. Boyle explained. "For a little while, you won't be able to swallow your saliva." Then he turned to the black nurse and said, "Give me the charcoal."

She handed him about a teaspoon-sized piece of black mush.

"What's that?" I managed to blurt out.

He grinned and began to sing: "Love Potion Number Nine."

Another time it would have been funnier, but I didn't mind. The little black nurse got a chuckle out of it, and I had a feeling she was the one it was intended for.

"This is going to taste delicious," Dr. Boyle said as he pushed the charcoal down my throat. "But this will absorb the rest of what's in your stomach. It'll also make you cough a little."

In addition to his impeccable bedside manner, the young doctor had a gift for understatement. I coughed so hard and so long that I thought my whole stomach was going to come up. But soon—soon to anyone who was watching, at least—it was all over. I had been through hell and lived to tell about it.

While I was lying there, Dr. Boyle cleaned the wound on the back of my head and put a bandage on it. "Lucky you've got a thick skull," he said. "Now I want to put you into intensive care, hold you overnight for observation."

"No," I said, "you can't do that. I've got to get out of here right away."

The doctor grinned. It was a charming smile. I figured it won him lots of points with the nurses. "You're not going anywhere tonight, Del."

"I've got to," I said. "I've got to get to that concert. I've got to talk to that cop."

Dr. Boyle handed me a wad of tissues to wipe my mouth with. I was drooling like a tired old dog.

"I'll get Brady. You can talk to him. But you're going to have to make a powerful case for yourself if you expect me to sign you out of here."

Officer Brady was surprisingly friendly to me when he returned to the room. "I found out something very interesting, Barnes," he said. "You told me you were worried about some guy named Darwin getting killed tonight. It turns out you were right. Chuck Darwin was found dead in the Knickerbocker Hotel on Walton Street an hour ago. Only he wasn't killed. He committed suicide."

"What?"

"That's right. He shot himself in the head with his own gun. And right before that, *he* killed a guy. Pushed him out a window on the twelfth floor."

"Who?" I demanded. "Do you know who?"

"Yeah," he said, looking at a small notebook. "Gerry Stillman. The guy's name was Gerry Stillman."

23

I t took almost an hour before I was able to leave the hospital. After pumping me full of liquids intravenously, Dr. Boyle permitted me to sign out AMA—against medical advice. He laughed when I pointed out that this was the same abbreviation as the American Medical Association.

"That's not just a coincidence," he told me. "It's more appropriate than you might imagine."

While I was getting primed for my return to the real world, Officer Patrick Brady was on the phone getting the lowdown on the murder of Gerry Stillman and the suicide of Chuck Darwin from the homicide detective investigating the case. I was amazed to learn that it was only quarter to ten, but my sense of time had been incredibly distorted by my roller coaster ride through hell. It seemed as if weeks had passed since my visit with Elmore Jackson earlier that day.

Brady told me what he had learned while we drove up Clark Street to the Park West, the concert hall on Armitage Avenue where Roots was playing. Since the show had started at eight o'clock, there was still time to pick up Jack the Knife and Kid's mother—unless they had split town before the concert. That prospect seemed highly unlikely, as it would only cast suspicion on them. With me out of the way, they had at least until the next day to make their escape.

Based on the description that Brady had gotten from the homicide detective, I determined that it was Gerry Stillman Sr. who had been pushed out of the window of the Knickerbocker

Hotel. The place was located on Walton Street, right across from the Drake, where the members of the band and I were staying. When the police searched Chuck Darwin's pockets, they found Stillman's room number at the Knickerbocker written down on a notepad from the Whitehall Hotel. When they checked over at the Whitehall, they located Sylvia Darwin. She told them that Gerry Stillman had called her husband shortly after six o'clock, and Chuck had gone to the Knickerbocker to meet him. She also told them that Darwin had been very depressed about the deaths of his two sons and had it in his mind that Stillman was somehow responsible. She didn't know why Stillman had called, but said that Chuck was agitated when he left their hotel.

"Do you know what time it was when Darwin killed himself?" I asked Brady.

"Yeah. Somebody in the room next door said they heard a gunshot at quarter to seven."

"Did they see anybody getting away?"

"You kidding? In this city? Who would've dared to look? We're lucky they even bothered calling the police. Most people don't even do that."

I nodded and slumped down in my seat. I was so tired, I could've fallen asleep right there in the car. In my exhausted mental state, I couldn't quite put together the pieces of the puzzle. Every time I thought I could, one of the pieces just didn't fit. If Chuck Darwin had died shortly before seven, I didn't see how Jack the Knife could have killed him. By that time, Jack should have been at the concert hall. And if he wasn't, it was probably because he was busy dropping me off in the vacant lot at the corner of Halsted and Division.

"What makes you so sure this guy Jack Mitchell killed Darwin?" Brady asked.

I gave him an abbreviated version of the story. I told him about Chip Darwin's death onstage in Madison, then related what I had learned about Bumblebee Mitchell's suicide years before. I told him that Kid's mother held Chuck Darwin responsible for her husband's death and had sworn revenge.

"And when you went to confront her, that's when he smacked you over the head and stuffed you full of drugs."

"Yeah, that's right."

"You should've come to us then. It would've saved you a lot of trouble."

"Next time I'll know better," I replied.

"Your story certainly gives us a motive, but Detective Conroy—that's the name of the guy who's investigating—says it looks like a suicide to him. This guy Darwin was shot with his own gun. So unless he killed himself, that means somebody must have taken the gun away from him. How do you explain that?"

"I can't," I replied. The wheels of thought were spinning too fast in my head now to make any sense of anything. I wondered if Chuck Darwin really had killed himself and murdered Gerry Stillman after all. Somehow I didn't think that was too likely. There was one other possibility, but it was so scary to me that I didn't want to mention it to Brady yet. Despite the lesson I had learned, I still wanted to check out that one myself.

"I've got an explanation," Brady said. "Let's say this guy Mitchell has a gun. He goes to the hotel, pulls it on Darwin and Stillman, then searches Darwin and finds his gun. He pushes Stillman out the window, then shoots Darwin. It's a frame job."

"I don't know." I shook my head. I told Brady my doubts relating to Jack the Knife's busy schedule. "And how would Jack have known what hotel Stillman was staying at?" I asked. "How would he have even known that Gerry Stillman was in town?"

"I don't get it," Brady said. "First you say you're convinced that this Mitchell is going to kill Darwin. But now that Darwin's dead, it sounds like you're trying to convince me he didn't have anything to do with it."

"It's complicated," I said. "I'm just not sure about anything anymore."

"Maybe the old lady did it, this Amazing Grace," Brady said.

"I don't know. Maybe." Despite what Elmore Jackson had told me, I just couldn't visualize Kid's mother actually killing someone.

"Well, we'll get a much better idea of what's going on after we pick them up and ask them a few questions."

"Did Darwin leave a suicide note?" I asked. We were pulling up to the Park West. It was beginning to rain.

"No. Conroy said they didn't find one. But that doesn't mean anything. Some people don't leave anything. Other people, they write a whole book."

"Chuck Darwin was the kind of guy who would write a book," I said.

As we got out of the car, Brady said, "By the way, Barnes, I'm sorry about slugging you back at the hospital. I thought you were just some crazy guy on drugs."

"At the time, that's exactly what I was," I replied.

There was one squad car and one unmarked but obvious police car parked at the curb. Two cops in uniform were chatting with a pair of plainclothes cops outside the concert hall. I hung back while Brady approached them.

"Has Conroy arrived yet?" he asked one of the plainclothes cops.

"No, not yet." He's supposed to be here shortly. I'm his assistant, Detective Del Greco."

Brady nodded. "The guy we're looking to pick up is the drummer in the band. This fellow here will point him out to us, then you guys can cover the exits. I think it would be a good idea to get some more backup."

"I already took care of that," Del Greco said. "Help's on the way."

As we entered the lobby, I could hear Tina Darling belting out "Hit the Road, Jack." She wasn't exactly Ray Charles, but considering the circumstances, it struck me as a powerful number.

Del Greco flashed his badge at the guard by the door and asked how much longer Roots would be playing.

"They just started their encore. They should be finished in ten minutes."

The Park West was a glitzy venue, closer in size and format to a club than a concert hall. The audience was seated at tables and booths that stretched across the hall in semicircular rows. The rows were banked like an auditorium so that the people sitting farthest from the stage also had the highest seats. Two stairways on either side led to a balcony, where there were more tables. All the tables and booths were filled, and there was a standing-room-only crowd packed four deep at the bar in the back. Even with a full house, it was the smallest crowd that Roots had played for.

The first aisle we came to was a wide arc that circled the tables on the main floor and led down to either side of the stage. We headed down to our right. As we neared the corner of the stage, I thought I could see Jack the Knife looking out at us, but that might have been my imagination. It was hard to tell in the dim lighting. I scanned the crowd for Kid's mother, but I couldn't spot her.

Once the cops had a look at Jack Mitchell, Del Greco sent three of them outside to cover the main exit and the side exits. "Be careful," he warned, "this guy could be armed."

"He will be armed," I said. "He'll be carrying a pair of switchblades. He uses them for drumsticks."

"What?" Brady peered up toward the stage. "Damn if you aren't right," he said.

The band finished the Ray Charles cover, then went right into "No Time for Tears," a cut from their album. It was a slow number, designed to quiet down the audience. Based on the crowd's reaction, I figured they'd have to play a few more numbers before anybody would be ready to leave.

"Let's go down to the dressing room," Del Greco said, heading past the exit sign into the back. "We'll nab him in the back when they're done playing."

As we approached the door to backstage, Tommy Ventura stepped outside. "Del, where you been, man? Marcy's been looking all over for you—she's real upset."

"Tommy, if I tried to explain it to you, it would take longer than a Dead concert." I introduced him to the two plainclothes cops. "He'll take you backstage," I said.

"Sure, man, but what's going on?" Tommy asked.

"They're here to get Jack the Knife. It looks like he killed Chip Darwin. He damn near killed me."

"I don't believe it," Tommy said.

"Believe it," I replied. "Do you know where Marcy is?"

"Yeah, sure, Del." Tommy looked like a kid who had just found out there wasn't a Santa Claus. "She's down in front on the other side of the stage."

Just then, Artie Crosby peered out from the door to the dressing room. "What's going on?" he asked.

"Jack the Knife tried to kill Del," Tommy said. "He's the one that killed Chip. The cops are here to get him."

"What? That's crazy."

I wasn't about to waste my time trying to explain things to Artie Crosby. As far as I was concerned, he could read about it in the morning paper. I made my way back out to the main floor. Through a throng of people dancing in front of the stage, I could see Marcy and Max on the far side. I waved to them, and Max saw me. He tapped Marcy on the shoulder and pointed in my direction. As soon as she saw me, she broke into a smile and began pushing her way through the crowd.

I met her halfway, and put my arms around her like the circle 'round the sun, as the old Memphis Jug Band song goes. I closed my eyes as she nestled against me and concentrated on blocking out the sound engulfing us. For one fleeting moment, I imagined I could hear her heart beating. I wasn't going to let this one get away.

"Oh, God, I'm so glad to see you," she said when we parted at last.

"Mutual, I'm sure," I replied in my best Bowery Boys accent. But I could hear my voice cracking, and I tried to remember the last time I had cried for joy.

"I got your message at the hotel, so I knew you were back. But then it was like you disappeared. We've been looking all over for you, but we couldn't find you anywhere. I was afraid something happened to you."

"You were right," I said. "Something did happen to me."

"What happened? Are you okay?" Max asked.

I looked at Marcy. "Now I am. Right as rain."

"It was so weird, I was so scared," she said. "Jack the Knife told us you came to his room looking for speed. He said you were drunk. I couldn't believe it."

"He had good reason to tell you that. He tried to kill me."

"What? You're kidding."

"I wish I were."

"Wait a sec," Max said. "Jack tried to kill you? I don't understand. What's going on?"

I shook my head. "I can't explain it all now, Max. Did you hear about Chuck Darwin?"

"No, what about him?"

"He killed himself, Max. Before that—"

"What? That's crazy. That can't be. I just saw him this afternoon. He was fine."

"I'm sorry, Max. He's not anymore. The police say he committed suicide. They found him in the Knickerbocker Hotel. In Gerry Stillman's room. He pushed Stillman out the window, then shot himself in the head."

Max shook his head. The blood rushed to his face, and he looked like he was trying to hold back tears. "I don't believe it," he said. "There must be some mistake."

Marcy put her arm around him. "Are you sure?" she asked me.

"Positive." I didn't think this was the time to discuss other possibilities. The fact was, Chuck Darwin was dead. It didn't matter just then whether he had taken his own life or somebody else had killed him to make it look that way.

"Oh, Jesus, I've got to call Sylvia," Max said. "Do you know whether or not she knows about it?"

"Yeah, she does. The police have already talked to her."

"Oh, God, I've got to call her. I've got to find a phone."

Marcy took my arm as we watched Max walk away with his head down. We moved to the right corner of the stage. "The cops are waiting for Jack in the back room," I said. "Have you seen Kid's mother?"

Marcy pointed across the club. "She was sitting on the far side, in the first row."

It was impossible to see through the crowd on the dance floor. Just then, the band finished its song. The crowd rose for a standing ovation. It seemed like sheer bedlam in the place but that could have been my state of mind.

"I don't understand why Jack tried to kill you. What exactly happened?" Marcy asked. She was shouting just to be heard above the din.

"It turns out Jack is Kid's uncle," I shouted back. "He was in the room when I went to talk to Grace. He slugged me, stuffed me full of speed, and dumped me in some lot." As I listened to myself, I realized I was starting to talk like a cop.

"God, that's terrible." Marcy shivered and pressed up against me. "Was Kid in on it, too?"

"I don't think so. I sure hope not."

We watched the members of the band leave the stage. From the level of crowd noise, I expected them to play one more encore. I wasn't sure whether Kid, Tina, and Jack would go all the way back to the dressing room or if they'd just wait in the wings. I wondered again whether Jack had seen me. If so, that would take the element of surprise away from Brady and Del Greco.

I felt a tug at my sleeve and turned to see Tommy Ventura. "I had to get out of there, man," he shouted. "Cops give me the creeps."

I nodded as a fresh cheer went up in the crowd. Tina and Kid were coming back onstage to play another song. But I couldn't see the drummer.

"Where's Jack?" I yelled at Tommy.

"Beats me. Maybe they nabbed him already."

But they hadn't. As Kid picked up his guitar, he was looking toward the wings. He walked toward the side of the stage. Tina had a puzzled expression on her face as she watched him. It appeared that Kid was talking to somebody. No doubt it was Uncle Jack. He knew something was up.

Kid nodded, then moved back to the center of the stage and began playing the intro to "Walk Don't Run" by the Ventures. The crowd began to cheer wildly, and it was at that moment that Jack Mitchell made his move. He lurched out from behind the curtain at the far side of the stage and jumped down to the dance floor.

"There he goes," I shouted to Tommy. But the roadie was already in pursuit, pushing up the aisle that formed a semicircle around the seats. I took off after him.

I looked to my right and saw Jack the Knife taking a shortcut through the crowd, hurtling over a table of his fans and cutting toward the main aisle on the other side of the club. A lot of people were standing now, no longer paying any attention to Kid Lee's thunderous guitar licks. I lost sight of Jack as I chugged up the opposite aisle, pushing and shoving my way past people with their necks craned to see what was going on. I was so damn tired that I felt like I was running through sand.

As I reached the second to last tier of tables, I caught sight of Jack again, running behind the back row. When he reached the main entrance, at the top of the arc, Tommy Ventura was waiting for him. Jack stopped in his tracks, then slashed at the roadie with one of his custom drumsticks. I remembered Tommy saying that he wouldn't want to mess with Jack, but he was clearly one tough customer himself. Tommy showed surprising agility for such a big guy, sidestepping the thrust of the knife and grabbing Jack by the forearm. He pulled Jack's wrist up behind his back and managed to wrest the knife from him, but Jack swung wildly with his other hand. Tommy grimaced in pain and clutched at his thigh. One knife he could deal with, but two knives was pushing his luck.

Jack Mitchell regained his balance. For a fleeting second, I thought he was going to slash at Tommy again. Instead, he charged out toward the lobby. Tommy lunged and grabbed one of Jack's ankles, upending him as he pushed through the glass doors leading to the lobby. The drummer took a headlong dive and ended up on the floor.

A pair of uniformed police officers stationed out in the lobby rushed over to Jack's side. One of the cops pulled out a pair of handcuffs, but Jack the Knife wasn't ready to be tied down just yet. He got to his knees with forearms raised. He flailed with his elbows as he leaped to his feet, nailing both surprised cops in one motion. They don't do it any better than that in the movies.

Jack ran out the main door with Tommy Ventura and me hobbling behind him. He was in the clear now, at least for the time being. There was no way we would be able to catch him. But Jack had no way of knowing that. The rain outside had increased to a downpour, and he sloshed out through the puddles with his head down. I yelled to warn him as he burst out into the street, but he didn't hear me. Or maybe he was just going too fast to stop in time.

The car hit him broadside and knocked him up in the air like a beach ball. He seemed to hang there for a moment, suspended in time, floating like a balloon, carried along by the momentum of impact. He landed twenty feet down the street. The car dragged him twenty more.

Tommy and I arrived at Jack's side before the driver could get out of the car. He was a middle-aged guy in a suit, and I could tell he had stopped for a drink that had turned into six drinks on his way home from work. There was liquor on his breath, and plenty of it. But I'm not sure even a sober person would have been able to stop in time.

"Somebody call an ambulance!" Tommy screamed at the crowd of people gathered outside the concert hall.

"I think it's too late for an ambulance, Tommy," I said as I leaned over Jack's crumpled body. The big guy wasn't making a sound. His head was turned at such an awkward angle that I felt sure his neck was broken.

"It almost looks like he's smiling, doesn't it?" Tommy said.

Yes it did. And there was something else that caught my attention. Jack the Knife was still clutching one of his custom drumsticks in his hand.

"I never even saw him," the driver of the car slurred.

We ignored him. Just then I became aware of somebody else standing by my side. It was Max. He was shaking his head.

"This is a nightmare," he said, "a goddamn nightmare."

"It's Chicago, Max," I replied. "It's the third city on the tour all over again."

24

It was complete chaos outside the Park West for almost an hour. As people poured out of the concert, they were confronted with the spectacle of at least half a dozen police cars with their dome lights flashing, a monumental traffic jam marked by the continuous blare of car horns, and a swarm of onlookers seeking to satisfy their morbid curiosity. Add to this a blinding thunderstorm, and you get some idea of just how confusing the whole scene was.

Some of the police began lining the curb with wooden sawhorses to restrain the crowds, while others went up and down the street rerouting cars and closing off the block. One of the cops spoke through a bullhorn, urging the crowd to move along, but most of the people had to be pushed before they responded to the order.

The gathering on the sidewalk swelled as more concertgoers exited the hall, forcing people huddling for cover under the marquee to spill out into the street. A scuffle broke out in the crush of bodies, and several cops swooped in to stop it, bowling innocent bystanders over in the process. I overheard a nearby cop call in on his radio for more backup, saying that a riot was about to ensue. I was afraid he might be right. With the disco demolition fresh in his memory, he wasn't taking any chances.

Through all the screaming and ranting, I heard a voice from the center of the mob shout, "Hey, dude, you break that radio and I'll break your face." A moment later, two cops emerged from the fray with Julius and Slim in tow. I didn't think it was a coincidence that the police had fingered two black guys as troublemakers in a crowd that was mostly white. But in Chicago, nothing surprised me. It was definitely not my kind of town. I was tempted to protest their arrest until I saw that the cops decided to let them go.

I was drenched to the bone by the time the ambulance arrived, but I was too tired and dirty and numb to care. Compared with the rest of what I had been through that day, a little water wasn't going to matter much. As the paramedics covered Jack the Knife with a sheet and began putting him onto a stretcher, I saw Marcy making her way toward us. She was accompanied by a policeman in uniform who was leading Grace Lee by the arm. I later learned that Marcy had spotted Grace in the crowd and pointed her out to the cop.

Grace kneeled over the stretcher and pulled back the sheet. She kissed her husband's brother on the forehead, then put the sheet over his face and got slowly to her feet. At that moment, she seemed very old to me. Grace closed her eyes, leaned her head back, spread her arms, and took a deep breath. She began to sing "Nearer My God to Thee."

Grace's voice boomed out over the noise of the crowd and echoed off the high-rise buildings on either side of the street. It was a repeat of her performance at Danny Darwin's funeral. As if by magic, the rain subsided to a soft drizzle and the throng of spectators gradually quieted down until the night was almost silent except for the sound of Amazing Grace. Marcy, Max, and Tommy all started to cry, and I could feel tears beginning to well up in my eyes. The paramedics, having already determined that Jack Mitchell was dead, waited until Grace was finished before they put Jack in the ambulance.

"Do you want to ride with him, ma'am?" a policeman asked Grace. "It's just around the corner."

"No," she answered quietly. "I best wait for my son. He's the only one I've got left anymore."

A cheer went up in the crowd, and I turned to see Kid Lee and Tina Darling stepping out into the street. They were followed by Artie Crosby and the two detectives, Brady and Del Greco.

Kid ran to his mother and put his arms around her. Tina, seeing the body covered by the sheet, let out a scream and began sobbing hysterically. Tommy limped over to comfort her, but she seemed not to notice.

Kid let go of his mother and moved over next to Tina. "Is he dead?" he asked.

"I'm afraid so," one of the paramedics replied.

"Can I touch him?" Kid lifted the sheet from the side and grabbed hold of Jack Mitchell's hand. "Uncle Jack, you were the best drummer that ever lived," he said. He turned to face his mother. "It's all right to call him Uncle Jack now, isn't it, Mama?"

Grace Lee nodded, and at last the floodgates of her sunken eyes burst open and unleashed a torrent of tears. She stepped toward her son and buried her head on his shoulder, weeping uncontrollably. Kid just stood there shaking his head and gazing silently at Uncle Jack.

Artie Crosby chose that moment to begin reading the riot act to the cops. "What the hell do you think you're doing?" he demanded. "You want to arrest this guy, so what do you do? You shoot him down without even giving him a chance to defend himself. I've heard about you guys in Chicago. You're not going to get away with it. I'm calling Chuck Darwin right this moment. We'll sue your ass."

"Who exactly is this schmuck?" Brady asked me.

"Artie, Artie, that's not how it happened, man," Tommy Ventura said. "He ran out into the street and got hit by a car. I'm the one that was chasing him. He stabbed me in the leg." Tommy angled to show the temporary bandage that one of the paramedics had wrapped around his thigh. "He tried to kill Del."

"What?" Kid said. "Uncle Jack tried to kill Del?" Kid looked at me straight on. "Why would he want to do that?"

"That's a lie!" Tina screamed. "Don't believe him, Kid. He's a liar."

I ignored Tina and fixed my gaze on Kid. "I think you should ask your mother, Kid," I said. "She can explain everything to you."

"Mama?"

Grace Lee pulled away from her son and gave me a look that made me shiver. "This is all your fault, Del Barnes," she said softly. "If it wasn't for you, none of this ever would've happened."

I didn't raise a word of protest. Ten years ago, something happened that was outside of my control. I took the blame for it anyway, and I had been carrying around the guilt with me ever since. This time, my conscience was completely clear. It was Grace Lee whose mind was twisted, not from drugs but from the blindness of revenge. I felt sorry for her, felt sorry for what she was going through, sorry for what she had been through. But I didn't feel any need to defend myself.

Just then, a red-haired guy in a suit walked up to our group. "What's going on here?" he asked.

"Hello, Conroy," Brady said. "Tough night, huh?"

"Tough ain't the word for it," Detective Conroy replied. "How're you doing, Patrick?"

Brady shrugged. "We got a real mess here." He nodded toward the ambulance. "That's the guy we came to pick up. He tried to make a run for it, and somebody ran him over with their car." Brady turned to face one of the uniformed cops. "Where's the driver? Did anyone talk to him yet?"

The cop pointed with his finger. "He's in the squad car over there. The guy's drunk as a skunk."

"I don't think it would have made any difference if he was sober," I said. I didn't like the idea of drunk driving, and if they wanted to take away the guy's license for the rest of his life, that was fine with me. But I didn't think he should be charged with vehicular homicide.

"Who's this guy?" Conroy asked Brady.

"This is Del Barnes. He's the one that came into the hospital."

"And you say he knows something about this Darwin thing?"

"What Darwin thing?" Artie Crosby demanded.

"Who are you?" Conroy asked.

"I'm the manager of the band. I work for Chuck Darwin."

"You don't work for him anymore," Conroy said. "Chuck Darwin's dead."

"What?" Artie Crosby let out a gasp. It was echoed by Grace, Kid, Tina, and Tommy.

"What the hell happened?" Artie asked.

"Looks like a suicide," Conroy replied. "Before he killed himself, he killed some guy named Gerry Stillman."

"What!?" There was another chorus of gasps from the people who hadn't already heard the news.

"That can't be," Artie said. "I don't believe it."

"You're not the only one," Conroy replied. He turned to Brady and nodded toward me. "So this is the guy with the story you said I should hear?"

"Excuse me, sir," one of the paramedics said to Conroy. "Can we take him away?"

Conroy deferred to Brady. "You done with him?"

"Sure, take him away," Brady said. "Where you going with him?"

"Around the corner to Grant."

Brady nodded, then spoke to Grace Lee. "We'll give you a ride over there in a few minutes, ma'am."

Grace Lee seemed not to hear him. She just stood there gazing at her brother-in-law as the ambulance pulled away.

"Why don't we go inside," Conroy suggested. "I want to hear what Barnes has to say."

We walked slowly through the crowd, which was finally dispersing. A few people called out to Kid and Tina, congratulating them on their performance. The compliments fell on deaf ears.

"Go away, folks, the show's over," Detective Del Greco said. "You can read all about it in tomorrow's paper."

"What does this have to do with the Darwin thing?" Conroy asked me once our group moved back inside to the lobby of the concert hall.

"At this point, I'm not sure it has anything to do with it," I said. "But I'm almost positive it's connected with a killing up in Wisconsin."

Conroy frowned and looked at Brady. "What am I doing here then?"

"Tell him why you thought there was a connection," Brady said to me.

"Well, it's a long story," I said, wondering where exactly to begin.

"Try to make it short," Conroy said. "I've had a long day."

I bristled at the cop's remark. "No longer than mine, I can assure you."

"Yeah, this guy's had a rough one, all right," Brady spoke up on my behalf.

Conroy shrugged, as if to give me a cue to start. I had the distinct feeling he'd just as soon declare Chuck Darwin's death a suicide, wrap things up in a nice neat bundle, and go home and watch TV.

"Chuck Darwin had two sons," I said. "One of them worked for the band and one of them played in it. They both died while the band was on tour. The first one died of an accidental drug overdose, but the second one, Chip, died onstage up in Madison on Tuesday night. It looked like a freak accident, but the police up there don't think it was an accident. I didn't think so either."

"What exactly is your relationship to this band?" Conroy asked.

"I'm a writer for a music magazine. I'm covering the tour."

"I'm the publisher," Max said in a weary voice. "He works for me."

"Go on," Conroy said.

"One of the women who was traveling with the band told the police that I was onstage before the concert in Madison, implying that I might have tampered with the equipment. Chip Darwin died when his amplifier fell on top of him."

"How did you find out that someone accused you?"

"The police investigator told me so. Anyway, I did some checking and that's when I found out that more than twenty years ago Grace's husband killed himself after an independent record agent signed him to a phony record contract and ripped off some of his songs."

"Hold on a sec." Conroy raised his hand impatiently. "I don't want to hear about what happened twenty years ago. I want to know about what happened tonight."

"I'm getting to that," I said. My voice was trembling. Marcy squeezed my arm to calm me down. "The guy they just took away in the ambulance was Grace's brother-in-law. It was his brother whose music got ripped off." All of my concentration was focused on trying to get the story out straight and clear, but I could still sense the shock registering among the members of the Roots entourage. "The man whose music was stolen was named Lee Mitchell. He was Kid's father."

"I get it now, man," Tommy said, looking at Kid. "That's why you called him Uncle Jack."

"Grace never knew the name of the guy who ripped off her husband—until a few months ago." I spoke to Grace now. "Isn't that right, Mrs. Mitchell?"

She nodded and more tears began rolling down her cheeks.

"That's why I suspected that Jack and Grace were plotting to kill Chuck Darwin. But first Jack killed his son, Chip."

"That's not true, that's not true!" Grace Mitchell wiped away her tears. "I admit we came here planning on killing Chuck Darwin. That's exactly what he deserved after he went and ruined my life. It was all his fault, causing my husband to go and kill himself. But we were never, ever planning on doing anything to his sons. I swear to the Lord."

I had come to realize that Kid's mother could be as dissembling and manipulative as any gangster who ever testified before a grand jury or any greedy music industry hack who ever signed some unsuspecting kid to a dead-end contract. Nonetheless I could sense that she was telling the truth.

"Aren't you the person who told the police in Madison that I went up onstage before Chip Darwin was killed?"

"I did nothing of the sort. Why in the world would I go and say that about you, after you being so nice to Kid and all?"

I stood there speechless, gaping at the faces around me.

"It looks to me like you had it all figured wrong," Conroy

said. "But *you*," he said to Grace, "what's this about you killing Chuck Darwin?"

"We didn't have a thing to do with that. I swear. I admit we were planning on it, but I didn't even know Mr. Darwin was dead until this police officer said so. You see, we were planning on doing it when the band got to Memphis. I thought that would be the sweetest revenge of all, on account of then Kid could get up and play right there in our hometown, just like Bumble used to."

"Who's Bumble?" Brady asked.

"That's the name of her husband," Marcy said.

"Not so fast," Conroy told Grace. I thought it was an ironic thing for him to say, considering the way he had been hurrying me along. "Maybe you didn't kill Darwin, but what about that brother-in-law of yours?"

"No, he didn't do it either, on account of he was otherwise occupied."

"And why don't you tell us what he was otherwise occupied *with*," Brady said. "Or maybe I should tell you myself. Your sweet brother-in-law didn't kill Darwin because he was busy trying to do in this guy." He hooked his thumb at me. "And you were an accomplice to it. I'm afraid I'm going to have to take you in anyway."

"But it was an accident," Grace protested. "I didn't want him to do it."

"An accident! You call slugging a guy over the head and then stuffing him full of drugs an *accident*? Lady, you've got problems. Big problems."

"But I'm sorry about it," she pleaded.

"Sorry about it! That's great. Why don't you tell *him* you're sorry. Then everything will be just peachy again."

Kid's mother obviously didn't grasp Brady's sarcasm. Her experience over the years had taught her a lot of things, but dealing with Chicago cops sure wasn't one of them. She turned slowly to face me, tears streaming down her face. "I'm sorry, Del," she said. "I truly am, from the bottom of my heart. And I'm sorry for what I said before about it all being your fault. I didn't mean that. I was wrong."

"Lady, you can apologize all you want, but we've still got to take you in." Brady looked flabbergasted by Grace's remarks, but that was nothing compared with his reaction to my response.

"Don't I have to press charges?" I asked.

"What? What the hell are you talking about? You mean you're not going to press charges after all this? She tried to kill you, goddamn it!"

"She didn't hit me," I said. "He did. She even told him not to. She tried to stop him."

"I don't believe you, Barnes. I don't goddamn believe you. I think you ought to go back to the hospital. I don't think Doctor Boyle got everything pumped out of your system. I think you're still loony on drugs."

"He ought to have his damn head examined is what I think," Conroy said.

"You're crazy, Barnes!" Brady shouted. "You're even crazier than *she* is."

"I'd just like some time to think about it," I said.

"Yeah, well you just go right ahead and think about it. You can take all the time you want." Brady motioned at the uniformed cop. "Why don't you take these people over to the hospital. I'm going home and get me some sleep."

"Me, too," Conroy said. "Next time you get some weirdo telling some crazy story, Brady, do me a favor: Call anybody you want, but don't call me."

I watched in silence as Brady, Conroy, and Del Greco filed out. Tommy, Kid, and his mother trailed behind them, followed by their hospital escort. Tina and Artie stayed behind.

"Just ignore those jerks," Marcy said. "You did the right thing. I'm proud of you."

I nodded and felt the lids closing over my eyes. Tomorrow morning, her comment would probably mean something to me. For the present, I was too numb to feel anything.

Max pulled his flask out of his pocket and handed it to me. "Here, have some bourbon," he said, "it's the universal antidote."

I didn't think anything would make me feel better, save

perhaps a week or two of sleep. I took a swig nonetheless. When the liquor hit my stomach, I felt like there was a roaring blaze down there. For a moment, I thought the bourbon was going to come right back up. It didn't. Maybe the charcoal absorbed it.

Max passed the flask around and everybody took a slug.

"What are we supposed to do now?" Tina asked.

"Somebody should go see Sylvia," Artie said. "Does she even know about it?"

"Yeah, I already talked to her," Max said. He looked at his watch. "I told her I'd be down to see her over an hour ago."

"Maybe we should get her some flowers," Tina said. "That always makes *me* feel better."

We were walking outside now. The crowd was gone, the show was finally over.

"Marcy's right," Max said, pulling me aside. "You did the right thing. The only mistake you made was getting too involved in this thing to begin with. You should've listened to me. This could've cost you your life. You're lucky it didn't."

"Max, the last thing I need from you right now is a goddamn lecture," I said.

That's the last thing I remember saying. We got into a taxicab and started back to the hotel. Before we got there, I fell asleep in Marcy's arms. For the first time since waking up an eternity ago, I was in the right place at the right time.

25

I woke up Saturday morning to the sound of an oldies radio station playing in the background and Marcy singing in the foreground. She was leaning over me, poised for a good-morning kiss, a cup of coffee in one hand. The song was "You Are the Sunshine of My Life." It was a nice awakening, an auspicious start to a day I was sure would eventually turn ugly. I gave her the kiss, took the coffee, and told her the feeling, as expressed by Stevie Wonder, was mutual.

"Sorry I had to wake you," she said. "You looked like you could have slept all day."

"You're right, I would have."

I sat up to take a sip of the coffee and felt the lump on my head beginning to throb. Or maybe it had been throbbing all night and I had been too dead to notice. As I turned on my side, I found out that the pain was not limited to one area of my body. My ribs were sore where Brady had planted his fist. My muscles ached from the stress of running and worrying and having my stomach pumped. Basically, my whole body was an exposed nerve, and the world around me was one extra-large dentist's drill set on very low speed.

I could tell from the clarity in her eyes and the bounce in her voice that Marcy had been awake for hours. "What time *is* it?" I asked through a yawn.

"Almost noon. That's why I decided to wake you up. We've got a big meeting to go to in a couple of hours. I wanted you to be ready for it."

Marcy dropped a copy of the *Chicago Sun-Times* on my lap. The story about Gerry Stillman's murder and Chuck Darwin's suicide was set out in a banner headline across the front page:

MUSIC BIGWIG KILLS EX-PARTNER, SELF

I put the paper aside. I wasn't ready to read all about it quite yet.

"There's a story on Jack in there, too," Marcy said. "It's way in the back."

I nodded and found out that was the worst thing I could do for my head. "Tell me about this meeting," I said. "Who called it? Max?"

Marcy smiled and shook her head. "No, I did."

"What for?"

"After last night, it seemed like there were a lot of loose ends to tie up. You may have been wrong about Jack and Grace being involved in killing Chip Darwin and his father, but you know as well as I do that Chip's death was no accident. And I don't believe for a minute that Chuck Darwin killed himself, either."

Marcy held out her hand and I squeezed it. "I didn't think you'd be in any shape to get started right away, so I took the liberty of setting things up myself," she said.

"You sure called that one right. I'm not in shape to do anything more challenging than swallow some aspirin and take a hot bath."

"We'll take care of that right now," she said. "I'm sure you'll want to look and feel your best for your old friend Detective Helga Schmitz."

"Helga Schmitz? You talked to her?" On the radio, Johnny Nash was singing "I Can See Clearly Now." It would take a while before *I* could say any such thing.

Marcy nodded and looked at her watch. "A couple of hours ago. She's on her way down here by now. I also went to visit your pal Officer Brady."

"My, you've been a busy girl. But I don't exactly think of Brady as a pal. I'm sure he thinks even less of me."

She smiled. "I turned on the charm. I can be very charming when I set my mind to it."

"Yeah, I've noticed that about you."

"You haven't seen me in action. I've never had to force it with you. It just comes naturally."

"Thanks," I said and took a sip of coffee. "So what did Brady have to say?"

"Not a whole lot. I did most of the talking. But at least he was willing to listen. I think I managed to raise his opinion of you again. He still thinks you're crazy for not pressing charges against Kid's mother, but I got him to at least see your side of things. At any rate, he agreed to come to the meeting. Detective Schmitz said she'd need to have somebody from the Chicago police there."

I shook my head in amazement and it felt like somebody was pounding on it with a sledgehammer. I was out of bed now and washing down the aspirin. "Who else is coming to this meeting?"

"Everybody who's connected with the band. It's going to be just like 'Perry Mason.' You know—lock everybody up in a room and solve the murder. And you, because you're so smart, get to play the part of Perry."

"I don't know if I'm ready for this, Marcy," I said.

She smiled. "Just call me Della, for Della Street. She was Perry Mason's gal Friday. And don't worry. You'll be ready."

"Okay, Della, tell me how you got everybody to agree to come to this meeting."

"That was a cinch. They're all feeling lost and bedraggled. I told them I wanted to take one last photo of our group. The only person who raised any fuss was Artie Crosby."

"That figures."

She smiled. "I charmed him."

"I'll bet you did. What I don't understand is why you seem so cheerful about all this."

"I feel bad about Jack the Knife. But I'm glad to find out that Grace and Kid didn't have anything to do with killing Chip. And more than that, I'm just happy that you're alive."

Marcy put her arms around me. "I was so worried about you yesterday, Del. I was afraid . . ."

She began to tremble, and the cheer disappeared from her face, washed away by tears that began to pour out of those beautiful blue eyes. I knew what she was afraid of. And she had good reason to be. I was lucky just to be alive. That thought started to cheer me up as I pressed against her.

"It's over," I said. "It didn't happen. I'm still here."

"I'm so glad. You don't know how happy that makes me feel."

"You're not the only one," I said, wiping the tears from her cheeks.

I followed Marcy into the bathroom as she turned on the water for my bath. "I stayed up late last night thinking about it," she said. "If Jack didn't kill Chip Darwin, I'm almost positive I know who did."

"Who's that?" I asked. I had a pretty good idea myself, but after being wrong about so many things the day before, I wasn't feeling real confident about my suspicions.

"Tina Darling."

Bingo. "That makes two of us," I said. I was a little dubious about whether Tina would have been able to push the heavy amplifier into position, but she had been fuming when she left the backstage area. The surge of adrenaline from her anger could have supplied all the extra strength she needed. Plus, she probably had been high on speed.

"I think I know who killed Chuck Darwin," I said.

"Who?"

"You're not going to like it."

"I don't care."

I told her about my conversation with Elmore Jackson, giving all the details I had left out when I spoke with Officer Brady the night before.

"It fits," she said, shaking her head.

"I don't think we should bring this up at your meeting," I said. "After the fool I made of myself last night, I don't want to involve the police until we can actually prove it. Plus I want to talk to him about it first."

"You didn't make a fool of yourself," she replied. "But how are we going to be able to prove it?"

"I guess we have to come up with a plan." I told her the one I was thinking about, and she added a few improvements.

"Are you sure it will work?" Marcy asked.

I shook my head. "I'm not even sure I'm right. There's only one thing I'm sure about."

"What's that?"

"I love you."

It was the right thing to say, but maybe the wrong time. She recoiled ever so slightly, then moved in closer and put her arms around me again. "I've still got a lot of things to sort out, Del," she said.

"I know you do."

"Let's not hurry things, okay?"

"Sure, I've got all the time in the world. I mean it. I'm willing to wait for as long as it takes."

"Thanks. It could be a long time."

"But I hope you don't mind if I hurry up with one thing."

"What's that?"

"I'd like to get this aching body into the tub."

"Be my guest," she said, sweeping her arm toward the door. "Take as long as you like. Just don't turn into a prune."

As I sank down into the hot water, I could hear Ray Charles singing "Georgia on My Mind" on the radio in the next room. His voice was deep and soothing, just like the water steaming the pain out through my pores. The song took me back, the way some old songs do, to a solitary moment, suspended in time.

It was Thanksgiving Day 1960 and I was driving with my mother and father and brother. I'm not sure where we were going, probably to my grandparents' house, but I do remember the last of the leaves swirling around the car, winter's chill in the air. I wondered what Georgia was like and thought it must be warm and friendly. I resolved then that someday I would explore the South. I was young then, seventeen years old. I would be attending college the next fall, and I recall feeling like I had my

whole life ahead of me. Since then I've always associated Ray
Charles with Thanksgiving, with my family.

But my pleasant little reverie soon wore off, as the song also
reminded me that I had to call my friend Marty Goldberg down in
Athens. I still had a lot of things to do. It was going to be yet
another long day.

26

It was a pretty sedate group in Chuck Darwin's suite at the Drake Hotel, when we all lined up for Marcy to take our photograph. The location of the meeting seemed a little odd, almost ghoulish, but Marcy said she couldn't think of another available room big enough to hold all the people. Sometimes you just have to work with what you've got.

The mood changed shortly after three o'clock when Patrick Brady and Helga Schmitz arrived, and it wasn't a change for the better.

"What're you doing here?" Tina Darling was the first to speak up.

"Isn't that the lady cop from up in Madison?" I heard Suzi Larsen ask her sister Vicki.

"I'm sure you all remember me," Detective Schmitz said.

It was apparent by the nodding heads that everyone did, though nobody issued a verbal acknowledgment. Based on my dealings with her, I didn't think Helga Schmitz had made many friends among the Roots entourage.

"Hello, Mr. Barnes," she said to me, putting out her hand and cracking a smile. "I heard you had quite an adventure yesterday."

"That's very true. How are you, Mrs. Schmitz?"

"I've been better."

Brady also extended his hand for a shake. "How's the head today?" he asked.

"Still there, still aching," I replied. "It's my ribs that are really bothering me."

He laughed. "The pain should go away soon. Probably by Christmas."

Tina, sensing that her first question would go unanswered, shot poisoned darts in Marcy's direction as she tried again. "I thought you said we were supposed to come here to get our picture taken."

Marcy answered with a smile. It could've been taken as a smirk, but I thought it made her look confident, beautiful. "Sorry," she said, "I lied."

"Yeah, what the hell's going on here?" Artie Crosby demanded.

Officer Schmitz raised her arms for attention. It appeared that Brady was content to let her take charge, just as he had let Conroy and Del Greco take over the night before. "We're still investigating the death of Chip Darwin in Madison on Tuesday night," she said. "Mr. Barnes and Ms. Hopkins thought they could shed some light on things if we all discussed it together. So why don't you all take a seat and relax and—"

"This is a bunch of crap," Artie snarled. "I don't have to sit here and listen to this crap."

"Take a seat, buddy," Brady barked.

"I don't believe it." Artie glared at the Chicago cop. "After all the trouble this guy's caused, you're gonna make us sit here and listen to him? I don't believe it. This guy's a jerk, he's a nobody."

"Hey, Artie, come on, man. Just sit down, okay? Let Del have his say."

I was glad to see that Tommy Ventura was still on my side. I was afraid he wouldn't be for long, not after we were done with Tina.

"Go ahead, Mr. Barnes," Schmitz said. "But try to make it brief. This *is* a bit unorthodox."

The Madison cop and Marcy took seats on one of the couches, while I remained standing beside Brady. Before I spoke, I looked around the room to make sure I had everyone's attention. Off in the corner, Max was smiling at me. When Marcy and I told him about the real purpose of the meeting, he had expressed his disapproval. But I knew he would support me to the bitter end. And I was certain the end would be bitter.

Artie and Tina had their heads down, sulking, but Kid, his mother, Tommy, and the Larsen sisters all had their gazes fastened on me. Grace hadn't said a word since the cops arrived, and I could tell she was nervous. She probably thought Brady didn't believe her story that she and Jack weren't involved in Chip's murder.

"The thing that convinced me someone had killed Chip," I began, "was that somebody with the band told Officer Schmitz that I went onstage before the concert. That wasn't true, so I figured somebody was trying to cast suspicion on me and deflect it from himself or herself. It turned out to be herself, because Mrs. Schmitz told me it was a woman from the band who had made the allegation.

"That puzzled me a bit at first, because I thought it would take somebody pretty strong, a man, to get that amplifier to budge. I talked to Tommy, and he said the only people who went onstage were Artie, Chip, Jack, Kid, and Grace. While checking on some other things, I found out that Chuck Darwin ripped off Kid's father years ago. I also found out that Grace had sworn revenge and that Jack was actually Kid's uncle. I spoke to a friend of mine who runs a club down in Athens, Georgia, and he told me Grace used to help Kid and Jack haul the equipment. So I figured that she, or she and Jack, had rigged the amplifier so that it would fall on Danny. I decided that Grace must have been the one who told Detective Schmitz that I—"

I stopped speaking when Kid's mother rose to her feet. "Now, Del Barnes, I told you we had nothing to do with that. We didn't do anything to that Darwin boy."

"Yes, I know, Grace. I was just laying things out, so it would be easier to understand."

"Well, you're doing a lousy job," Artie said. "I don't understand *any* of it. If you ask me, this whole thing's a waste of time."

"Nobody asked you, buddy," Brady said.

"My name's not buddy," Artie replied.

"His name's Artie," Vicki Larsen told the cop.

Brady smiled. "Thanks, miss. And what's your name?"

"Suzi Larsen. And this is my sister, Vicki."

Once again I had mixed up the Larsen sisters.

"Pleased to meet you," Brady said, then he nodded for me to continue.

I did so, focusing my gaze on Tina, but she looked away as soon as I made eye contact. "After last night, I realized the whole thing probably wasn't as complicated as I thought. It just seemed complicated, because so many people had motives for killing Chip. I think we all know that Chip wasn't the most popular guy in the band. But I began to think that Tommy might have been mistaken about who went onstage. Or"—I looked at the burly roadie head on—"I thought Tommy might have been lying."

"Wait a minute, man." Tommy got to his feet. "I've been nice to you, Del. And now you're calling me a liar?" The roadie was angry, but I could tell I was right.

"Yeah, I'm sorry, Tommy. But I think you did lie. I think you lied to protect Tina."

"Me? You're saying I killed Chip?" Now Tina stood up. She was shaking all over. "You're crazy. I knew you were a jerk from the first time I saw you. I was in love with Chip, you idiot."

"I know you were. Everybody who hung around with the band knew that. And that's why you were so mad at him the night of the concert. Because Chip had Vicki and Suzi sitting on his lap. You stormed out of that room, Tina. And Tommy wasn't watching the stage then because he was in the dressing room talking to Marcy and me. But when he went back out there, I'll bet he saw you onstage. He must've seen you up there, because when I asked him about it, he insisted that you weren't. He couldn't have been sure, because *he* wasn't out there. But he kept insisting—"

"Oh, this is totally crazy!" Tina waved her arms in disgust. *"You're crazy!"* she shouted.

"Yeah, leave her alone, man, she didn't do anything." Tommy looked like he was about to charge forward and put me through

the wall. He pointed his finger at me, in a classic Chip Darwin
pose. "And don't call me a liar, man. I'm warning you, Del."

Helga Schmitz sensed that things were getting out of hand and
had the good sense to take over for me. She spoke to Tina first.
"You say you didn't do anything, Miss Darling. Then what about
telling me that Mr. Barnes was up onstage? Do you deny that?"

"No, I told you that, I know. I just . . . I just made a
mistake, that's all. I thought it was him but it wasn't. Everybody
makes mistakes."

"Miss Darling, surely you don't expect me to believe that. You
know all the members of the band. I hardly think you would have
failed to recognize them."

"Okay, okay, I admit it. I just told you that because . . . I
wanted to get back at him, that's why. He went and blabbed to the
cops about us giving drugs to Danny. He started a fight with Chip
on the day of Danny's funeral."

I didn't feel any need to correct Tina's version of who had
started my altercation with Chip Darwin. Marcy apparently did.
"Chip started that whole thing, sister," she said. "And you know
it."

I looked to the corner, where Max was smiling and shaking his
head. I guess it was a good show—better than "Perry Mason."

Detective Schmitz resumed her grilling of Tina. "So you were
lying about that," she said. "And now do you want to tell me
where you went when you left the dressing room? You went up
onstage, didn't you?" Helga turned to Tommy, raising her voice.
"Didn't she?"

Tommy shook his head, just as Tina started to crack. "Okay,
okay, I went up onstage," she said. Her voice was hysterical now
and her hair was flying loose over her face. "But I didn't touch
Chip's amplifier. I couldn't have moved it. I'm not strong
enough. I didn't kill him!"

"That amplifier wouldn't have been so hard to move,"
Detective Schmitz said. "I know, because I tried it myself."
Somehow I didn't think it was exactly a fair test to match Helga's
musculature against Tina's, but I didn't say anything. "Besides,"

she continued, "it was really a matter of leverage. All you had to do was wrap the cord tightly—"

"I didn't do it!" Tina sat back down in her chair and began to sob. "Don't you understand?" she pleaded. "I didn't do it!"

Officer Schmitz shrugged and glanced at Brady. "I don't think you'll need the cuffs," she said.

Tommy took two steps forward and spoke quietly. "She's telling the truth," he said. "She didn't do it."

Schmitz looked the roadie over, as if she were assessing a cut of meat in the butcher shop. "And why do you say that?"

Tommy Ventura lowered his head. "Because I did," he said. "I'm the one that killed Chip."

"What?" Marcy let out a gasp, and the Larsen sisters joined her on backup. Kid and his mother appeared mystified, but they kept their thoughts to themselves. I looked over at Max. He was still shaking his head, but the smile was gone now.

Helga Schmitz did not seem shocked by Tommy's confession. I recalled Marcy's comment about instantly knowing Tommy had a crush on Tina because of female intuition. Helga had probably picked up on that as quickly as Marcy had.

"So you killed him," she said calmly. There was a trace of a smirk on her face. "Why don't you tell us about it."

Tommy looked at her, perplexed, but his eyes went back to the floor when he started to speak. "There's not much to tell," he said, buying himself a little time. "I just went up onstage and rigged the amplifier. That's all there was to it."

"Did you see Miss Darling when you were up there?"

"No. Well . . . yeah, I did see her, but not when I was up there. I made sure nobody was looking."

"Very smart. It's always a good idea to make sure no one's looking when you're trying to kill somebody. Why'd you do it?"

Tommy had to think about that one for a moment. "I *hated* Chip Darwin," he said at last. "I couldn't stand the way he was always pushing everybody around, giving orders. I couldn't stand the way he treated Tina. He treated her like dirt, man."

I looked at Tina, who was wiping her eyes and gazing at the

roadie with newfound admiration. "You killed him for me, Tommy?"

"Yeah, I did. That's right."

"Don't be a sucker, Tommy," I said.

He wheeled and pointed at me. "You shut up, Del. I've had about enough of you. I thought you were my friend."

"Well, that certainly wraps things up," Detective Schmitz said. She was smiling broadly now. She nodded toward Brady, who was taking out his handcuffs. He got up and put them on Tommy while reading him his rights. The roadie didn't put up any resistance. He just stood there glumly, staring at the floor.

As Brady started to lead Tommy from the room, Artie Crosby got up. "Hey, you can't do that," he said.

"What do you mean?" Schmitz retorted. "He confessed to a murder. This isn't a game. We're taking him to jail."

"But you can't do that. He's just a kid."

"Don't worry." Schmitz gave Artie that smug grin of hers. "He'll grow up fast in jail. All the kids do."

"But you can't do that!" Artie repeated.

"And why not?"

"Because . . ." Artie Crosby stared at his feet. He remained silent for a moment while everybody in the room focused on him. When he finally raised his head, there were tears in his eyes. He looked years older than he'd been when the meeting started.

"Because . . . I killed Chip Darwin," he said. "I killed the little snot-nosed sonofabitch. He was a *monster*, just like his brother, just like his old man. They didn't give a damn about anybody but themselves. They deserved to die, all of them."

Artie took a breath preparatory to launching into a tirade, but Detective Schmitz stopped him. "Don't say anything further, Mr. Crosby, until you get a lawyer."

"She's right, Artie," Max piped up from the corner. "Keep your mouth shut until you get some help."

The band manager nodded as his protégé, Tommy Ventura, walked over and put an arm around Artie's shoulders. "You're like a son to me, Tommy, you know that," he said.

"I know, Artie, I know," Tommy said. "I've learned a lot from you, man."

"I couldn't let you take the rap for it," Artie said. He glared at Tina. "Especially for that tramp. You stay away from her, understand? She's no good."

Tommy winced as Brady led Artie Crosby to the door. I didn't think any amount of fatherly advice could end Tommy's jones for Tina Darling. She'd have to do that herself.

As Artie walked past us, Officer Schmitz said, "Thank you, Mr. Crosby."

"You knew," I said to her, "didn't you? You knew all along that he did it."

She answered with her smug grin. "I knew, but I couldn't prove it."

"I had no idea," I said.

"Don't feel bad, Mr. Barnes," she replied. "I'm just smarter than you are, that's all."

27

The meeting left me emotionally drained, but the worst part of my day was yet to come. I was feeling so confused that I began to wonder if I should go through with our plan. If it worked, we would be able to prove who killed Chuck Darwin and Gerry Stillman. But in so doing, we would only bring more pain and suffering to people whom I thought deserved a better fate than the law would probably allow.

We had solved the riddle of Chip Darwin's murder, but I wasn't convinced we had really done much good. I didn't care for Artie Crosby, but I also didn't think he would kill anyone again. Putting him away for twenty years or the rest of his life wasn't going to solve anything. It wasn't going to bring Chip Darwin back to life.

I understood the frustration that had led Artie to kill the young guitar player, and I wasn't sure I wouldn't have done the same thing had I been in his place. But I realized this was nonsense after mentioning my doubts to Marcy—and getting a brief lecture in response. Maybe my brain was still mushy from my adventures of the day before. As Marcy pointed out, Artie Crosby had plenty of alternatives for dealing with Chip Darwin. He just happened to pick the wrong one, and now he would have to pay for it. There was no justification for killing another human being, unless your own life was in danger.

Marcy and I wandered over to the support group surrounding Tina Darling. We apologized for putting her through the wringer, but she was not in a gracious mood.

"Get away from me! Both of you!" she yelled. "I don't wanna have to see your ugly faces again."

"Yeah, you two should split, man," Tommy Ventura said. "Tina's still awful upset, and it's your fault."

"Okay, Tommy," I said, "but I'd like to talk to you for a minute as soon as you get a chance. It's important."

Tommy put his hands on his hips and answered with a scowl. "And what if I don't feel like talking to you, Del?"

I took two steps back as the roadie took one step forward. The last thing I wanted was a fight with Tommy Ventura. I'd rather get my stomach pumped again.

"Hit him, Tommy!" Tina said. "Flatten the jerk. You can do it."

I don't think anyone doubted Tommy's chances of success in unarmed combat with me. The only question was whether he was angry enough to actually start something. Unfortunately, he looked like he was giving it some thought. In another setting, I was sure I could have talked him out of it. But with his unrequited love interest urging him on, I didn't want to risk saying anything that might offend him.

"We better go," Marcy said, pulling at my arm.

"That's just what I was thinking."

As we turned away, Kid and his mother fell in step beside us, leaving Tommy and the unlikely duo of the Larsen sisters to comfort Tina. Max was waiting at the doorway.

"Don't feel bad, Del," Kid said. "It's not your and Marcy's fault. None of this would've happened if Tina hadn't gone and told that police lady you went up on the stage."

"Kid's right," Grace said. "She's just acting the part of the little princess."

"She doesn't have to act," Marcy muttered. "She was born into the role."

Behind us I could hear the little princess saying, "He's chicken, Tommy. He's scared of you. Look at him walking away like a little chicken." She even made a few chicken noises for effect.

I glanced back over my shoulder in time to see a red-faced

Tommy saying, "C'mon, Tina, cut it out. I don't wanna fight anybody."

"Well, it's been a rough one," Max said when we reached the doorway. He looked at his watch. "What do you say? I've got time for one quick drink down in the bar before I have to go." Max had told us earlier that he would be flying to Minneapolis with Sylvia Darwin later in the evening.

Kid's mother politely declined for herself and her son. Marcy shook her head.

"I'm buying," Max added, but the offer didn't change their minds.

"I'll need a few minutes, Max," I said. "How about if I stop up to your room in a little bit?"

"Okay, suit yourself. But I'm leaving in an hour, so you better get there soon." As Max, Kid, and his mother turned to go, Max said, "You're going to have a helluva story to write, Del."

I nodded. "And the whole story isn't even out in the open yet, Max."

"What do you mean?"

"I mean there's a lot more to it."

Max frowned. "I don't get it." He looked at Marcy. "Do you know what he's talking about?"

Marcy nodded. She looked like she was about to cry. I almost felt like crying myself.

Max looked at me expectantly. "You want to tell me, or do I have to guess?"

"Not now, Max. I'll talk to you upstairs."

Max shook his head. "For chrissakes, don't look so damn serious," he said.

Marcy and I waited in the hall and watched Max, Kid, and Grace walk toward the elevator. "What do we do now?" she asked. "We need Tommy's help getting a tape recorder if the plan is going to work."

"We could go buy one," I said. "Don't worry, I'll talk to him."

"You better have a baseball bat when you do."

"I don't think so. I have a feeling Tommy's opinion of Tina

might change pretty quick once he finds out what it's like to have her liking him.''

"I don't think we have that much time.''

The amount we had turned out to be enough. Just then, Tommy Ventura emerged from the suite. When the door opened, I could hear Tina and the Larsen sisters jabbering away inside. It sounded as if they were having an argument, but they could have been swapping stories about rock stars they had known and loved.

Tommy almost stumbled into us. "Oh, man, you're still here,'' he said. "I was just going up to your room to see you. I, uh, I . . .'' Tommy put out his hand. Mine was already waiting for him.

As we shook, he said, "I'm really sorry about what happened inside, Del. I don't know what got into me. I just got carried away, you know. I mean, Tina was so upset, and with Artie and all, I guess I just lost it.''

"Forget it,'' I said. "There's something going around. I'm just glad you didn't hit me.''

"Oh no, man, I never would've done that. I was just upset. You know how it is.'' Tommy took a deep breath. "Man, I feel sorry for Artie, man. You don't know what it feels like when they put those cuffs on you. It's like, I don't know, it's like your whole life's just passing you by.''

"It was awful,'' Marcy said.

"Yeah, you said it.'' Tommy shook his head, then asked what I wanted to talk to him about.

I told him what we needed and he said it would only take a few minutes to rig something up. Twenty minutes later, I was knocking on the door to Max's room. I was wired, with a mini-cassette recorder and a microphone the size of a fingertip.

There was no answer when I knocked, so I pounded a few times. Still no answer, so I tried the door. It was unlocked. I stepped inside the room and took a look around. The luggage was gone, so were Max's clothes. On the dresser, I found a note of thanks to the maid with a ten-dollar bill attached. Max has always been a generous guy. I called down to the desk and confirmed what I already knew: Max Horton had checked out ten minutes ago.

"He knows we know," Marcy said when I met her down the hall where she and Tommy were waiting. "Now what do we do?"

"We try another hotel," I replied.

28

It was a two-minute walk around the corner to the Whitehall Hotel on Chestnut Street. The desk clerk looked like the officious type who wouldn't reveal a guest's room number if you held a gun to his head, so I picked up a house phone. When the operator's voice came on, I said, "I'm calling for Sylvia Darwin. I don't know her room number, but I'm sure she's—"

"Five-sixteen," the operator volunteered. "I'll connect you."

I hung up before she could. We rode the elevator in silence until the door opened at the fifth floor.

"Are you sure you don't want us to come in with you?" Marcy asked.

I shook my head. "This is something I've got to do by myself."

"Maybe I should go in too, just to be safe," Tommy said. "What if he has a gun?"

"Max is scared of guns," I replied. "That's the irony of this whole thing. But I'd like you to stay right outside the door, just in case things get out of hand."

"Sure thing," Tommy said.

They waited around the corner while I knocked on the door to Sylvia Darwin's room. "Yes, who is it?" she asked.

I could have said I was a delivery boy, but I decided to play it straight. "It's Del Barnes, Mrs. Darwin."

The door opened wide enough for Sylvia Darwin to peek out. "Yes, Del, how are you? Can I help you with something?"

"I came to see Max," I replied.

"Max? Why, he's not here, Del. I don't know where he is. I'm sorry."

I put my hand on the door with enough force to stop her from closing it. "I know he's in there, Mrs. Darwin."

From inside the room, I heard Max's gravel voice. "Better let him in, Syl. I'll have to talk to him sooner or later. It might as well be sooner."

Sylvia Darwin opened the door wide and backed away as I stepped into the room. Her blond hair was tied back in a ponytail. She was dressed in black, of course, but it was a dress that served to remind anyone who saw her that she had once been a bombshell. To some guys, like Max Horton for instance, she still was.

Max was lounging on the couch, working on a martini. He forced a sheepish grin and motioned for me to sit on a chair across from him. "You couldn't listen to me, could you?" he said. "You couldn't let sleeping dogs lie."

I tried to grin, but I couldn't. There was a lump in my throat as I said, "Sorry, Max."

He held up his drink. "Happy hour. You want one?"

"Yeah, a double."

Sylvia walked to the mini-refrigerator and got out ice for my drink. On a portable radio on the night table, Blondie was singing "Heart of Glass."

"I'd like to talk to you alone, Max," I said.

"There are no secrets between me and Sylvia," he replied. "What's on your mind?"

"This is really hard for me, Max."

"It's even harder for me, pal."

I nodded. "As you know, I spoke with a guy named Elmore Jackson yesterday. In case you don't remember him, he used to own a club down in Memphis where Bumblebee Mitchell played."

"I remember him, all right," Max said.

I took my drink from Sylvia Darwin, who sat down on the couch beside Max and took his hand. "When I talked to him on the phone, Elmore couldn't recall the name of the guy who ripped off Bumblebee Mitchell,'' I said. ''But he was sure he could remember the guy's face. So I went down to Memphis and—''

''You did *what*?'' I caught Max in mid-swallow and he almost spit out his drink.

''I went to Memphis,'' I said.

''And you paid for it with your own money, I hope.'' Max tried to force a smile.

Sylvia was having no such luck. She frowned and said, ''He knows more than you thought he did, Max.''

Max squeezed her hand. ''Let's see how much he knows.''

''Sure, Max,'' I said. ''It was my money. When I got down there, Elmore Jackson said he remembered the name of the guy after all. It was Chuck Darwin. Funny thing, though. When I showed him a picture of you guys, the person he identified wasn't Chuck. It was you, Max. You and Stillman and Darwin were all down there together. But it was you who ripped off Kid's father. You're the one who returned to the club a couple nights later and signed him. And then you gave him Darwin's name.''

Max was squirming a bit now, and Sylvia looked like she was about to faint. She got up off the couch and mixed herself a drink. Max told her he wanted another.

''That's an interesting story, Del,'' Max said, ''but I'm afraid no one would ever buy it. Who's going to believe that some old coot's memory is that good? It happened twenty years ago, for chrissakes.''

''I'm glad you mentioned that, Max. I hope you don't mind if I make a phone call.''

Max looked puzzled but said, ''No, go right ahead.''

As I dialed Marty Goldberg's number, I continued to talk. ''One thing I didn't understand was how Grace Lee located Chuck Darwin after all these years. By chance, I found out from a guy I know who owns a club in Athens that Gerry Stillman had been down there scouting Roots. It was shortly after then that Kid and Jack showed up at Darwin's office. But it didn't make any sense that Stillman would send them to see Darwin. He would've signed them to a contract—''

Marty Goldberg answered the phone before I could finish the sentence.

"Marty, this is Del Barnes," I said.

"Yeah, Del, how you doing?"

"Fine, Marty. I've got a quick question for you."

"Shoot," he said.

"Did you get that magazine I sent you?"

"Yeah, sure did. I got it right here. I haven't had a chance—"

"I'd like you to open it up and turn to page four," I said. "Do you see where it says, 'From the Publisher'?"

"Yeah, okay, I'm with you. Sounds like you're a bit rushed up there, Del."

"I am, Marty. Sorry." I was staring at Max as I spoke. He was still trying to hold a smile. "Now I want you to look at the picture of the guy—"

"Yeah, that's the guy. That's Gerry Stillman. He's the one that came into the club. . . . But wait a minute. The caption under the picture says it's Max Horton. There must be some mistake or—"

"No, that's right, Marty. That's exactly what I wanted you to check. Thanks a lot."

"Hey, wait a sec, when are you coming down to visit?" Marty blurted just before I hung up.

"In a few days, Marty," I said.

"You serious?"

"You can book it."

There wasn't even a trace of a smile on Max's face when I put down the phone.

"They may not believe Elmore Jackson," I said, "but Marty Goldberg saw you at his club only a few months ago." I stared at Max for a long moment. I loved this guy and I hated for it to come to this. But I had felt it coming for a few days now. Ever since I found out Max owned a piece of Roots, I had a sinking feeling that I just couldn't shake.

"Okay," he said at last. "So you can prove that I was down there asking about the band. So what? That doesn't prove I did anything wrong. It was just a joke."

"It's not very funny, Max, none of it. I can't believe you ripped off Kid's father. I thought you were the only trustworthy guy in this whole stinking business."

"Well, you were wrong. But let me tell you something, pal. Now it's my turn to talk." Max pointed his finger at me. "I'm not proud of what I did. In fact, I'm ashamed of it. So ashamed that I was almost relieved when Richie Randall got killed in that car accident. He would've gone on to record more of Bumblebee Mitchell's songs, but after he died I didn't do anything with them. I could've sold them. I could've gotten rich in this business. I could've been a fat cat, just like some of these other guys. Guys like Gerry Stillman and Chuck Darwin. Do you know how many guys they ripped off? Do you have any idea how many songs *they* stole?

"I suppose you never made any mistakes in your life. Oh no, not Del Barnes. You never did anything wrong. I saved your goddamn life. I pulled you out of the cut-out bin. And this is the thanks I get?"

I shook my head. I could feel tears welling up in my eyes. "Okay, Max, you're right, I understand that. I shouldn't be so damn self-righteous. But that doesn't justify murder."

"Murder! Who did I kill? Tell me who I killed!" Max was standing up now. "And don't give me any of that crap about murdering Kid's father. I'm not responsible for that any more than you're to blame for that plane going down."

I knew he'd bring up the crash. But he was right. He never blamed me. He didn't have to. I took care of that myself.

"Let's see," I said as Max sat back down. "Chuck Darwin, Gerry Stillman. They died yesterday. Does that refresh your memory?"

"Chuck Darwin killed Gerry Stillman," Max said. "And then he killed himself."

"I don't think so, Max. That's not how it happened."

"Oh no? Okay. Then you tell me how it happened."

"You were here with Chuck and Sylvia yesterday when Gerry Stillman called. Something must have jogged Stillman's memory. He must have figured out who Kid Lee was. Or he figured out

something that was going to be damaging to you. Stillman told
Chuck he had to see him. He didn't tell Chuck everything over
the phone, but he told him just enough so that you knew
something was up.

"I couldn't figure out at first how you got Chuck's gun away
from him. Then I realized Chuck didn't take his gun with him. I
realized that Sylvia was in on it with you. She gave you the gun,
Max, and you followed him over there and killed both of them."

Sylvia looked at Max nervously, but Max stared at me. "Good
try, Del, but you're wrong," he said.

"He knows too much, Max," Sylvia said. "He's too close."

I studied Max's face, then Sylvia's. Only then, when I saw the
icy chill in her eyes, did it finally dawn on me. As I had told
Tommy Ventura, Max was scared of guns.

"*You* did it!" I said to Sylvia.

"That's right, Del, I did it." Now that it was out in the open,
now that the cards were on the table, Sylvia Darwin's pretty lips
began spreading into an expression that approximated a smile. It
was a smile that made me shiver. "You want to know *why* I did
it?" she asked.

I could only nod. I was too shocked to speak. But in a way, I
was relieved. The revelation restored some of my faith in Max.
Not all of it, of course, but enough to make me realize that he was
not a cold-blooded killer.

"Chuck Darwin was one of the most insensitive, selfish,
money-grubbing, egotistical men who ever walked on this
earth," Sylvia said. "He was ruthless, conniving—"

"You married him," I said.

"That's right. I married him. I was pregnant, so I married him.
We didn't think of having abortions in those days, not like *your*
wonderful generation, Chip and Danny's generation. I didn't
know any better, so I tried to make the best of it, tried to have a
family. But you don't know what a holy hell it was to live with
that man. And my sons. *My* sons. They both took after him,
spoiled brats, nurtured along by him, of course. He turned those
kids into greedy little monsters, mirror images of their father.

They were just like him. And all the while . . . all the while, I
was in love with Max Horton."

Sylvia took Max's hand and smiled at him.

"You two have been involved for a long time then," I said.

Max actually grinned. "Fifteen years now."

"Sixteen," Sylvia corrected.

"But why didn't you just get a divorce?"

Sylvia shook her head. "That wouldn't have worked. I hung in
there, for Chip and Danny's sake. I thought it was the right thing
to do. But Chuck, you see, he knew about us. It was Gerry
Stillman who told him. Chuck was always jealous of Max. He
would've screwed me out of every cent I had coming. Max didn't
care about the money. But I did. I worked for that money. Believe
me, I worked for it. It was a matter of principle."

It was far too late to explain to Sylvia Darwin the difference
between principle and greed. Perhaps she understood the difference once. Maybe living with Chuck Darwin had warped her
view.

"Chuck really was a cheap sonofabitch," Max said. "You
wanted to know about me having a conflict of interest owning a
piece of the band? Well, the only reason Chuck cut me in was
because he wasn't sure the band would take off. If he had been
sure, he would've kept it all for himself. But he was too damn
cheap to take the risk."

"That's right," Sylvia said. "The world won't miss him. I
know I sure won't."

"What about Gerry Stillman?" I asked. "You killed him,
too."

"Oh, he was a swine, just like Chuck. They were both cut
from the same cloth."

"How long had you been planning to kill him?" I asked.

"We weren't planning on it. Max thought Grace Lee would do
it for us. But then Gerry Stillman got in the way. I knew we
couldn't wait any longer. After Danny and Chip were killed, I
didn't have anything left to lose."

"But didn't you wonder if your plan was backfiring? I mean

when your sons died? Weren't you afraid that Grace was killing *them* instead?"

"I talked to her," Max said. "I talked to her right away after Danny died. I told her I knew who she was. I told her I wouldn't stand in her way if she wanted to get even with Chuck Darwin. But I told her that shouldn't have anything to do with Danny and Chip. She said she didn't have anything to do with it. I could see she was telling the truth."

"And that's why you kept telling me to back off," I said.

"Yeah, that's right. But you wouldn't listen to me. You had to play investigative reporter. You couldn't leave well enough alone." Max lit a cigarette. "Well, I hope you're happy now."

"No, I'm not, Max. And you know it."

"So what're you planning to do? Go to the police? They're going to have a hard time believing your story. We'll deny it. You can't prove it. Neither can they."

I reached in my pocket and pulled out the tape recorder. "It's all here on tape, Max," I said.

"Oh, you dumb asshole. You stupid asshole." Max wiped his hand over his face and took a swig of his drink. But Sylvia was not taking things sitting down. She leaped up and lunged for the tape recorder, but I pulled away.

"Give me that!" she screamed.

She tried to pry my fingers apart, but it was no use. I'm not a tough guy, but I've still got strong hands from when I played guitar. She gave up after a few minutes, then fell back on the couch, exhausted, sobbing.

Max put his hand on Sylvia's shoulder to comfort her and tried friendly persuasion on me. "You know that's not admissible as evidence in court, Del," he said.

"I know. But it'll keep the cops after you until you break."

"We'll leave the country," he said.

"It's a free country, Max. You can do what you want. If they don't catch up with you, it's fine with me. I'd almost prefer it that way, in fact."

"How about if I buy the tape from you?"

I shook my head. "You don't have enough money."

"Maybe we do," Sylvia said. "How much do you want?"

"He means that he can't be bought," Max explained.

"Silly," she said, turning to Max. "Just like you." She started crying again and began fumbling in her purse for a tissue. "We've got to stop him, Max."

Max sighed. "I know we do, honey. You got any ideas?"

"How about *this*?" Sylvia produced a tissue from her purse, but that wasn't the only thing she pulled out. She was holding a gun.

It was a small gun, but any gun can do a lot of damage at close range. I was at close range.

"Hand over the tape, Del," Sylvia said.

I realized she had already killed her husband and Gerry Stillman, but that had all been an abstraction for me. Now, as I looked into her eyes, I could clearly see that she was capable of murder.

I handed it over, cassette recorder, microphone, and all.

"Smart," Max said. "That's the smartest thing you've done all day. Now take some smart advice. Get out of here. Forget everything. Forget you ever knew me."

I nodded and began to get up.

"No," Sylvia said. She was still pointing the gun at me. "We can't let him get away."

"What do you mean?" Max said. "Let him leave. He won't say anything." To me, he said, "You won't say anything, right, Del?"

"No," I said, "I promise." And I meant it. At that moment, I wasn't thinking about anything except getting out of that room alive.

"Put the gun away, Syl," Max said. "That thing scares me."

"It's too late," she said. "He knows too much. We've got to get rid of him."

I stood there frozen, looking from the shiny metal barrel of the gun to the steel-trap glare of her eyes.

"No, Syl," Max said. "It'll be okay. I'll talk to him. He'll listen to me."

But Sylvia Darwin wasn't listening to Max. She was off in

another world—an ugly, irrational world where people do ugly, irrational things.

I shivered as she pulled back the trigger. I realized that my number was finally up. I thought about yelling for Tommy Ventura, but it was too late for that. My only chance was to lunge for the gun.

Before I could make my move, Max beat me to it. Once again, the only guy I ever trusted in the music business saved my life. But this time, it cost him his.

Max stood up as soon as he heard the trigger click back. "For chrissakes, don't do it, Syl!" he pleaded. For a fleeting moment, I thought he might be able to change her mind. I was wrong.

Max lunged in front of her just as the gun went off. It was a sharp, popping sound, quieter than I thought it would be. He staggered back against me, clutching his heart. Sylvia recoiled, raising her hands for an instant, allowing me just the moment I needed. I charged forward, pushing Max aside and leaping at the gun over his shoulder. As I lurched ahead, I grabbed hold of Sylvia's wrist with both hands, twisting it until the gun came loose.

My momentum knocked me to the floor and I landed on top of the gun. Sylvia Darwin landed on top of me. She began beating me over the head with her fists, shrieking, "It's your fault! I hate you! It's your fault!"

Within seconds, Tommy Ventura came crashing through the door. Tommy pulled Sylvia off me, and I crawled to Max, who was slumped against the couch. Blood was gushing from his chest, more blood than I had ever seen before.

It's strange what captures your attention when everything is crazy around you. During our conversation, I had completely tuned out the radio, but now I could hear it loud and clear. The song was "Accidents Will Happen," and Max heard it, too.

As I leaned over him, he asked me, "What's that kid's name?"

"What kid?" I asked.

"The kid . . . singing on the radio."

"That's Elvis Costello."

"He's going to be a big hit," he said, struggling for a breath. "I can spot them, you know. I've always had the knack."

"I know, Max," I said. Another time I would have made a wisecrack. I would've told him that he was too old for the business. I would've told him that the new kid was already a big hit, that he was arguably the leader of an entire movement called New Wave. Max would've shrugged. He would've made his own wisecrack in response, and then we would've laughed.

I was crying now, crying hard, crying because there would be no more laughter between us.

"You're the best, Max," I said. "I'm sorry. I'm really sorry."

"Forget it," he said. "It's only rock 'n' roll." He winced as he tried to take another breath, a precious breath. "How about . . . a drink, Thelonius?" He tried to force a smile. "I'm buying."

By the time I handed him his glass, he was already dead.

29

I t seemed like an eternity passed before the police carried Max away and led a dazed and bedraggled Sylvia Darwin from the hotel room. All the while, I answered their queries until my head was spinning and my mouth was dry. When it was finally over, Tommy, Marcy, and I walked back to the Drake Hotel bar in silence, then began drinking in earnest.

"It's not your fault, Del," Marcy said. "You can't blame yourself."

"Just watch me," I replied, downing a double bourbon as if it were a glass of soda water.

"Marcy's right, Del," Tommy reassured me. "It's just like after Chip was killed, man. Remember what you said to me that night? We can't control these things, man. They just happen, that's all. There's nothing we can do about it."

Deep down inside, I guess I knew Tommy was right, but that consolation didn't ease the pain and guilt that were surging to the surface. It was Chicago all over again, demons swirling all around me. Just when I thought I had conquered them, they were back for another battle. And this time, I didn't have my guard up. They were winning the war again.

I wanted to be left alone, didn't want to talk to anybody, didn't want to listen. I was lousy company. After an hour or so, Tommy gave up and went to find Tina. A while later—I don't know how long it was—Marcy left, too. She was depressed about Max, disgusted with me. Every attempt she made to reassure me, I challenged. Every gesture of affection and support, I rejected.

Finally she just threw in the towel. I was morose, immersed in self-pity, not even thinking about what she was going through. She told me she'd see me upstairs, but I never showed. I had my wish to be alone, and I made the least of it.

I stayed in the bar until it closed, drinking one for Max, one for me. When they finally threw me out, I staggered around the neighborhood until I found an all-night drugstore that sold liquor on Rush Street. I got a bottle of bourbon, and the next thing I knew I was back in my room. I didn't know how I even found my way back to the hotel. Maybe I got some help from a Good Samaritan. Maybe I followed the tracks of my tears.

It wasn't until I woke up the next morning that I remembered bumping into Joe Boyle, the doctor from the emergency room. He was the one who helped me get back to the hotel. He had been with the cute nurse, the one who had helped me up after Officer Patrick Brady put his fist through my ribs. They had just gotten off duty, but they ended up working overtime on my behalf. It seemed like I had been getting a lot of help lately. And I hadn't been showing much appreciation for it.

I thought I should write Dr. Boyle a thank-you note, write to the AMA and tell them what a swell guy he was. More than that, I thought I should probably get out of Chicago as soon as I could.

Marcy came to my room around ten o'clock. She had been the most help of all. She didn't look happy to see me, but I could tell she was relieved that I was all right.

"I looked in on you earlier," she said, "to make sure you were okay. I stayed up half the night worrying about you."

My first thought was to tell her that I was a big boy, that I could take care of myself. But sometime during the night, I had stifled the urge to lash out thoughtlessly in anger. Maybe I had drowned it in the bourbon. Maybe my wits were so dulled by my hangover that I couldn't muster the requisite energy for a glib response. Or maybe, just maybe, I had learned something.

"I owe you an apology," I said.

"Not me," she replied. "I'll be just fine. But you owe yourself one. You're too damn smart to wallow. You ought to stop feeling sorry for yourself and try doing something nice for someone else."

I nodded and felt my head throb. As I reached out to give her a hug, she pulled back from me. I shivered at the thought that the damage I had inflicted the night before might be permanent. I couldn't remember exactly what I had said. I only knew that when I'm morose and drinking, I can be pretty ugly.

"It's not over, is it?" I could hear my voice trembling.

"No, not unless you want it to be."

"I don't."

"Good. I don't either. But I've got one at home that's difficult enough to deal with. I don't want to be with you when you're acting like you were last night."

"Last night was an exception," I said. "I'd like to say that it won't happen again, but I just don't know. I'm sorry. I just had to get it out of my system."

"I know you did." She sat down beside me and put her arms around me, "like the circle 'round the sun," reprising the old Memphis Jug Band tune.

I held Marcy close, and she started to cry. "I guess I've got to get it out of my system, too," she said.

We ordered breakfast from room service with an extra pot of coffee, and I broke my vow of penance by allowing myself the luxury of aspirin. It finally dawned on me that the habit was less Spartan self-denial than it was self-pity.

We took a hot shower every half hour.

Around three o'clock, Kid Lee knocked on the door to my room. "I came to say good-bye to you, Del," he said. "Marcy, too, if she's around."

"Oh yeah, she's here," I said. I shook Kid's hand and told him to come in, but he said he had to leave soon. Marcy came over and joined us at the door.

"Well, it's been a real pleasure getting to know you, Kid," I said. "And it's been truly amazing to see you play."

"That's right," Marcy said. "Do you know what your plans are yet? Are you going back home with your mother?"

"No, Mama already left with Uncle Jack on the train. I'm

hoping maybe I can get together another band. Do you think I've got a chance, Del?"

"Are you kidding? Every record company in the country is going to be after you."

"That's good." Kid hesitated for a moment, shifting his weight from foot to foot in the doorway. "I got another question for you, Del."

"Sure, Kid, what is it?"

"Well, Mama says I got to get a manager. She says she's getting too old for going on the road and stuff. So I thought maybe I should ask you. You see, I want to have somebody I can trust, and after what happened to my daddy . . ."

"Sure, Kid, I can check into it for you. I'm positive we can find you somebody good."

"Okay, thanks." Kid started to turn away, then looked at his feet and stopped. "That's not what I meant, Del."

"What is it, Kid?"

"He means he wants *you* to be his manager, dummy," Marcy said.

"Me?" I'm not ordinarily a greedy sort, but I have to admit that for a fleeting moment I did see dollar signs flashing before my eyes. "Is that what you mean, Kid?"

He nodded. "Well, at least if you'd *think* about it."

"Of course I would. How can I reach you?"

Kid smiled. "Well, we're going on a vacation now—out to California." He glanced over his shoulder, and I realized why he hadn't entered the room. There was someone waiting for him outside.

I opened the door wider and saw Vicki Larsen standing in the hall. "This is my girlfriend, Suzi," Kid said sheepishly. With a fifty-fifty chance, one of these days I had to get the Larsen sisters' names right.

"Of course," I said, glancing sideways at Marcy. She was wearing a grin wider than the Santa Monica Freeway.

"That's great," she said. "I'm happy for both of you."

"So am I," I said. "But, Kid, just don't let Tommy Ventura know about it."

"Huh?"

I figured Kid was baffled by the inside joke and I realized I probably shouldn't have said anything.

He turned and looked out into the hallway, then looked back at me. "Why not?" he said. "Tommy's coming with us."

Just then, Tommy Ventura stepped into view from his hiding place out in the hall. His face was redder than a beefsteak tomato. Apparently, he had developed an appreciation for groupies since we had last seen him. The other Larsen sister—Vicki, it had to be—was standing beside him. They were holding hands.

Tommy put out his free one. "How are you feeling today, Del? Man, you were really working on a bad one last night."

"Much better, Tommy," I said. "I'm sorry about being so obnoxious."

"That's okay, man. I understand what you were going through. Max was like your mentor, just like Artie was to me."

I nodded. Max Horton, Marcy Hopkins. I clearly had a better deal than Tommy Ventura.

"What about Tina?" Marcy asked. Realizing that she might be touching a sensitive nerve, she quickly recovered, adding, "I mean, is she okay?"

"Oh yeah, she's fine. She's off with her new boyfriend—some guy who plays in a band. I think they want her to jam with them." Tommy shrugged. "Well, I guess we better be going. We gotta get to the airport."

"Just a second," Suzi Larsen said. "I have to get Del's autograph."

"My autograph?"

"Yeah, she collects them," Kid said. I could see his eyes rolling behind the lenses of his glasses, an indication that he was already perplexed by one of his girlfriend's foibles.

Suzi took out a small spiral notebook. "Once a rock star, always a rock star," she said, giggling. "It doesn't matter how old you are."

"Thanks," I said, flipping through the pages of the writing tablet. It was an impressive collection—from heavyweights to lightweights, has-beens to never-weres. I asked if there was a special section for one-hit wonders.

"Uh-uh," she said. "Just do it here under S."

I didn't ask why, I just signed my name: "To Suzi—Best wishes always, Del Barnes."

When I was done, she squinted at the scrawl. "Barnes?" she said, puzzled. "I thought your name was Del *Shannon.*"

Marcy laughed. "Just how old do you think this guy is?"

We watched them stroll down the hall, hand in hand, four kids on a double date. Marcy and I had a date of our own. We got out of downtown and found a saloon on Diversey Avenue called Lawry's that had seventy-five-cent beers and the best fried chicken you'll ever eat. Then, at long last, we had a good night's sleep.

We stayed around the next morning to tie up loose ends, taking care of arrangements for Max, making calls to people back at the magazine. There was still plenty left to do, lots of hurdles to jump, obstacles to climb. But for now, my vacation had officially begun.

As I drove Marcy to the airport, I took a swing through one of the bad neighborhoods of the city.

"Where are we going?" she asked.

"I've got to make a quick stop," I said, pulling over at the corner of Halsted and Division.

"Here?"

"It will only take a minute."

I glanced around the abandoned lot and saw him sleeping behind one of the concrete dividers holding up Ogden Avenue. At least I hoped he was only asleep. It turned out he was.

As I approached, he looked at me with his one big sad eye. He licked at my hand, then I held out the ham sandwich that I had wrapped up from lunch. He ate it in about five seconds— mustard, mayo, lettuce, and all.

"This is only lunch, pooch," I said. "Tonight you'll be eating barbecue."

He followed me back to the car and didn't hesitate to hop into the backseat.

"What's this all about?" Marcy asked. "What are you doing?"

"I thought over what you said about doing something for someone else," I replied. "This is a thank-you present for Elmore Jackson. I think it'll cheer him up. I have a feeling the pooch won't object, either."

I got Marcy to the airport just in time for her to catch her flight. When I got back out to the car, I started to feel lonely. But the feeling passed pretty quickly. After all, I wasn't alone. I was with man's best friend.

I flipped on the radio just in time to hear Ray Charles singing "I Can't Stop Loving You." It was an auspicious start to the vacation I'd always wanted to take. I was heading south, where it was warm and friendly. It was still a few months until Thanksgiving, but I got a jump on thinking about all the things I had to be thankful for.